Brodie's Gamble

MacLarens of Boundary Mountain

Historical Western Romance Series

SHIRLEEN DAVIES

Book Two in the MacLarens of Boundary Mountain

Historical Western Romance Series

Avalanche Ranch Press, LLC
PO Box 12618
Prescott, AZ 86304

Brodie's Gamble is a work of fiction. Names, characters, places, and incidents are either products of the author's imagination or used facetiously. Any resemblance to actual events, locales, or persons, living or dead, is wholly coincidental.

Book design and conversions by Joseph Murray
at www.3rdplanetpublishing.com

Cover design by Kim Killion, The Killion Group

ISBN: 978-1-941786-35-2

Books by Shirleen Davies

Historical Western Romance Series
MacLarens of Fire Mountain

Tougher than the Rest, Book One
Faster than the Rest, Book Two
Harder than the Rest, Book Three
Stronger than the Rest, Book Four
Deadlier than the Rest, Book Five
Wilder than the Rest, Book Six

Redemption Mountain

Redemption's Edge, Book One
Wildfire Creek, Book Two
Sunrise Ridge, Book Three
Dixie Moon, Book Four
Survivor Pass, Book Five

MacLarens of Boundary Mountain

Colin's Quest, Book One,
Brodie's Gamble, Book Two

Contemporary Romance Series

MacLarens of Fire Mountain

Second Summer, Book One

Hard Landing, Book Two
One More Day, Book Three
All Your Nights, Book Four
Always Love You, Book Five
Hearts Don't Lie, Book Six
No Getting Over You, Book Seven
'Til the Sun Comes Up, Book Eight, Releasing
2016

Peregrine Bay

Reclaiming Love, Book One, A Novella
Our Kind of Love, Book Two

The best way to stay in touch is to subscribe to my newsletter. Go to *www.shirleendavies.com* and subscribe in the box at the top of the right column that asks for your email. You'll be notified of new books before they are released, have chances to win great prizes, and receive other subscriber-only specials.

I care about quality. If you find something in error, please contact me via email at shirleen@shirleendavies.com

Description

Brodie's Gamble, Book Two, MacLarens of Boundary Mountain Historical Western Romance Series

"Every book of Shirleen's never fails to draw me in and make it impossible to put down until I devour it!"

Brodie MacLaren has a dream. He yearns to wear the star—bring the guilty to justice and protect those who are innocent. In his mind, guilty means guilty, even when it includes a beautiful woman who sets his body on edge.

Maggie King lives a nightmare, wanting nothing more than to survive each day and recapture the life stolen from her. Each day she wakes and prays for escape. Taking the one chance she may ever have, Maggie lashes out, unprepared for the rising panic as the man people believe to be her husband lies motionless at her feet.

Deciding innocence and guilt isn't his job.

Brodie's orderly, black and white world spins as her story of kidnapping and abuse unfold. The fact nothing adds up as well as his growing attraction to Maggie cause doubts the stoic lawman can't afford to embrace.

Can a lifetime of believing in absolute right and wrong change in a heartbeat?

Maggie has traded one form of captivity for another. Thoughts of escape consume her, even as feelings for the handsome, unyielding lawman grow.

As events unfold, Brodie must fight more than his attraction. Someone is after Maggie—a real threat who is out to silence her.

He's challenged on all fronts—until he takes a gamble that could change his life or destroy his heart.

Brodie's Gamble, book two in the MacLarens of Boundary Mountain historical western romance series, is a full-length novel with an HEA and no cliffhanger.

Visit my website for a list of characters for each series.
http://www.shirleendavies.com/character-list.html

Acknowledgements

Thanks also to my editor, Kim Young, proofreader, Alicia Carmical, and all of my beta readers. Your insights and suggestions are greatly appreciated.

As always, many thanks to my wonderful resources, including Diane Lebow, who guides me through my social media endeavors, my cover designer, Kim Killion, and Joseph Murray who is a superb at formatting my books for both print and electronic versions.

Brodie's Gamble

Prologue

York, Pennsylvania
1858

"Hold him down." The tallest of the boys put his hands on his knees and bent over, laughing at Brodie MacLaren, who glared back as he tried to free himself. Sixteen years old, tall and strong for his age, it took five boys to hold him down—six if you counted their leader, Horst Ackermann, the oldest of the bunch.

"Did you think you could pass through our neighborhood without paying for the privilege?" Horst glanced at his friends. "These arrogant Scots believe they can go anywhere they please."

Brodie's body twisted in rage, his face red with anger. "It's a free country. I can go anywhere I want."

"Well, you can't go through here without paying the toll." Horst rifled through Brodie's pockets, knowing he'd left his Saturday afternoon job an hour before. Finding what he sought, Horst gripped the coins, holding them in the air. "Look here. Appears we will have a fine time tonight."

The boys loosened their hold on him long enough for him to wrench his hands free. Jumping to his feet, he kicked the knee of one boy, slamming a fist into another's face, sending both crumbling to the ground. That was all the satisfaction he got before his arms were, once again, wrenched behind him.

"It's a miserable group of lads who steal." His defiant yell earned him several fists to the face and stomach.

Horst counted the coins, then looked at Brodie's bleeding face.

"You know nothing of misery, MacLaren. Stay out of our part of town. And if you run to the sheriff, we'll find you again and it won't end so well."

A last retort died on his lips as a final blow to his head blackened Brodie's world.

"There'll be no going to the law and no retaliation, lads. You're to quit the job, Brodie, and I'll hear no argument." Brodie's father, Ewan MacLaren, stood a few feet away, as his wife, Lorna, washed away the blood on Brodie's face, then bandaged the cuts.

"But, Da, we need the money, and I like working for the gunsmith." Brodie's protests fell on deaf ears.

"Aye, and look what happened." Ewan looked around the room at the oldest MacLaren cousins, Colin, Blain, and Quinn. "I'll be talking to my brothers about this, so don't be going against what I'm saying. You four are to stay away from Germantown. Am I clear, lads?"

Shoving hands into their pockets, each nodded.

"Good. Now, be gone with you. Brodie needs to rest."

Sending glances to Brodie before they left, Colin, Quinn, and Blaine walked out, stopping a hundred yards away to huddle together.

"What do we do, Colin?" The youngest of the four, Blaine, always looked to his older brother, the oldest of the male cousins, for guidance.

"We wait for Brodie to heal, then go after Horst and his lads." Colin's steely voice held a firm conviction when he'd made up his mind about something. "Uncle Ewan means well, but he doesn't know what we face at school and whenever we go to town. Attacking Brodie is the last of it. I'll not be having my family threatened and robbed."

"The punishment will be severe." Quinn glanced behind him, confirming their uncle had not come outside.

"Taking your punishment has never bothered you before," Blaine joked. Of all the cousins, Quinn snubbed authority more than any of them, uncaring of the penalty doled out.

"I didn't say it would bother me." He slapped Blaine on the back of his head and laughed. "I agree with Colin. It's time someone stood up to Horst and there are no better lads to do it than us MacLarens." He sobered as he considered Brodie's reaction. "You know he'll want us to hold a trial."

Colin let out a breath. "Aye. It's his way."

"We take Horst, the four of us have a trial, then we teach him a lesson." Blaine grinned, glad to have contributed.

Colin nodded. "It's settled then. We wait for Brodie to heal, then do what's needed."

"You don't need to get in the middle of this, lads. I can take care of Horst." Brodie crossed his arms, wincing as pain from two broken ribs shot through him.

"Not by yourself. We've a plan and we're going through with it." Colin's calm resolve made him the perfect leader of the cousins.

"I won't have you acting the same as his gang of hooligans."

"We plan no beating, Brodie. The four of us will wait for him after school, get him away from his lads, and question him." Colin glanced at Quinn and Blain, who nodded in agreement.

"He won't confess."

"Aye, Brodie, he will. It's his arrogance that will fail him. When it does, we dispense the punishment." A smile crossed Colin's face at what they'd planned.

"I don't know, Colin. As much as I want justice, and my money back, I don't want us to turn into savages like him and his lads. We came to America to rid ourselves of tyranny and punishment without being allowed to defend ourselves."

"That was one reason, Brodie. Mainly, we came because we might have starved to death if we stayed. Do you remember the nights we fell asleep with wee amounts of food in our bellies?" Quinn asked.

"Aye, I remember."

"And do you remember the raids when neighboring clans swooped in to burn our crops and kill our families?" Quinn's gaze hardened, remembering the violence. "We canna let it happen here by brutes such as Horst. He needs to be taught a lesson, and we MacLarens are the ones to give it."

"Are you with us, Brodie?" Colin stepped up to him, placing a hand on his shoulder.

Brodie nodded, his face a mask. "Aye. I'm with you."

"There he is." Blaine and the others waited on the trail Horst used each day to go home. His family wasn't farmers or ranchers. Instead, his father and uncles were harness makers, farriers, and tool makers. When he and his boys weren't harassing or threatening others, Horst joined them to learn the trade. He had little respect for those who worked the land or weren't of German descent...and he had no problem acting on his disdain.

Horst whistled as the trail crossed over a stream, then made a sharp turn at a brick building used for storing tools. He didn't see the hand shoot out to wrap around his arm until he landed on the ground.

"What's going..." His voice faded as he stared into the faces of the four MacLarens.

Without uttering a word, Quinn grabbed Horst's arms, Blaine stuffed a rag in his mouth, then Colin and Brodie picked up his legs, carrying him into the building and locking the door. Setting him on the floor, they tied his hands together, then his legs, and hoisted him up to rest against a stack of wooden crates.

Colin crossed his arms, letting his gaze roam over Horst, then shook his head. "You aren't too bright of a lad, are you, Horst?"

The rag stifled his scream as his eyes widened in what could've been fear or anger. Either was fine with Colin.

"You see now, Horst, when you attack one MacLaren, the rest of the family believes it's our God-given right to discover why. Did Brodie attack you first? Did he steal something of yours? Perhaps the lad smiled at a girl you like." Colin walked up to him, leaning into his face. "We are not animals, Horst. Before we decide if there is to be retribution, we need to know the reason you beat Brodie, then stole his money."

Blaine stepped forward, removing the rag from Horst's mouth.

"Now is your chance to say your piece. Me and the lads are willing to listen." Quinn crossed his arms and leaned against a wall.

Horst's eyes darted from one boy, then to another, his gaze resting on the door.

"Ah, now, laddie, that would be a mistake. You *will* be leaving here, but not until you've answered Colin's questions." Brodie's smile was feral as he took in the sight of a trembling Horst. "You don't seem so brave when you don't have your lads about you. Lucky for you we aren't like them."

"I don't have to tell you anything." Horst's face twisted into a scowl before he spat on the floor.

"True, but then we'd be thinking you have no sense and I, for one, think you're smarter than that."

"I don't know, Brodie. Seems the lad's as dumb as a post." Quinn crossed his arms, laughing.

Horst uttered a stream of curses, trying to lunge toward Quinn, tripping over his bound ankles and landing on the floor.

"See, Brodie. Dumb as a post."

"Enough, Quinn," Colin broke in. "Answer the questions, Horst, so we can get back to our chores."

Horst glared up at them from the floor, his face the color of a ripe plum.

"We don't like you MacLarens. You Scots always think you're better than us, flirting with the girls and taking our jobs." He nodded at Brodie. "You shouldn't be the one working for the gunsmith. It should be one of my boys taking home the coin. We hate your kind."

"So you decided beating Brodie and stealing his pay was a fair way to get back at us?" Colin's gaze narrowed, his face turning to stone at the venom in Horst's voice.

"And I don't regret it. He deserved it for talking to Polly, taking her attention from me."

Quinn shot a look at Brodie. "Polly is it now?"

"Nae. I spoke to her a couple times. It's of no importance." Brodie turned his attention back to Horst. "The pay you stole *is* of importance and I'll have it back."

Horst tilted his head and laughed. "Too late. The money's gone, MacLaren."

"Well then, since you admit to stealing and beating Brodie, there'll be a need for retribution." Colin paced in a circle, as if considering what would be appropriate. "Lads, what do you think?"

"Aye, he's admitted it right out," Blaine agreed, taking a stand next to Colin.

"I'm with Blaine." Quinn stepped next to his two cousins.

"Brodie?" Colin asked.

He stared at Horst, pitying the boy who allowed hatred and jealousy to rule his life. "We can't let him do this to others."

Colin and Quinn jerked Horst up off the floor, leaned him against a wall, and stepped aside.

Colin rolled up his sleeves, locking a cold gaze at the prisoner. "Horst Ackermann, you've admitted to the crimes, been found guilty, and have shown no remorse."

"Wait," he screamed, horror twisting his face. "You can't kill me."

Quinn laughed. "Sure we can."

"But we won't," Brodie smirked. "Right, Colin?"

"Not this day, laddies." Colin glanced at Horst, whose body began to shake. "Remember, you brought this on yourself."

Quinn doubled over, holding his stomach to contain his laughter. "I wish we could have stayed to watch. It's sure they'll be looking at Horst in a different way after today."

The others joined him as they pictured the way they'd left Horst in the building. They'd stripped him down to nothing except his drawers, then leaned him against a post. Tying his hands together, they wrapped the rope around a nail above his head, securing it with a well-placed knot. Last, they tied his legs to the bottom of the post.

"You're certain the message you sent went to Polly's home?" Blaine asked Colin.

"I am."

"An invitation from Horst for Polly and her friends to come see the surprise he'd created." Blaine shook his head as he gulped in large amounts of air. His eyes watered from laughter. "Quinn's right. I wish we could see their faces."

"It's good you warned the lad once more about what would happen if they bullied anyone else. I believe he may have gotten the message, Colin."

Colin nodded, although his face remained passive. "We'll see. It's a stubborn boy he is." Settling a hand on Brodie's shoulder, he leaned toward him. "Are you satisfied?"

"Aye. It was a wise plan and I'm grateful for your help."

"Ach. If it had been up to me, me and the lads would've taken him behind a barn and settled it the old way. You, with your sense of justice, encouraged us to do it the right way. Someday, lad, I believe you'd make a fine sheriff."

Brodie burst out laughing at the ridiculous suggestion of becoming a lawman. "The day I start wearing a badge is the day you can put me in the ground because it is for certain I would've lost my mind. Come on, lads. It's time we get home before the family sends out a search party."

Chapter One

Conviction, California
October 1864

"Sheriff, you gotta come quick. Those Olsen boys are causing all kinds of trouble at the feed lot outside of town."

Sheriff Brodie MacLaren sighed. He had a long night and rough morning. Now this. His best deputy had left town to follow the woman he loved to San Francisco, and another one had taken time off to help an uncle on his ranch for a few weeks. Brodie had fired another deputy for being drunk on the job, and suggested the final one leave due to his strong loyalty to Sheriff Yost, the man Brodie replaced. He needed men who were loyal to him and the town, not ones who brooded over the fact they believed they were a better choice for the job than Brodie.

All of this left him alone to watch over the riverfront community of over four thousand until he could find replacements. He'd been sheriff for a few weeks. So far, the ones who'd applied for the deputy openings didn't match his requirements—proficient with a gun, previous work as a lawman, a desire to become a part of

Conviction, and an unflappable sense of right and wrong. Brodie either had to loosen his standards or broaden his search. He'd chosen the latter.

"What are they up to, Jack?" Brodie sized up the young man who'd wandered into Conviction a year before. He swore he didn't have a first name. Locals referred to him as Jack-of-all-trades Perkins, but most just called him Jack or Perkins. Regardless, he knew more about what went on around town than anyone else, including Brodie.

"No good, I can tell you that."

Brodie stood, crossing his arms and pinning Jack with a cold stare.

"Hell, Sheriff. They're doing what they usually do. Taunt someone until he's angry and takes a swing at 'em. Then someone else jumps in, and before you know it, it's a doggone brawl."

Shaking his head on a groan, Brodie strapped his gun belt on and grabbed his hat.

"Do you want me to come with you, Sheriff?" Brodie grinned at the eagerness in Jack's voice. He had a habit of following Brodie around like a ranch dog. His zealous attitude sometimes got in the way, but proved to be a big help when Brodie needed someone to act as a messenger or keep watch on prisoners in the jail.

"Tell you what, lad. I've got Bob Belford sleeping it off in a cell. It'd be a big help if you'd wake him up and take him home to his wife."

"Sure, Sheriff." Jack beamed at what he considered an important chore, something Brodie would normally have a deputy handle—when he had one. "Maybe I could be your deputy. I mean, you know...until you find the right man. I could even wear a badge."

Brodie put a hand on Jack's shoulder. "Lad, the best way to help is to continue with what you already do for me. We keep it between us. A secret between the two of us."

Jack's eyes grew wide, his excitement rising. "You mean like a spy?"

"Aye. Do you think you can do that for me?"

Jack straightened his shoulders. "Yes, sir. You can count on me, Sheriff."

Brodie breathed a sigh of relief, then remembered he was about to head into a firestorm at the feed lot. His days never failed to surprise him.

Brodie wiped the sweat from his brow, sliding his gun into its holster.

"Jack shouldn't have sent you out here, Brodie. I told him I could handle those Olsen boys." Stein Tharaldson held the shotgun easily in his huge hand. Towering over Brodie, and most men within fifty miles, Stein ran the feed lot and store with firm control. Congenial, even jovial most of the time, Brodie knew he possessed a keen mind and, if pushed too far, a fierce temper.

"Where are they?"

"Ran off the moment I lifted the shotgun. I never seen men run so fast and far in such a short time." Stein's deep, rumbling laugh had the sheriff chuckling with him. Sobering, he glanced at Brodie. "I wanted to get at least one of them in the backside—teach them both a lesson."

He had no doubt Stein would have done it without a lick of remorse. "Did they draw their guns on you?"

Stein laughed again, shaking his head. "They have dirt for brains, but knew enough not to risk their lives by pointing a gun at me. The Olsens pick on weaker prey, those they can push around. The oldest started an argument with an old rancher I've known a long time. One of his ranch hands got in Olsen's face, then all hell started. That's when I came out with my gun."

Brodie pushed his hat back on his forehead, looking up at the sky. He should go after the Olsens, charge them with disorderly conduct and whatever else he could to get them off the streets. There were enough witnesses.

"Do you want to press charges?"

"Not this time, Brodie. I've got enough to do without going through a trial once the circuit judge decides to make a visit." Stein pulled on his reddish-blond beard. "I will if they cause trouble again."

"It's your decision, but I expect you to let me know if they threaten you or your customers again. I can't let you take the law into your own hands, Stein."

He studied the sheriff a moment. They'd known each other since the MacLarens came to the area and started their ranch, even sharing drinks with Brodie at Buckie's Castle Saloon on many occasions. Brodie had to know he'd do what was needed to protect what was his.

"I won't lie to you, Brodie. I'll do what needs to be done. If it's before you can get here, so be it."

Brodie let out a slow breath. He knew Stein wouldn't back down from a fight to safeguard those who mattered to him, which included the townsfolk he'd known most of his life.

Brodie took a path along the water as he rode back to the jail, pulling his collar up to fend off the late October chill. Glancing at the bustling port, he marveled at how many people came through town. Some stayed, but most left.

Nestled between the Feather and Boundary rivers, Conviction began as a small settlement in 1840. Riverboats from San Francisco and Sacramento brought miners, settlers, gamblers, and vagabonds, swelling the population from a few hundred to thousands in less than a decade.

Watching a riverboat unload its passengers, his thoughts returned to hiring deputies. He couldn't continue putting in twenty-hour days much longer. The city fathers posted notices in Virginia City, San Francisco, and Sacramento. He needed men with experience who'd want to make the rapidly growing frontier town their home.

Taking off his hat, he resettled it lower on his forehead, wincing as he passed the Gold Dust Hotel. Colin and Sarah had ridden into town the day before, leaving a message on his desk at the jail saying they expected him to join them tonight for supper. He hadn't responded.

The family hadn't been happy with his decision to accept the job as sheriff rather than do what they expected and continue working the ranch. According to his father, as the oldest of Ewan and Lorna MacLaren's six children, he had responsibilities he'd abandoned by accepting the badge.

A cold knot settled in his stomach each time he thought of how not one of his family had supported his decision. Not even Colin, Quinn, or Blain—cousins who were more like brothers— had stepped forward in his defense. As much as he wanted to see Colin and Sarah, he didn't look forward to sitting through supper with Colin berating him for his decision.

Dismounting outside the jail, he walked in on leaden feet, wanting nothing more than to lay down in one of the cells and sleep. Sitting down at the desk, he picked up the message from Colin, knowing he had no choice but to join Sarah and him for supper.

Pushing up from the desk, he grabbed the keys before heading to the back. Four cells lined the back wall. During his weeks as sheriff, he'd never had more than two people locked inside.

The cell where Bob Belford had slept off his drunken night was in good order. The furniture consisted of two beds, a small desk, and a chair. More than in most jails. He suspected Jack had something to do with nothing being amiss. *Perhaps the lad* would *make a good deputy.* The thought brought a smile to his lips. Turning toward the front, Brodie let out a deep sigh, knowing he had to send a message to Colin.

"Let's go to lunch, then see if we can find him." Sarah MacLaren glanced at Colin as he escorted her downstairs to the hotel dining room.

A large town by most frontier standards, Conviction boasted four hotels. All offered meals, although the quality had always been best at the Gold Dust.

This afternoon, though, Colin found it hard to enjoy his venison stew and biscuits. His mind kept returning to Brodie and how much he missed him. Perhaps his cousin would listen to reason and return home. He couldn't imagine running the ranch without him.

"Look there." Sarah stared out the window at the jail.

Turning in his chair, following her gaze, he saw Brodie ride up on Hunter and dismount. Scanning the boardwalk, he tipped his hat at a passing couple, then disappeared inside the jail.

"At least we know he's in town." Colin finished eating, pushing his plate away, noticing Sarah watching him. "What?"

"You don't plan to charge over there and demand he come home, do you?"

"As much as I'd like to, no. We'll invite him to supper, find out if he's met the new neighbor south of us, and that's all. No matter how much I don't like or understand it, I know it's his decision."

Walking across the street, Colin noticed several more stores than he'd seen on his last trip to town, and new buildings seemed to be going up on every corner. The hotel clerk mentioned two more saloons and a few shops would be moving into the spaces. The growth made him realize how much Conviction needed a strong sheriff. As much as he didn't want to admit it, he knew Brodie would make an exceptional lawman, better than anyone Colin could think of.

Opening the door to the jail, they spotted Brodie walking from the back where the cells were located.

"I wondered when you two would be coming to pay me a visit. Good afternoon, Sarah." Brodie brushed a kiss across her cheek before setting the keys on his desk, shifting to look behind Colin. "Quinn didn't come with you?"

"Not this trip. Sarah and I rode in alone. We're hoping you can take time to join us for supper tonight."

"We'd like to spend time with you, Brodie. Please say you will." Sarah reached out, taking his hand and squeezing it.

He sent her a broad smile, unlike the wary welcome he'd offered Colin. "I'd like to meet you for supper, as long as you don't try to change my mind about taking the sheriff's job." He nodded toward a couple chairs.

"You keeping busy?" Colin asked, pulling out a chair for Sarah.

"You'd be surprised—"

Brodie's head snapped around as the door burst open and a woman he'd never seen dashed inside. Taking deep breaths, she looked out the window, then turned toward Brodie, gasping for air.

"Can I help you, ma'am?"

"Are you the sheriff?" She turned to glance out the window once again.

"Aye."

Shifting back toward him, she wrapped her arms around her waist, eyes wide. "I hope you can help me. I think I killed my husband."

Chapter Two

Sarah's shocked expression mirrored Colin's and Brodie's. The woman looked to be no more than seventeen years old. She wore a thin coat over a calico dress with a ruffled collar and white pinafore, which seemed more suitable for a much younger girl. Wisps of dark red hair, falling loose from what appeared to be a hastily prepared bun, set off clear blue eyes and framed a pale face dotted with freckles.

If the distress on her face wasn't so acute, they might have mistaken her for a woman not quite right in the head. Her trembling body, shaky breath, and wide, frightened eyes spoke of a woman ready to break.

Striding to her, Brodie took her elbow, guiding her to a nearby chair.

"Sit down and tell me what happened, Mrs..."

"King. I mean, Stoddard." She closed her eyes and took a deep breath. "Yes, Stoddard."

Brodie glanced at Colin and Sarah, not sure what to make of her confusion.

"Is it King or Stoddard?"

She gripped her hands together in her lap, squeezing tight, forcing herself to relax. Looking at Brodie, her breath caught. His intense moss green eyes were rimmed with black and dotted with golden flecks. At the moment, they bored into hers, making her squirm in the chair. Swallowing the lump in her throat, her gaze roamed the room, stopping briefly on the stove and gun rack before returning to Brodie.

"It's Stoddard now, but not by choice."

His brows lifted. "And your first name?" Brodie prodded, trying to keep his patience.

"Marguerite, but everyone calls me Maggie." Her quiet, nervous laugh was out of place given the announcement she'd made. "My mama used to call me Princess Maggie King. It seems so silly now." She let out a low sob before covering her mouth with a shaky hand. A moment passed before she spoke again. "My maiden name is King."

Neither Stoddard nor King meant anything to Brodie. "Sarah, would you mind pouring Mrs. Stoddard a cup of coffee?"

Sarah rushed to the stove, grabbing a dented tin cup, filling it to the top. Glancing down at the murky liquid, she wondered how long it had been sitting in the pot. Shrugging, she knelt down next to Maggie.

"Here you are, lass. It may help you calm yourself." Sarah held out the cup, grateful when Maggie took it from her hand.

"Perhaps it would be best if Sarah and I left—" Colin began.

"No." Maggie's eyes widened in alarm as she reached out to grip Sarah's arm. "Please don't go."

Sarah patted her hand. "I won't go, not if you'd like me to stay." She sent an apologetic look to Brodie, surprised when he returned a grateful smile.

Pulling up a chair, Brodie sat facing Maggie. He leaned toward her, his arms braced on his thighs. "All right, Mrs. Stoddard. You said something about killing your husband?"

She nodded, not looking at him.

"Why don't you tell me what happened."

Biting her bottom lip, she shot a quick glance at Sarah, who nodded her encouragement.

"Arnie came home drunk and angry."

"Your husband's name is Arnie?" Brodie asked.

"He's not my real husband. Arnold Stoddard is his full name, but he prefers Arnie."

"All right. You can tell me why he's not your real husband later. So, Arnie came home drunk last night."

"It was very late. Arnie said someone at Buckie's Castle cheated him out of most of his money. He was too drunk to stand. He took his bottle of whiskey, walked into the bedroom, and passed out. When he woke up this morning, he drained the rest of the bottle and started yelling, grabbing me and shoving me around."

Brodie had noticed the dark bruise on her cheek. "Is that when you got that?" He indicated the spot on her face, anger swelling in him at what the man had done.

"Yes. When he's drunk, which is most of the time, his temper takes over. I never know what he'll do." She looked at him, her face showing no emotion. "When he'd leave for town, I'd pray he wouldn't come home." Sitting back in her chair, she sucked in a breath and closed her eyes. Opening them, she continued. "I know it's wrong, but I hated Arnie, hated the way he treated me, hated what he...what he..." Her voice caught on a sob. Burying her face in her hands, she tried to stop the tears.

Standing, Sarah wrapped an arm around her shoulders. "It's all right, Maggie. Take as much time as you need."

A few minutes later, she dropped her hands. "We aren't married, Sheriff. Not properly."

Brodie pondered this a moment, needing to understand what she meant. "Why were you with him then?"

Her face drained of color as she caught her bottom lip in her teeth. "It's been close to two years now. My family traveled from Illinois to Colorado after my father sold our farm and bought a business in Denver. When we arrived, my father met with the banker who helped him with the purchase. That's when he found out there were problems. I didn't understand what happened. All I remember is my father being very angry and my mother trying to calm him down. One night, they left the hotel room, leaving me to watch my two younger brothers." She swiped at the tears on her cheeks, pain filling her red-rimmed eyes. "I woke in the middle of the night to find two men in the room. My parents' bed was empty and my brothers were sound asleep. Before I could say a word, the men gagged me and used something to knock me out."

"Chloroform?" Colin guessed.

Maggie shrugged. "After several days of traveling, we ended up in Nevada. They stowed me in a cabin, checking on me a couple times a day. It must have been at least five days later when they returned with three other men. One was Arnie Stoddard. He paid the men before loading me onto a wagon.”

“He *paid* for you?” Brodie couldn’t hide his disgust. “Forced you to live with him?”

She nodded, unable to meet his gaze. “Arnie told me if anyone asked, I was to say we were husband and wife. He said if I didn’t do what he ordered, I’d be sorry. I tried once to get a message to a family we met on the trail. When Arnie found out, he beat me until I couldn’t stand.” She sucked in a shaky breath. “I didn’t try again.”

Sarah placed a hand on her stomach, nausea sweeping through her at what the young woman had endured.

Brodie stood, pacing toward the cells, trying to sort out what Maggie revealed. She’d been wronged, kidnapped, and forced to live with a man as his wife. He could understand the rage she must feel, the need to seek revenge and get away. Did that rage include murder? Turning back to her, his features dispassionate, he sat back down, leaning close.

“Tell me. Why do you think you killed him?”

“I hit him on the head. He fell to the floor and didn’t move.”

“Did you check to see if he was still breathing, if he had a pulse?” Brodie rested his arms on his knees, his gaze never wavering from her face.

"I didn't want to get too close. If he was alive, I knew my life wouldn't be worth as much as your stale coffee." Her face colored. "No offense, Sheriff."

"None taken." Brodie chuckled, acknowledging the quality of the lukewarm brew. "So you left."

"As fast as I could and came here. It took a bit of time since we live so far back in the hills." She stood. "Do you need to arrest me?"

Putting his hands on his knees, Brodie pushed up from the chair, his face softening. "No, Mrs. Stoddard. Not until we learn if you really did kill your husband."

"You want me to go back to the cabin?" The shocked look in her eyes spoke louder than any words. "I can't."

"I'm afraid you don't have a choice, Mrs. Stoddard."

"It's Maggie King, and why don't I have a choice?"

He sighed. "Because you confessed to possibly killing your husband and I have to find out if you did."

"He's *not* my husband," she ground out, frustration now warring with fear. "He kidnapped me, made me do things..." Her voice cracked. She squeezed her eyes shut, covering her mouth with her hand.

No matter her tale or how much he wanted to believe she hadn't killed him, Brodie had a job to do. Ignoring her outburst, he continued. "He may have just been knocked out. By the time we arrive, I wouldn't be surprised if Arnie is long gone. You need to show me where the cabin is located, and I'd rather you do it willingly."

"How about Colin and I go along?" Sarah suggested.

"*Nae*," both men said simultaneously.

"You'll not be going this time, Sarah. I'll ride along in case Brodie needs help."

"But Colin—"

Wrapping an arm around her waist, Colin pulled her close. "There'll be no arguing on this. We don't know what happened and I'll not put you in danger. We'll get this done, then meet you at the hotel for supper." He kissed her temple.

Her eyes sparked as she pushed him away. "You'll not be treating me like a child, Colin MacLaren. I can ride and shoot as well as anyone."

Colin and Brodie laughed at her overblown boast.

"Sarah, lass, you can ride and shoot a gun. It's your aim we question." Flashing her a cocky grin, Colin turned to Brodie. "You ready?"

Brodie glanced at Maggie, seeing rage and fear in her eyes. He hoped she'd give him no trouble.

"Come on, Mrs. Stoddard. It's time we discover if you really did kill your husband."

Maggie's stomach churned the entire ride to the cabin. She didn't have a horse, so Brodie had settled her in front of him, an arm holding her tight to his chest. It wasn't the closeness she minded. His warm body helped protect her from the chilling winds whipping through the trees. What bothered her was the way her body responded to being held so close, almost intimately, against him.

And the way he continued to call her *Mrs. Stoddard.*

"Do we continue on this trail?" Brodie's warm breath caressed her neck. He should be ashamed, knowing quite well what he was doing, but couldn't seem to muster any guilt at the way her body trembled against his. She probably wasn't even aware of her effect on him or how much he enjoyed it.

"About another mile, then the trail narrows as we get closer to the cabin." Adjusting herself in front of him, she heard Brodie groan. "I'm sorry. Did I hurt you?"

Brodie gritted his teeth, pulling her tight to stop her from squirming. Maggie's voice held no trace of mockery, and he realized she had no idea how his body had responded to her slight movement.

He sucked in a breath. "No. I'm fine." It had been a stupid idea to have her ride in front of him. He told himself the decision saved time by not having to locate and saddle a horse for her. Feeling moisture building along his brow, Brodie acknowledged the real reason. He'd been fascinated by her from the moment she'd stormed into the jail.

The mere presence of a woman had never affected him the way Maggie did. No matter how much he pondered the reason, he couldn't come up with a satisfactory answer. Yes, even with her disheveled appearance, she was pretty—beautiful in fact. The ordeal she'd been through, the fear he saw on her face, enraged him. Her determination to report what happened, even if it meant going to jail, moved him in a way he couldn't define. He'd never met a woman who seemed so innocent, so full of contradictions. Perhaps his attraction was pure fascination and nothing more.

"There." Maggie pointed to a rundown cabin hidden in the trees ahead.

Colin arrived first, dismounted, then drew his gun. A moment later, he helped Maggie to the ground and waited for Brodie.

"Show us where you left him." Brodie stepped toward the open door, then stopped as he glanced around the interior.

Maggie moved in front of him, then drew back, a hand coming to her throat.

"He's gone." Turning in a circle, she scanned the room. "He was right there." She pointed to a spot close to the fireplace.

Kneeling down, Brodie touched an almost dry stain on the floor. Rubbing it between his fingers, he glanced up at Colin. "Appears to be blood."

Colin continued to search, finding nothing. "If he were bleeding, he would've left a trail. I don't find anything."

"Let's take a look outside." Brodie led the way to the back of the cabin, searching the bushes, around the woodpile, and inside a poorly maintained stable. Pushing his hat back on his head, he furrowed his brows. "You probably knocked him out. Once he regained consciousness, he got on his horse and rode out."

Maggie nodded, hoping it were true, believing she couldn't be that lucky.

"Brodie," Colin called from behind the stable. "There's something you need to see."

Maggie followed, stopping when she saw what appeared to be a shallow grave.

Colin picked up a handful of dirt, letting it fall through his fingers. "Fresh. My guess is it's a few hours old. If it were longer, there'd be a crust on top from last night's drizzle, and possibly animal markings."

Brodie's blood went cold at the discovery. He'd hoped whatever they found would clear Maggie. The mound of dirt before him didn't bode well for her.

"I'll get a shovel." Brodie continued to survey the area as he walked back to the stable.

"Get two, Brodie. I'll look for a blanket."

Maggie continued to stare at the mound of dirt. It hadn't been there when she fled and ran toward Conviction, leaving Arnie's crumpled body on the floor of the cabin.

Weeks ago, after a fight with Arnie, his younger brother, Joel, had ridden off. She didn't want to think about the reason for their fight, knowing he'd left because of her. Arnie would've killed him if he'd stayed. After Joel left, Arnie sent their middle brother, Syd, to San Francisco. He hadn't returned.

"You'll need to step away."

Maggie startled at Brodie's voice, his appearance pulling her from thoughts of Joel and Syd. Without a word, she moved several feet away, watching as the two men began to dig. It didn't take long before they spotted clothing, the body lying face down. She stifled a gasp, her body going still when she recognized the shirt Arnie had been wearing.

"Do you recognize him?" Brodie asked, seeing her ashen expression.

"It's Arnie." She backed away, shaking her head, glancing between Brodie and Colin. "He was in the cabin when I left. How could he be here? I don't understand."

Brodie didn't know what to make of her claim of possibly killing Arnie, then finding his body buried behind the stable. Kneeling down, he brushed away more dirt before his gaze caught sight of a wound on the back of his head where Maggie had landed her blow. Turning the body over, he sucked in a breath.

"Colin. Take a look at this."

Bending down, Colin stared at Arnie's face, which was bludgeoned beyond recognition.

Glancing over his shoulder, Brodie confirmed Maggie hadn't tried to get away. He wondered what thoughts were running through her mind as she looked at the body of the man who'd caused her so much pain. A man she may have murdered.

Brodie stood, brushing dirt from his pants, then his hands.

"How many times did you say you hit your husband?" he asked Maggie as he moved toward her.

"He was *not* my husband," Maggie hissed, then calmed herself, knowing getting angry with the sheriff wouldn't help her at all. "Once, on the back of his head."

"You didn't hit him anywhere else?"

She tried to glance around him at the body, but he blocked her view.

"No, it was once. I'm certain of that."

"What did you use?"

"The first thing I could pick up—my iron skillet. I don't understand, Sheriff. Are you saying he was hit more than once?"

"I'll look inside for the skillet, Brodie." Colin gave him a meaningful glance as he left them alone.

Maggie watched him walk away, fear gripping her.

Brodie crossed his arms and studied Maggie, waiting until she swung her gaze back to his.

"We're going to take the body to town for the doctor to examine, then you're going to tell me again what happened this morning."

"But, I—"

Brodie held up a hand to stop her at the same time Colin walked toward them, an iron skillet in his hand.

Brodie's steely gaze bored into hers as he pulled a set of handcuffs from a pocket. "Marguerite King Stoddard, I'm placing you under arrest for killing your husband, Arnold Stoddard."

"Wait." She shot a look at Arnie's body, her stomach roiling at a face so smashed no one would be able to recognize him. She tried to twist away as Brodie grasped her arm. "I hit him on the back of the head, not his face."

"We'll talk about it in town," Brodie answered.

"No." She ripped her arm from his hand, then walked to the shallow grave and pointed. "I didn't do that to him. I hit him once and he dropped to the ground. We were inside the cabin, not outside."

"Enough. You'll have your time before a judge." Brodie gripped her tighter this time. "I don't want to hear any more lies, Mrs. Stoddard. No matter what he did to you, I'll expect the truth about how he died."

"I came to you, told you what I did. I didn't do what you see there." Panic rose as tears welled in her eyes. "You have to believe me."

Yanking her around to face him, he grasped her shoulders. "I don't need to believe anything, Mrs. Stoddard. You're the one who'll have to tell a judge and convince a jury. Until then, you'll be a guest in my jail."

Chapter Three

"Are you sure about this, Brodie?" Colin lowered himself into a chair as Brodie walked in from locking the cell door behind Maggie.

Tossing the keys on his desk, he let out a heavy sigh. "What would you have me do, Colin? She admitted hitting him, thought she'd killed him."

"Aye, she admitted hitting him on the *back* of the head. Do you think she bludgeoned him, dragged him outside, and buried him?"

Removing his hat, Brodie ran a hand through his hair. It had taken both of them to carry the body into the doctor's office so he could provide his opinion on the man's death and check for other wounds. Brodie guessed the man had been a little under six feet tall and well over two hundred pounds. About five-foot-five and whisper thin, he'd be surprised if Maggie weighed more than a hundred twenty—much too small to carry Stoddard outside. Although he hadn't studied the area as he should've, there was no indication Arnie had been dragged from the cabin.

"I don't know and it's not my job to decide. She'll get a trial when the judge comes to town. The jury will determine her fate, not me." As much as he believed what he said, he also knew another trip to the cabin was needed to discover what had been missed.

"When is the judge expected?"

"A few more weeks." Sitting down, he pinched the bridge of his nose. "I could take her to San Francisco for trial, but I've no one to keep watch on the town while I'm gone." Strumming his fingers on the desk, he looked past Colin when the door opened.

"I heard you arrested a woman, Sheriff." Jack strolled inside, shutting the door and taking a seat as if he were an actual deputy.

"Don't you have work to do somewhere else, Jack?" Exhaustion forced Brodie's patience to a thin line.

"Nope. Thought I'd help you out. You know, like watch the prisoner while you have supper."

"A wonderful idea, lad." Colin stood, ignoring Brodie's fierce expression. "Sarah is expecting us for supper. It will be good for you to get out of here for a while."

"He's right, Sheriff." Jack flashed him a smile.

Brodie sent each an exasperated glare. "You don't go anywhere while I'm gone, Jack. Don't go back to the cell to talk to her, and do not, under any circumstances, unlock the cell. I'll bring her supper when I return. Do you understand?"

Jack almost danced with excited energy. "I sure do, Sheriff. I'll stay right here at the desk until you get back. You can count on me."

Slamming his hat down on his head, Brodie walked toward the door. "Don't let me down, or this will be your first and last day sitting at that desk."

Slapping Brodie on the back, Colin chuckled as they crossed the street. "So is this what you expected when you took the job?"

"Hell no. Drunks, an occasional theft or mischievous prank, saloon brawls, certainly cattle rustling. A woman murdering her husband never crossed my mind."

"According to her, she wasn't married to Stoddard, not legally anyway." Colin sobered as he thought through what he knew. "A good lawyer could weave a tale of her being justified in getting away by any means necessary. Being kidnapped, held as a prisoner, and beaten wouldn't sit well with people around here. Do you know of a good lawyer in Conviction?

Someone who's defended someone for murder and not just public drunkenness?"

"No. It appears I'd better start looking." As the sheriff, he couldn't do much to help her, other than gather all the evidence he could find and locate a decent lawyer. The rest would be up to her.

Brodie opened the door of the restaurant, seeing an anxious Sarah perched on the edge of her chair. A broad smile flashed across her face when she spotted them. "The lass is glad to have you back, Colin, although I don't know why." For the first time all day, he relaxed. The peaceful moment didn't last long.

Waiting until they took their seats, Sarah speared Brodie with an icy glare.

"I hear you arrested that poor girl for killing the man who kidnapped and forced himself on her."

"Can we let Brodie eat before rounding on him, lass? It's not been a good day for him, either." Colin leaned over to place a kiss on her cheek.

"Not a good day? Maggie King is sitting in a cell for doing what was right, and Brodie is sitting in a nice restaurant." Sarah sucked in a breath, then let it out in a slow whoosh, sending Brodie a conciliatory look. "I know you must do your job, but I don't have to like it."

"Aye, you don't have to like it, and neither do I. You and Colin were both there when she confessed. I've no choice now that we found a body." He nodded when the server arrived with two whiskeys for Colin and him, and a switchel for Sarah.

Stirring her drink made of water, vinegar, honey, and ginger, she took a sip and smiled. "I would ride all the way to town just to get a glass of this."

"Not drinking whiskey tonight, Sarah?" Brodie asked, nodding toward her glass. "I've never known you to pass up a whiskey when you're off the ranch."

Colin picked up Sarah's hand, brushing his lips across her knuckles. She nodded at his unasked question.

"We have news." Colin settled her hand in his lap, waiting for Brodie to respond.

Brodie's hand stilled as he glanced between the two. "What news?"

"Sarah is with child." Colin's broad smile lit his face.

His eyes widening, Brodie stood, walked around the table, and leaned down to kiss Sarah on the cheek, then clasped Colin on the shoulder.

"It is not just news. It's *magnificent* news. I'm certain the family is excited."

Colin shook his head. "We came to town to see the doctor and make sure what Sarah thought was true. We've yet to tell the family."

Sitting back down, Brodie picked up his glass for a toast. "Then I'm honored to be the first to know." After being almost shunned for weeks by his family, Brodie couldn't explain what it meant for him to be the first to learn they were having a baby. "To Sarah, Colin, and the wee bairn."

Sarah blushed as she took a sip of her drink.

"The doctor told you not to drink whiskey?" Brodie asked, setting his glass down.

"Nae." Sarah shook her head. "He said an occasional sherry or wine could be medicinal. The man was not so approving of whiskey. I don't much like sherry or wine so..."

"You drink it when Kyla pours you a glass."

"Aye, Brodie. To be polite. And don't you be telling Kyla that or there'll be hell to pay." Sarah sent him a withering glare. She loved Colin's mother and never wanted to hurt her feelings.

"You know Ma wouldn't care if you told her. Maybe it's time you confess about the sherry." Colin leaned back as the server set down their meals of sliced beef, roasted potatoes, beans, and biscuits.

"Aye. The best time would be when you tell everyone about the baby," Brodie suggested, cutting into his roast. "Catch her at a good time."

They ate in silence, enjoying the meal and each other's company. After the waiter delivered dessert and filled their coffee cups, Brodie's face grew serious. He leaned forward, lowering his voice.

"Maggie will need a lawyer and I've no idea what to tell her."

"Surely there is someone in town who can take her case." Colin sipped his coffee, glancing over the rim at his wife, a warm sensation growing deep in his belly. He wanted to finish supper, then take her upstairs and into their bed.

"There are three I know about. The best one is August Fielder."

"Aye. Everyone knows Fielder is the best, but I've heard he's so busy with his other businesses he never practices anymore."

"I've heard the same. There is one who moved here from back east a year ago. He's older and spends most of his time playing cards and drinking at Buckie's. The other hung up a shingle, but no one knows anything about him, except he's from Louisiana." Brodie rubbed his chin, studying the liquid in his cup. It wasn't his place to track down a good lawyer. His job was to hold her for trial, nothing more.

"You don't sound comfortable with either." Sarah sat back, folding her arms over her stomach.

"I don't have to be comfortable. Mrs. Stoddard does."

"Why do you insist on calling her by the name of the man who hurt her when she's made it clear they weren't married? The least you could do is call her Maggie King, as she's asked." Sarah still felt raw about the young woman being jailed, even though she understood Brodie's reasons.

"Agreed, lass. I'll do my best to remember." He'd made it a point to call her Mrs. Stoddard. Doing so helped him keep his distance and perspective. Neither Sarah nor Colin knew about or would understand the attraction he felt for Maggie, the strong need he had to protect and take care of her. A need that could get him in trouble if he acted on it. It would take all his willpower to douse his growing desire and stay away from her until the judge came to town.

"I'll send inquiries to San Francisco and Sacramento. Maybe a lawyer there would be willing to travel here and defend her, although I doubt she has money to pay." Colin drained his coffee and set the cup aside.

"Nae, don't waste your time. The lass has no money and few, if any, friends. I can ask around about a lawyer. Surely there are others besides the two I know about. I'll also send a telegram to Denver. She may have family looking for her." Brodie pushed his chair back and reached into his pocket.

Colin held up his hand. "I'm paying for supper tonight. You need to get back to the jail and make sure your new deputy is doing his job."

"You don't need to tell me, and he isn't a deputy—yet. As I said, it may be his first and last chance at being in charge of a prisoner."

MacLaren's Circle M Ranch

"Come on, Bram. Brace up the end so I can secure it." Quinn groaned under the weight of the large log. One of his younger brothers, Bram, worked alongside him, as did Brodie's younger brother, Fletcher. The addition to one of their barns was long overdue. "That's it, lad."

"I thought you said this part would only take a couple hours." At eighteen, Fletcher stood almost as tall as the oldest MacLaren cousins, including Brodie.

"You complaining already? Wait until we get to the hard part." A year older than Fletcher, Bram flashed him a smile as he stepped away, slapping his hands on his pants.

"And where are Cam and Sean? Shouldn't they be helping?" Fletcher referred to his other cousins, Camden and Sean.

"Stop your whining, Fletch. You know both are with the herd. They'll be here when they can." Quinn looked at what they'd accomplished, shooting a satisfied grin at Blaine.

Brodie, Colin, Quinn, and Blaine had grown up practically joined at the hips. Camden, Bram, Fletcher, and Sean were similar, seldom separated, and now of age to take on more responsibilities.

"We may have this finished before Colin and Sarah return." Blaine scooped water from a nearby pale, poured it over his head, then shook his hair. The cold October air should've made him shiver. Instead, he felt refreshed.

"Ach." Quinn stepped away, too late to miss being sprayed with water. "Watch what you're doing." Shoving Blaine's shoulder, he laughed. Sobering, he remembered all the good times he'd shared with the oldest cousins. He missed Brodie, and with Colin married, he didn't have much free time.

"Well, look there." Blaine pointed to the trail from town. "Looks like Colin and Sarah."

"Aye, it's them." Quinn tugged his hat lower on his forehead and turned toward the others. "All right, lads. Let's finish this last part then get back to the other chores."

"I wonder if he spoke to Brodie." Of all of them, Blaine understood his cousin's need to fulfill his dream of being a lawman. He might not have gone searching for work as a sheriff or marshal, or even a Texas Ranger, but he'd accepted the job when offered, disappointing his parents and surprising many in the family.

"Appears we'll be finding out." Quinn set down the tool he'd been holding, straightening when the wagon came to a stop. "Welcome back."

Colin acknowledged the greeting then jumped down, reaching up to help Sarah. Setting her on the ground, he turned to survey the log addition, walking around to study what they'd accomplished since they'd left.

"Looks good, lads. When will you finish?"

"Two more days if we can get the laddies here to work harder." Quinn shot a glance at Bram and Fletcher.

"Aye, if we can get Cam and Sean to stop what they're doing long enough to do some real work," Bram joked, noticing something in

Sarah's expression he hadn't seen before. "What is it, lass? Are you feeling all right?"

She placed a hand on her stomach and swayed slightly, her face going pale.

"What is it?" Colin's expression grew serious as he wrapped an arm around her waist and pulled her to him.

"Ach, it's nothing. I'm just tired and a bit chilled. I'd better go inside and lay down for a spell." Her strained smile didn't make Colin feel any better.

"I'll go with you."

"Nae. It's right there." She nodded to the large house about thirty feet away. "You stay here and help. I'll be fine. I promise."

Colin watched her leave, concern wrapping around him.

"What's going on?" Blaine stood beside him, following his gaze, seeing the worry etched on his brother's face.

Colin saw Quinn's brows furrowed and motioned him over. "We've not told Ma yet, so don't say anything. Sarah is with child. It's one reason we went into town. To see the doctor."

"Congratulations, brother." Blaine clasped him on the shoulder, his voice low so the others wouldn't hear.

"Are you pleased with the news, Colin?" Quinn moved to stand in front of him, his face neutral.

"Aye, I am. It's just..."

"She'll be fine, if that's what concerns you. You know the women won't let anything happen to her or the baby. Ma may not even let Sarah out of her sight."

"I know, Blaine, but ..." Colin drew in an unsteady breath. "So much can happen."

"Are we going to get back to work or are you laggards going to leave it up to Fletch and me?" Bram's question had the three turning away from the house.

"Who are you calling a laggard?" Quinn mumbled a few choice words as he returned to work.

"They're right," Colin said, following Quinn. "We should do as much as we can before Ma calls us for dinner."

"Wait, Colin." He turned back around at the question in Blaine's voice. "Did you see Brodie?"

"Aye. Let's finish, then I'll tell you lads all about our visit."

"He arrested a *woman*?" Blaine almost choked on the words.

"It doesn't sound like he had much choice." A slow smile crossed Quinn's face. "Is she pretty?"

"Does it matter?" Colin asked, shaking his head.

"Well, is she?"

Colin sighed. "Yes, quite pretty. But don't go telling Sarah I said that."

"Ach...you know I won't. Her being beautiful is going to muddle Brodie's mind. A female in jail for killing a man who kidnapped and who knows did what else to her."

"*Possibly* killing a man, Quinn. We found him in a shallow grave with his face bashed in. She swears she hit him once on the back of the head, then ran. Brodie had to weigh her story against what we found. From what I saw, he had no choice, lads." Colin picked up a handful of dirt, letting it sift through his fingers. "It's a mess is all I'm saying."

They sat on the ground with their backs against the barn wall, each with a cooling cup of coffee in hand. Dinner had gone much as Colin expected after they made the announcement about Sarah being pregnant. His ma, Kyla, yelped with surprise, as did the rest of those at the table. When dinner ended, and over Sarah's and Colin's protests, she declared supper would be a special affair with the entire family invited—and she expected the cousins to spread the word.

Colin had smiled at his mother's enthusiasm. As tired as Sarah was, he knew she wouldn't spoil Kyla's plans. If her mother-in-law wanted a celebration for the coming baby, so be it.

From where the men sat by the barn, Colin could see their upstairs bedroom window, knowing Sarah would be sound asleep. Before nodding off, she'd left firm instructions for him to wake her at least two hours before supper. It was certain he'd hear of it when she woke to find her directive had been ignored.Quinn shifted on the hard ground, bending his knees to rest his arms on them. "I should ride into town. It's been too long since I spent time with Brodie."

"Although he said nothing, I believe he's missing the family. I'm certain he'd welcome company, even a lad as tiresome as you." Colin laughed when Quinn reached over to thwack him on the back of his head.

"I need to make a trip into town for supplies. You can ride along, Quinn." Blaine stood, dusting off his backside. "It's time I got back to work. You reprobates can stay and talk if you've a mind."

Quinn stared after Blaine, cocking a brow at Colin. "Reprobate?"

Colin chuckled. "Seems my younger brother has gotten to the letter *R* in the dictionary."

"I wish he'd finish it," Quinn muttered. "I'm tired of him calling me something and me having no idea what it means."

Chapter Four

"Ach. Where is that girl?" Quinn's mother, Audrey, stood with hands on her hips, staring out at the open pasture. "Your sister is trying my patience."

"She tries everyone's patience, Ma. I'll ride out, see if I can find her." Quinn glanced at the other men who'd come in from their work to get ready for the lavish supper Kyla had prepared.

"Nae. You'll not go." Audrey crossed her arms, her eyes flaring in frustration. "If she gets lost or hurt, it will be the lass's fault. As much as she's been warned, Heather is determined to go her own way."

"Alone." Caleb Stewart wiped his wet hands on his pants, as frustrated as Audrey when it came to Heather.

He'd been part of the original wagon train the MacLarens took when they left Pennsylvania. The MacLarens had split off to finish their journey to Northern California, while Caleb's family ended up in Oregon. They'd reconnected when Colin came for Sarah, the MacLaren cousins inviting him to journey to Circle M Ranch at the base of Boundary

Mountain. He'd jumped at the offer and now found himself one of few outsiders who worked alongside the MacLarens. A job which included almost daily contact with Quinn's younger sister, Heather.

"Aye, Caleb. The lass is set on besting the men, no matter the task. Well, I've lost my patience with her." Audrey turned, stomping back into the kitchen to join Kyla and most of the female MacLarens to finish supper preparations.

"I'll go after Heather, Quinn." Caleb held up a hand when Quinn began to protest. "You live in the same house with her. No sense in you incurring her wrath, listening to her complain and storm around while everyone's trying to stay out of her way. At least I'm able to bunk down wherever I choose." Caleb strapped on the gun belt he'd hung on a post. "Besides, I think I know where she is."

"And how is that?" Blaine asked from a few feet away.

Caleb scratched his head, a sheepish grin crossing his face. "We had a bit of a disagreement over a few cattle she thought had crossed onto the neighbor's land. I disagreed with her. The tracks indicated the steers had wandered into a ravine. She'd have none of it and took off. My guess is she's camping out, embarrassed about being wrong, waiting to ride in when we're all asleep."

"Stubborn wench," Quinn muttered. "She hates being wrong about anything. If Da were still alive, she'd get a good talking to, or worse, for the way she behaves. If it weren't for Ma, I'd leave her to get into any trouble she wanted—as long as it didn't affect the rest of us."

"You say that now, but you'd be the first to protect her if she were in real trouble." Blaine understood how Quinn felt about Heather. Most of the family felt the same. "I'll ride with you, Caleb. You shouldn't be facing her alone."

"I won't argue with you, Blaine, but I'll go alone. The woman is a frustrating lass. Does she scare me? Not at all, although she does get my blood boiling, and not in a good way." Walking toward the barn, Caleb glanced over his shoulder. "Save me some food, lads. I'll be back as soon as I can—with the missing MacLaren."

"Hungry?" Brodie carried a tray laden with food toward the cell, noting his question had no effect on Maggie. "It's beef stew and biscuits." He set the tray down, then put the key in the cell door. "I'm going to unlock this, so don't do anything foolish."

The last remark got her attention and she swiveled around to face him. The icy glare didn't surprise Brodie as much as the way she stepped forward, as if she planned to walk right through him. Instead, she stopped a foot away, hands fisted on her hips.

His gaze raked over her. With all she'd been through—the long journey to town on foot, the events at the cabin, being locked in a cell—Maggie was still the most beautiful woman he'd ever seen.

"Sheriff, are you afraid I'll overpower you and escape? After all, I *am* a dangerous woman."

She hadn't intended her bravado to have much of an impact on the young lawman, so it surprised her when he reached out to grip her wrist, drawing her to within inches of his face.

"I'd be careful about how you approach a man wearing a gun, Mrs. Stoddard. Some might take it as a threat."

She gasped. The words were soft, almost intimate, as his warm breath washed across her face.

"This will go better for both of us if you keep your distance from me." Brodie stared into the clearest blue eyes he'd ever seen, seeing them widen at the same time she tried to pull free of his grip. He held her firm, not wanting to let go, a heat he hadn't expected coursing through his body. Feeling a bead of moisture form on his brow, Brodie dropped her wrist. "Am I making myself clear?"

Moving away, he watched as she rubbed her wrist, knowing his grip hadn't been painful. He wondered if she'd felt the same unsettling sensation he had at their touch, and if she were trying to rub away the unwelcome awareness.

Taking a step away, she swallowed the lump in her throat, willing her voice to sound calm and strong. "Quite clear, Sheriff." She backed up to the far wall, allowing him to set the tray on the bed.

"You should eat it while it's hot." He glanced up in time to see her tongue dart out to moisten her generous, raspberry-colored lips. The intense urge to grab her, haul her to him, and taste her sweetness crashed over Brodie, prompting him to stagger backward. He let out a breath, hoping she couldn't detect the war raging within him or the effect she had on him.

Maggie glanced at the food, then back at Brodie, her face showing no emotion or recognition of Brodie's desperate state. Turning her back to him, she stared up at the window a foot above her head.

"I wouldn't think about trying to escape. You wouldn't get far."

Shutting and locking the cell door, Brodie stared at her, wishing she'd turn around, display more of the spunk she'd shown a few minutes before. Letting out a sigh, he left her alone, hoping she'd take his advice and eat.

Maggie heard his retreating footsteps, letting the air whoosh from her lungs as her shoulders relaxed. She'd meant to goad him, push a little, demonstrate how much she hated him. His resulting response took her by surprise, his touch overwhelming her, causing her stomach to flip.

Arnie had been her only experience with men. Over the months she'd been under his control, he had come to her a dozen times, drunk, crude, and always rough. He'd always left her with a sick feeling in the pit of her stomach, wanting nothing more than to scrub her body clean, removing any trace of what they'd done. The fact there'd been no children from the disgusting encounters had been a blessing.

She didn't know what to expect of other men, wondering if Arnie's actions were normal. So many nights, she lay awake, wishing he'd drink himself into a stupor and never wake up, never again force her to submit to his demands. One particular night, his brutality had been absolute, leaving her with a broken arm, swollen face, and bruises across her chest and arms. Arnie's brother, Joel, had tried to help her, receiving a licking from Arnie for his efforts.

The difference in the brothers confused her, as did the change in moods she saw in Sheriff MacLaren. One moment, his light touch and soft words gave her comfort. Other times, his harsh tone and severe manner had her believing he was no better than Arnie.

"Arnie," she snorted. If only she'd been able to get away, leave him and the terror behind, she wouldn't be sitting in this cell, at the mercy of a man who knew nothing of what she'd experienced.

Closing her eyes, Maggie sat down on the thin pad, inhaling the aroma of cooked beef. Her stomach rumbled. Placing a hand over it, she realized it had been over a day since she'd eaten. As much as she wanted to fill the void inside her, she pushed the tray away, feeling too nauseous to swallow. She'd felt woozy and unwell since Arnie let out a groan and slipped to the floor of the cabin. Thinking the law would understand her position and protect her, she foolishly sought their help. Maggie had never regretted anything more. Now she sat in the jail, a prisoner of a by-the-book lawman. A man who sucked all the air from around her whenever he was near, making her heart beat uncontrollably.

Spending hours alone in a cell allowed for much reflection. After considering all that had happened, Maggie knew she needed two kinds of defenses. One for the death of Arnie, and one to shield her from the growing attraction to the hard-nosed sheriff.

Brodie slid the key onto the hook, then collapsed into a chair. Rubbing his eyes, he chastised himself for what he'd done in the cell. Although new to the job, he'd had his share of overnight guests in the jail. Each had been treated with respect, fed, and allowed to walk around out back after taking care of business. His behavior toward Maggie, a frightened young woman, had been inexcusable.

The moment she'd stepped within his reach, he'd felt a strong craving to wrap an arm around her waist and draw her to him. Her length to his, chest to chest. The rush of desire sweeping through his body when he gripped her wrist stunned him. He may not have as much experience with women as others, but he'd never felt anything like the strong craving burning through him.

Burying his face in his hands, he let out a groan. He needed sleep...and more help. Leaning back in the chair, he closed his eyes, willing himself to forget the woman in the cell a few feet away and concentrate on finding at least one new deputy. Instead, his head spun with visions of the red-haired prisoner with the clearest blue eyes he'd ever seen. Eyes a man could get lost in, making him act in ways he'd later regret.

Pulling out a drawer, he grabbed the few responses he'd received from his latest telegrams to nearby towns. He read through each, setting them aside before picking one back up to read again.

Ex-Union officer. Skilled with gun. Experienced lawman. Looking for work out west. Contact me at Bellamy Hotel, Independence, Missouri. Nathan Hollis.

Brodie pulled out the pocket watch his father had given him the year before. Ewan's father had given it to him when he was Brodie's age. Whenever he held the precious timepiece, Brodie's chest constricted, knowing it was a distinct honor to own it. Staring out the front window, he thought of his mother and father, wondering if they would ever accept his desire to become a lawman. They hadn't tried to contact him or send a message since the night he'd announced his decision. He prayed they'd eventually come around.

"Evening, Sheriff." Jack came bursting into the office as if he belonged there. "Anything I can do to help out tonight?"

No matter his reservations, Brodie had to smile at the young man's enthusiasm.

"You came at the right time, lad. I need someone to keep watch on Miss King while I send a telegram."

Jack rubbed his jaw, his brows furrowing. "I think the telegraph office is closed for the night."

"I'm certain that's true. I also know where to find the clerk." When he'd accepted the badge, Brodie had made it clear to Ira Greene that the telegraph office was never closed when he needed to send a telegram. "Keep away from the back, Jack. All I need you to do is talk to anyone who comes in while I'm gone."

"Don't worry, Sheriff. I'll take care of everything."

Aye. That's what worries me, Brodie thought as he grabbed his hat and stepped outside.

"Sheriff, are you out there?" Maggie stood, her hands grasping the bars. "Sheriff MacLaren, I need to speak with you."

Jack sat straighter in his chair, torn about what do. Brodie hadn't been gone long, but he had been specific about not going back to the cells. Considering it a moment, deciding it would be best to wait, he settled back into his chair, folding his hands on the desk.

"Sheriff, I really must speak with you."

Jack mumbled a curse. Certainly the sheriff wouldn't get mad if all he did was find out what she wanted and tell her he would return shortly. He wouldn't take the keys with him—just poke his head around the corner. Feeling better, he glanced around the corner, seeing Maggie gripping the bars with both hands.

"Sheriff MacLaren isn't here, but he'll be back in a bit." Satisfied, he turned to leave.

"Wait. I need help."

The anxiety in her voice worried him enough to shift back around. Jack looked at her, an eyebrow raised in question.

"I, uh...need to use the privy." A red blush crept up her face, her knuckles turning white as they held the bars.

"Well now, I, um...I think you should wait for the sheriff." Flustered, Jack took a step away.

"Deputy, you don't understand. I've been waiting for hours. Please, won't you help me?"

"Look, miss, the sheriff was real clear that I'm not supposed to go near the cell. He'd be darn mad to come back and learn I let you out to use the privy. Sorry, but you'll just need to wait."

"Deputy, *please*." She could feel her face heat. Even with Arnie, she'd never begged to get her business done. "The sheriff doesn't need to know. I promise I'll be quick."

"Ah, hell," Jack muttered, shaking his head.

"I won't say a word to him if you don't." She let go of the bars, letting her arms drop to her sides. "Please, Deputy. It won't take long."

Taking a deep breath, Jack got the keys, then grabbed a pair of handcuffs, sliding them into a pocket. Pulling open a drawer, he picked up a gun Brodie kept in the desk, praying he was making the right decision.

"Don't you try anything. If I suspect you're trying to bamboozle me, you'll be back in this cell and I'll tell the sheriff myself." Jack meant it. If she did anything suspicious, he'd have to tell Brodie, no matter the consequences. "Step back."

"Thank you." The relief in her voice sounded genuine as she moved away.

Holding the gun in one hand, he unlocked the cell. "Here. Put these on." He tossed her the handcuffs.

"But—"

"Don't argue. The sheriff will be back soon and I can't take a chance of you trying to get away." Jack waved the gun a couple times, then glanced over his shoulder. "You'd best hurry or I'll change my mind."

Working fast, she clasped them on each wrist. "All right. Can we go now?"

"It's out that way." Jack nodded to the back door.

Dashing to it, she fumbled with the knob, surprised at how easily it turned.

"Down those steps and out back. I gotta warn you not to try anything."

Stumbling in the dark, she walked behind the jail, spotting the enclosed wooden structure a few feet away. Glancing around, she noted the dark and isolated area around the privy, the door facing away from the jail. Brush and trees surrounded the wooden structure, allowing for some measure of privacy. Not fifty feet away, she saw a livery, knowing there were always horses kept in the stables in back. She could either be hung for stealing a horse or for murdering Arnie. With a horse, she might get far enough away to save herself.

Memorizing what she saw, Maggie pulled the door open and disappeared inside. A few minutes later, she emerged, flashing Jack a grateful smile.

"Thank you, Deputy. I don't know what I would've done if you hadn't agreed to help me."

Jack flushed at the compliment, glancing away, clearing his throat. "Uh, sure..." Waving the gun toward the jail, he stepped behind her, praying Brodie hadn't returned while they were gone.

Maggie walked back into her cell, then turned when she heard it lock behind her.

"Now, put your hands through the bars and I'll unlock the cuffs." The gun shook slightly in one hand as he tried to use the key, not quite getting it to work.

"You may need both hands," Maggie suggested, her mouth curving into a grin.

Jack looked at her, knowing he'd never get her out of those cuffs using one hand. He set the gun and cell keys on the floor behind him.

"Keep your hands where they are, but step back," he ordered, his voice unsteady.

She did as he asked, holding her arms straight out in front of her, creating a distance of a foot between her body and the bars.

Working fast, he unlocked the handcuffs and stuffed them into a pocket before picking up the gun and cell keys. He shot her a quick glance, then returned to the front of the jail.

"Thank you, Deputy. You don't know how much I appreciate your help."

Looking back around the wall, Jack nodded, hoping Brodie wouldn't find out.

Maggie lowered herself onto the uncomfortable mattress. Satisfied she'd learned what she needed, a smirk crossed her face as she processed the possibilities. Soon, she'd be out of there, and it couldn't happen fast enough.

"I can't believe I'm hauling you in here twice in one week, Bob." Brodie walked into the jail, dragging Bob Belford by the collar toward one of the three empty cells. Hefting him onto the bed, Brodie turned the lock, then shook his head. "Does your wife know you're in town drinking?"

Bob rubbed his eyes, trying to focus, his face falling. "You aren't going to tell her, are you, Sheriff?" His slurred words confirmed how much the man already had to drink.

"Who's running the ranch while you're sitting in here sleeping off the whiskey? Your oldest lad is only twelve, right?"

Bob's face lit up. "Thirteen." He said it as if it were justification for his actions. "His brother is almost eleven. Right big boys, too, Sheriff."

Crossing his arms, Brodie stared at the man. The same age as Brodie's father, he owned a sizable spread a few miles south of town. Word was he'd run into trouble, lost some land gambling, lost cattle to rustlers, and now spent a good deal of time drinking at Buckie's Castle. Before he could say more, Bob collapsed on the bed, already snoring.

For a moment, Brodie had forgotten about the woman one cell over. He shot a quick glance at her, seeing her gaze locked on him, her face impassive and cold. As much as he knew Maggie must hate him, he couldn't shake the way her presence affected him. Like a moth to a flame, he was drawn to her, tempted to do things that didn't fit with his position, certainly getting him fired if he acted on them.

He took a step closer to her cell. "Are you doing all right, Miss King?"

She didn't answer, staring a few more seconds before turning her back to him.

Sighing, his shoulders slumping, he walked to the front. Jack had left his seat behind the desk and now sat in a chair by the stove.

"Any problems with the prisoner?" Brodie asked as he removed his gun belt and sat down.

Jack shook his head, looking like a dog shaking off a coat full of water. "Not a peep. Quiet as a mouse. So quiet, I got a little bored sitting around. She's—" Jack stopped when Brodie held up a hand.

"I understand, Jack."

Jack nodded, then jumped up, heading for the door. "Guess I'd better get going. Got lots to do."

Brodie cocked his head as his brows furrowed. "It's after dark, Jack. What are you planning to do?"

"Uh, well...sleep. Yep, it's past my bedtime. Have a good night, Sheriff."

Brodie stared at the closed door, wondering what was going on with him. Although he worked hard and most people liked him, some called Jack addle-brained. Brodie didn't approve of the description and didn't agree with them. Still, something wasn't right with him tonight.

Pushing up from his chair, he marched to the cells, taking another look at Maggie. She sat on the edge of the bed, head bent, hands in her lap. He stood silent, knowing she didn't know he watched. Twice, she stroked her face, and he wondered if it were tears she swiped away. The despondent pose pierced his stoic nature. Swallowing the hard knot in his throat, he turned, pacing back to the front. He could not...would not let her get to him.

As much as her suffering cut deep, causing him to doubt her guilt, he had no proof anyone else had killed Arnie. No footprints, tracks, or evidence anyone else had visited the cabin. And she'd admitted hitting him. Still...

Slumping into his chair, Brodie scrubbed a weary hand down his face. He wanted to believe in her innocence. Opening a drawer, he pulled out a piece of paper and pencil, then started jotting down notes. An hour later, he dropped the pencil, pinching the bridge of his nose. Something didn't make sense. Tomorrow, he'd ride back to the cabin, take a long, hard look around, and hopefully find what he and Colin had missed the first time.

A warning rang in his head. It wasn't his job to find evidence to clear Maggie. He'd done what the town paid him for—use the facts to arrest and jail a suspected killer. It would be up to a good lawyer, not Brodie, to obtain her freedom.

Unfortunately, looking at what he'd written down, all his instincts told him her story was accurate and pointed to her innocence. If he didn't act, any additional evidence could disappear—washed away by rain or obscured by animal tracks. The job fell to him.

Looking around the corner and glancing at her cell, his heart seized at the sight of Maggie curled up on the hard bed, her hands tucked under her cheek. Stepping closer, he could hear her ragged breathing, her breath hitching in her sleep, her body trembling.

Entering the cell, he lifted the edge of the blanket, pulling it over her. The instant his fingers brushed across her shoulder, she tensed, her body beginning to shake. He waited until she stilled, then brushed a strand of hair off her face. She started, turning onto her back, her arms flailing.

"No. Don't." Her panicked voice accompanied her hands punching into the air, as if she were fighting someone off. "Stop...don't touch me." Her words were slurred, yet Brodie understood them. His stomach tightened at the reason for her nightmare.

"Maggie, darlin', wake up." He bent over, stroking her hair. His touch caused her to rear her arm back and swing at him. Leaning to the side, he barely avoided her landing a punch to his jaw. "Maggie, it's a dream. You need to wake up."

Knowing he might be risking a black eye or broken nose, he sat on the edge of the bed. Still asleep, a captive of whatever dream claimed her, she reflexively pushed herself back against the wall.

Stroking her back, he whispered to her in the Gaelic, knowing she'd never understand him. They were words his mother had used when he was young and had nightmares. He stopped for a moment when her body convulsed once more, a pitiful whimper escaping her lips.

Unable to hold back, he wrapped his arms around her, lifting and settling her on his lap. To his surprise, her body relaxed against him, her fingers gripping the front of his shirt.

"There now, lassie. You'll be all right. It was a wee dream." Knowing it was much more, he cursed the man who caused her to carry such a burden. Rocking back and forth, he listened as Maggie's breathing calmed, her body settling into him as if she were meant to be there. A feeling he'd never known ripped through him and all he wanted was to stay there all night, his arms wrapped around her, protecting her.

The frightened woman, who worked to be brave during the day, couldn't control her reactions as she slept. As strong as she tried to be, Maggie King fought demons from her past and a far from certain future. He knew she was scared, and with good reason.

If found guilty, it would be doubtful a judge would order her to hang, but she would spend the rest of her life in prison. Ironic. She'd gone from an innocent young lady to being the prisoner of a man who abused and mistreated her. Now, in her quest for freedom, she'd most likely become a prisoner again. This time, there'd be no escape.

Brodie couldn't let that happen. He had to find a way to help her, prove her innocence. A cold resolve washed over him. It was time someone stepped forward to help her. No matter the consequences, Brodie promised himself he wouldn't stop until he discovered the truth about Arnie Stoddard's death.

Chapter Five

Brodie jerked, reaching for his gun as the door to the jail slammed open. With the bright morning sun behind them, blinding him, he couldn't make out the identity of the two figures standing in the doorway.

"Whoa, Brodie." Quinn stepped inside, his hands raised when he saw the gun pointed his way. "It's your family, come to check on you, lad." A broad smile crossed his face when Brodie walked around the desk, his arms outstretched.

He wrapped Quinn, then Blaine in a quick embrace before stepping back to look at them.

"It's good to see you two scoundrels." After the visit by Colin and Sarah, he'd hoped the rest of the family would come around, pay him a visit. Brodie couldn't believe how good it felt to see his cousins after weeks of silence.

"Scoundrels are we now?" Quinn laughed, slapping Brodie on the back. "I'll have you know we've been shouldering your work and our own since you left."

"Quinn is right," Blaine added, his eyes flashing as he looked around the jail. "Appears you've made no changes since they ran Yost out of Conviction."

The mention of the former sheriff had Brodie wincing. "Aye. I've had little time and no budget. Seems I'll live with it as it is for a while." He motioned to the chairs. "Have a seat and tell me what brings you to town."

"Besides you?" Blaine chuckled.

"I'm flattered, but know you wouldn't have made the trip just to see me." Brodie leaned back in his chair, lacing his hands behind his head.

"Right, but you are the main reason we came *today*. It's been too long and you've made no attempt to come to the ranch. Blaine and I drew the short straws, so it fell on us to make certain you've not gotten yourself into trouble." Quinn shot a look at Blaine and winked.

Brodie held up his hands. "All right. All right. I know I should've ridden out to see Da and Ma, if not the rest of you miscreants. Unfortunately, I've lost my deputies. All the work falls on me."

"Aye, that's what Colin said. Have you had any luck finding replacements?" Quinn leaned forward, resting his arms on his legs.

"There doesn't seem to be much interest in a town as small as Conviction when there are jobs in San Francisco and Sacramento. From what

I've heard, the pay is quite a bit more in those towns."

"So is the danger." Blaine stood to walk around. "At least you aren't risking your life every day in Conviction."

The words had no more than left his mouth when the door burst open, Jack rushing inside.

"Sheriff, you gotta get over to Buckie's Castle." He stopped when he spotted Quinn and Blaine. "Uh…"

"Go ahead, Jack. You've met my cousins, Quinn and Blaine."

"Uh, sure, sure." His head bobbed, a habit when he was excited. "Sheriff, they got trouble at Buckie's."

Sighing, Brodie stood, walking to the door. "What kind of trouble?"

"Some gambler came in on today's riverboat from Sacramento. He's been winning big." Jack looked around, thinking they understood his meaning.

"And?" Brodie prompted, raising an eyebrow.

"I mean *real* big, Sheriff. So much so, they're accusing him of cheating. They got him up against a wall and mean to either hang or shoot him."

Brodie didn't say a word before grabbing his hat and storming outside.

"We're coming, too." Quinn stood, tightening his gun belt, seeing Blaine do the same.

"Want me to stay here, Sheriff? Keep watch on the prisoner?"

"Aye, Jack," Brodie called over his shoulder. "Like before, do not talk to her. If she needs anything, she'll have to wait for me."

"Sure. You know you can depend on me." Jack's grin had Brodie stopping.

"I mean it. You're not to go back there. No matter what."

Jack's eyes flashed before he dropped his gaze to the floor and nodded.

Before Brodie could say anything else, gunfire drew his attention to the saloon. He ran down the street as a second shot rang out, Quinn and Blaine steps behind him. He stopped and spun to face them.

"This isn't your job, lads. I can deal with whatever is happening."

"It's a gang of men, Brodie. You can't face them alone." Quinn's hand rested on the butt of his gun.

"Quinn's right, Brodie. You can't go in there by yourself. Besides, there's nothing you can do if we follow you inside." Blaine's smirk set Brodie off as much as Quinn's fingers twitching on his gun.

Muttering a curse, he dug into his pocket, taking out two badges and tossing one to each man. After Stein Tharaldson suggested he might need to deputize men quickly, he'd carried them as a precaution for weeks. He'd thank Stein later.

"If you're determined to help, you go as my deputies. When it's over, I want those back. I'm going in the front. You two enter through the back. You'll go through a storeroom before entering the bar—"

"We *know* the saloon, Brodie. You're wasting time." Quinn glared at him, ready to deal with whatever was going on inside.

Spinning on his heels, Brodie dashed up the steps and glanced over the top of the double swinging doors. A lone man stood against the wall, guns in both hands pointing toward a crowd of men, two clutching wounds.

"Now, gentlemen, I've already told you. I don't cheat. Never have. There's no need when you possess the skills I do." He flashed a cocky grin, earning him a round of jeers. "As much as I'd like to stay, chat with you charming fellows, I'm afraid this party needs to end." He edged along the wall toward the doors, already aware someone stood outside, guessing it to be the sheriff or one of his deputies. Focusing on movement in the crowd, he stopped, his voice hard. "No one move. There are already two men injured because of your actions. I don't want to shoot anyone else." Waiting until the men backed up, he continued, stopping a foot away from the doors, his gaze still focused on the men inside. "I know you're outside, but I'm not the one you're after. He's standing at the back of the group of men, his back to the bar. He has a dark mustache and short beard, and is wearing a white shirt, brown hat, and coat. Check his pockets. You'll find all you need to arrest him for swindling people out of their hard-earned money."

Brodie stiffened. "I'm Sheriff MacLaren, and I'm going to tell you what you're going to do." He raised his gun, pointed it at the door, and waited.

"I'm afraid I can't oblige you, Sheriff. My job has been to identify the person fleecing funds from unsuspecting gamblers. I've led him to you. Your job is to make an arrest and send him to trial."

The utter confidence in the man's voice stunned and intrigued Brodie. He'd taken control inside the saloon, extricating himself from a dangerous situation, and sounded as if he had no doubt Brodie would believe all of it.

"Who are you?" Brodie pushed one of the doors open enough to spot his prey.

Without taking his focus off the men inside, the man slammed the other door open and slipped out.

"Samuel Covington. Soon to be ex-Pinkerton agent." Glancing over the top of the doors, he lowered his guns, settling them in holsters on each hip. "Appears your men are inside. Perhaps you'd care to join them." Sam turned to leave before feeling Brodie's hand on his arm and seeing the gun the sheriff still held.

"Hold on there, lad. First, you need to show me some type of identification from Pinkerton. Then you'll come back inside with me and identify the man you're accusing of fleecing people. Afterwards, you and I are going to have a long talk." Brodie nodded toward the saloon. "After you."

"And I was so hoping for a quiet lunch," Sam grumbled as he strolled back into the saloon.

Brodie read the telegram from Allan Pinkerton, then passed it to Quinn and Blaine. All of them had been skeptical of Covington's claim of being connected to the agency, even after arresting and searching the man he'd indicated was behind a series of cons covering the area between Newcastle, Sacramento, San Francisco, and Conviction. The discovery of a journal, indicating dates, locations, and amount earned, now rested in a locked drawer in Brodie's desk.

"It says here, *amount earned*. Shouldn't it say stolen?" Quinn smirked.

"For con artists such as David Meeks, the line between earning money and taking it is quite slim. In fact, it is non-existent." Sam leaned back in his chair, crossing his arms. "They do it for the rush, the excitement, not for the end result of money in their pockets."

"Seems odd the money wouldn't be the main factor." Blaine read the telegram once more before handing it back to Brodie.

"Oh, they definitely want the money, but what drives them is the challenge of outsmarting someone else. Meeks and other con men need to prove they're smarter than those who would stop them." Sam winced at the gnawing sensation in his stomach, followed by the unmistakable rumble of hunger. "That's why Pinkerton sent me out here last spring. To prove Meeks wrong by catching him." Standing, he stretched his arms above his head, then cast a look at Brodie. "If you have no further questions, I believe I'll take my leave."

"Hold on, Covington. You said something about becoming an *ex*-Pinkerton agent. What did you mean by that?" Brodie fiddled with the edge of the wanted poster of David Meeks he'd found buried in a drawer.

"I'm taking a leave from the agency. Allan has dominated my time for several years and now is my chance to explore other opportunities."

"In law enforcement?"

Sam's bark of laughter reverberated against the hard walls of the jail. "Not if I can help it."

Brodie nodded. "If you change your mind, come see me. I'm looking for a couple good deputies. The pay isn't great, but it comes with an apartment and monthly food allowance. Might be a way to pass your time in Conviction while helping the town."

Sam narrowed his gaze and studied Brodie, his face neutral as he considered the proposal. "I do understand your predicament, Sheriff, and will be happy to send any prospects to see you. For now, however, I'll have to pass on your generous offer." Settling his hat firmly on his head, he nodded at the three men. "Gentlemen, it's been a pleasure. Perhaps we'll run into each other again."

Quinn waited until Sam closed the door, then turned back to Brodie. "Too bad. He would've made an excellent deputy."

"I'm not giving up yet. Anything can happen before Covington leaves town." A slow smile spread across Brodie's face. *Aye, just about anything.*

Brodie paced back and forth in front of his desk, aware of the dire situation. He had four cells. Three of them were filled, although Bob's wife would be coming to fetch him in the morning. He expected the U.S. Marshal within a few days to transport David Meeks to San Francisco. From there, Brodie didn't care what happened to the man, as long as he never returned to Conviction.

He ran a hand through his hair, then massaged his temples. The slow rise of a headache had started minutes after Quinn and Brodie had left for the Circle M Ranch, promising to ride back on Saturday. He didn't know if he was the reason for them returning so soon or because of the excitement of what had happened today. It didn't matter. Any visit by his family was cause to be thankful.

The dilemma he faced, the reason for his extreme concern, sat alone in cell one. Maggie said little, asking for nothing except an occasional trip out back, but her piercing blue eyes shot daggers through his heart each time their gazes met. He had to find a way to get back to the cabin. Her guilt or innocence, the difference between years of languishing in a filthy prison or a lifetime of freedom, might hinge on what he found.

Resting fisted hands on his hips, Brodie looked up at the ceiling, then let out a slow breath before walking back to the cell.

"Miss King?"

Maggie glanced up, her gaze fixed on some point behind Brodie, as if she couldn't bear to look at him.

"I, uh...came to see if you needed anything. Food, water, a trip out back?"

Resting her hands on either side of her, she pushed up from the bed, walking the short distance to face him.

"A trip out back would be good, Sheriff. Thank you."

He didn't handcuff her or draw his gun. Nothing she'd done indicated a desire to run, escape her confinement in the small cell. Still, he walked by her side, ready to reach out and grab her if she made any move to get away.

Taking care of her business, she stepped out of the privy, looking up at the late afternoon sky. It would be a few hours before complete darkness fell, revealing a thick blanket of twinkling stars. This had always been her favorite time of day, when daylight began to fade. Now it did nothing for her except signify all she'd lost and how her life had changed. Shaking off the morbid thoughts, she glanced at Brodie.

"How long have you lived in Conviction, Sheriff?" She walked along the back wall of the jail, breathing in the fresh air, once more noting anything that might help or hinder her when she did make her escape.

"My family's had a ranch northwest of here for over five years."

She leaned against the wall of the jail, letting her palms brace herself against the rough wood.

"I know about your cousin, Colin, and his wife. There are more of you?"

Brodie chuckled, crossing his arms over his chest, letting his gaze rake over her. Her cheeks reddened at his unconcealed appraisal, but she didn't look away. Instead, she met his assessment with one of her own, her mouth turning up at the corners as her gaze wandered over his slim hips, broad chest and shoulders, settling on his full mouth. Heat flashed through him at the look of approval on her face.

As if they both realized what was happening at the same moment, Brodie stepped a few feet away, Maggie pushing herself from the wall.

Clearing his throat, Brodie fought to remember her question. "Aye, lass. There are quite a number of MacLarens. Two more cousins visited today. Quinn and Blaine. Along with Colin, the four of us used to be closer than..." Pausing, he rephrased what he'd planned to say. "We've been almost inseparable our entire lives."

They both seemed to relax, continuing their brief stroll behind the buildings.

"What changed?"

"Colin married Sarah. I took the job as sheriff." He shrugged, accepting the sad truth. "We aren't laddies any longer, dependent on each other as we once were."

Clasping her hands behind her back, she nodded. "I suppose so. I often wonder what my brothers are doing, wonder if they've changed much. It's been less than two years, but still..."

"How old were you when you met Stoddard?" He hadn't meant to ask the question, didn't need to know more about her than he already did. Maggie's age didn't matter. It only mattered that he held her as a suspect in a murder.

"Eighteen. I'm twenty now." She spoke with a staid calmness, as if detached, speaking of someone else. "I wish I could tell you the time flew by, but that would be a lie." This time, her voice held the bitterness he expected. Closing her eyes to still the moisture beginning to pool, she sucked in a deep breath.

He didn't know what triggered his quick response—her shaky voice, the tremble of her body, or the tears she couldn't hide—but he reached out, wrapping his arms around her and drawing her close. Splaying his hands across her back, he rested his chin on top of her head as she settled her cheek against his chest.

"Shhh, lass. He can no longer hurt you." Brodie's heart pounded, his chest tightening at the same time he tried to provide her comfort. He couldn't imagine the horrors she'd been through. If Arnie weren't already dead, it would've taken all the strength Brodie possessed to not kill the man himself. Feeling the tears soak through his shirt, he drew back, lifting her chin with a finger.

"You must try to believe it will be all right, Maggie."

Her glassy blue eyes stared up at him as the faintest sliver of hope crossed her face. A hope he could encourage or dash with a rash word or careless gesture.

"Do you truly think it will work out for me?"

Brodie didn't know what more to say. Instead, he did the most foolish thing imaginable. Lowering his head, he brushed a gentle kiss across her lips, feeling her tense, then relax against him. He kissed her again, losing himself in the taste and feel of her.

Awareness of the colossal mistake he was making sliced through Brodie an instant before he tightened his hold, fitting Maggie snuggly to his body, his lips pressed against hers, claiming her mouth with fierce desire.

Her heart thundered and stomach churned as Brodie continued his gentle assault. The warmth of his body, the hardness of his chest and muscled arms sheltered her at the same time heat ripped through her, as if she were engulfed in a circle of flames.

Brodie couldn't get her close enough. He wanted to lift her into his arms, carry her to his bed, and lay her down. Kiss every inch of her body, caress…

He pulled back, his abrupt departure causing her to whimper as she buried her face against his throat. They had to stop. *He* had to stop. The madness, which gripped him moments before, gave way to guilt and self-loathing. How could he have surrendered so completely to the charms of one woman? A woman who'd done nothing except look to him for help?

Setting her aside, he straightened, steeling his features. "We need to go back." He could see the slight shiver of her body as she swayed toward him. "Now, Miss King. You need to get back in your cell, and I need to get back to my work."

The hurt in her eyes did nothing to dispel the remorse he felt. He'd crossed a line, and he could blame it on no one except himself.

Chapter Six

Brodie tried to concentrate on the telegram left on his desk while he'd been outside, moments away from ravaging Maggie. It had been almost two hours since he'd locked her back in her cell. Two hours of self-recrimination and doubt. Glancing up as the door opened with a rusty creak, Brodie wasn't surprised to see Jack walk inside, a hesitant smile plastered on his face.

"Got done with my work a little early, Sheriff. You need me to watch the back while you grab supper?"

"Do you know how to use a gun?" Brodie walked around the desk, pulling out the extra Colt pistol. "A gun like this one?"

The question caught Jack by surprise. He quickly recovered, the tentative grin bursting into a full-fledged smile.

"I sure do, Sheriff. My pa taught me how to use a gun, rifle, and shotgun. Been shooting since I was, well...maybe this high." He raised his hand to about three feet above the floor.

"Do you have one of your own?"

Jack's smile faded, his gaze dropping to the floor. "No. Can't say that I do."

Brodie checked his pocket watch, then walked to the front window and glanced outside. "We have a little bit of daylight left. Come on out back. I want you to show me what you can do with this gun."

Fifteen minutes later, the two walked back inside, Brodie still stunned from what he'd seen and Jack with his chest swelling. The noise had been enough to gather a curious crowd of onlookers, who watched Jack pick off one target after another. Their jaws slack, murmuring amongst themselves, Brodie knew the young man had won some much needed respect from the locals.

"Told you I could shoot, Sheriff."

"Aye, you did, lad." Brodie set the gun back in the drawer and slowly closed it, his mind already made up. "You're right. I need to get some supper. When I come back, we'll talk about your new job as deputy."

Brodie pulled his hat lower on his forehead. He'd already buttoned up his jacket as tight as he could, but still felt the brisk breeze whip around him. The early morning mist turned to a light drizzle as he rode out of Conviction and toward the trail leading to the Stoddard cabin.

Once Jack had settled down from his elation at being Conviction's newest, and only, deputy, he'd offered to stay the night to keep watch on the prisoners, allowing Brodie to get some much needed sleep. At first he'd declined, saying he needed Jack in the morning so he could ride to the cabin. In the end, Jack's persuasive protests and Brodie's exhaustion won out, allowing him a few hours of rest before waking at dawn.

"The U.S. Marshal could come anytime to escort Meeks to San Francisco. With Bob gone, all you'll need to do is watch after Miss King. Nothing's changed, except you'll need to accompany her outside when needed. I should be back by noon."

"Don't worry, Sheriff. I'll take care of everything while you're gone." Jack's head bobbed up and down as he spoke, the grin from last night still plastered on his face. With a nod, Brodie had left, not sparing a glance at the cells.

He needed the long ride to clear his head, figure out how he'd lost control. The cold air slicing through his clothes was a welcome distraction, keeping him focused on the journey instead of Maggie. *Maggie,* he thought, a flash of pain gripping his chest.

The confusion on her face when he'd let her go and stepped away kept him awake a good portion of the night. Ignoring the dazed expression and pain sparking in her eyes, he'd taken hold of her elbow, guiding her into the jail and back to her cell, then locked the door before she had a chance to say a word. Although it bothered him more than he wanted to admit, he'd kept his distance. He refused to make the same mistake again, no matter how perfect she felt in his arms.

Rounding the last corner, he spotted the cabin ahead. It looked the same as a few days before when he'd come with Colin and Maggie. Unless there was other family, which Maggie hadn't mentioned, he wouldn't expect anyone else to make the journey to such a remote spot.

Reining Hunter to a stop, he swung to the ground, loosening his coat as the sun's rays pierced the clouds. He scanned the area around the cabin. Nothing moved and he noticed no new tracks since the last visit. Throwing open the front door, he stepped inside, his gaze landing on the spot where Maggie said she'd hit Arnie. Sunlight washed over the area, making it easy to search for any traces of evidence they may have missed.

Brodie knelt down next to the spot he'd first seen blood. It had dried and seeped into the rough wood floor. The size of the stain seemed normal for a gash on the back of his head, but too small for the damage done to Arnie's face. If he'd been killed in the cabin, there would've been much more blood and a definite trail leading outside.

The doctor told Brodie it would've been unlikely Arnie died from the injury to his head. Extreme pain for days, wooziness for several hours, but not death. His face was another matter. The amount of blood loss would've been critical. The doctor believed the crack in his skull, across the middle of his forehead, killed him.

Brodie thought the beating had to have taken place outside. Stepping out the door, he walked the path to where they found the shallow grave. Maggie would've had to carry him out or drag him through the front door, around to the back of the cabin, and behind the stable.

He guessed Maggie weighed no more than a hundred twenty pounds. The doctor said Arnie weighed over two hundred. That ruled out her carrying him. The only way for her to move the body would've been to drag it, yet he couldn't find any markings to support that conclusion—no trail of blood and no evidence a trail had been obscured by brushing it away.

Brodie also reminded himself she'd run for hours to reach Conviction and report what happened. Maggie had been so frantic when she rushed into the jail, he wondered if she even realized what she'd said—admitting she may have killed Arnie. Fear, exhaustion, her first taste of freedom in almost two years—all of that could have contributed to her blurting out a confession.

His instincts, combined with what he'd figured out today, told him Maggie was innocent of dealing the fatal blow to Arnie Stoddard. Knocked him out? Yes. Killed him? Doubtful. Brodie believed a good lawyer could piece together a defense any jury would accept.

A bigger mystery remained. Who arrived at the cabin after Maggie left, and why did they want Arnie Stoddard dead?

Maggie had tossed and turned on the thin, uncomfortable bed all night. Images of Brodie leaning over her, lowering his mouth to capture hers, then pulling away in horror woke her more than once, her clothes soaked, head swirling. The look he'd given her when he'd broken their kiss haunted her. Disgust and pity passed over his face before he'd taken her by the elbow, roughly guiding her back to the jail and her cell.

Opening her eyes to the sound of men talking, she swung her feet to the floor and sat up. Rubbing her eyes, she concentrated on the voices, recognizing Brodie and Jack whispering. All she could make out was Brodie saying he expected to be back by noon.

Drawing her knees up to her chest, she moved back against the wall, closing herself off from everything around her, much as she did while living with Arnie. It was her fantasy world. One she created in order to disappear from the grim reality of what had become her life. Nothing had changed since Arnie died. She still found herself retreating, locking herself off from the rest of the world and the pain it caused. The only way she'd experience peace was to escape. Get as far away from Conviction, and Brodie MacLaren, as possible.

Maggie let out a relieved breath at the sound of the front door closing. Brodie had left, leaving Jack in charge. She smiled, realizing her chance may have come sooner than she expected. An hour passed before she heard the voice of a man she didn't recognize. Within minutes, Jack and the other man, a U.S. Marshal, unlocked David Meeks' cell, escorting him by gunpoint to the front. No one spared her a glance, as if she were invisible. She wished it were true.

Hearing the men leave, she walked to the front of her cell, wrapping her fingers around the bars.

"Deputy?" She waited a moment, then tried again. "Deputy, are you out there?"

"Just hold on a minute. I'm coming." Jack came around the corner. "Been a right busy morning, Miss King."

"I saw you take Mr. Meeks out."

"Yep. That U.S. Marshal arrived right on time. Now, what can I do for you?"

Maggie nodded toward the back.

"Oh, sure. I'll just get the key." A few seconds later he returned with the key in one hand, Brodie's extra gun in the other. "You just step back until I get this door open."

"Thank you, Deputy." Maggie smiled sweetly as she walked past him and out the door to the privy. Glancing around, she saw a few people milling about at the far end of the alley, but they weren't paying them any attention. "I won't take long."

Walking around to the door that faced a large stand of trees, she stepped inside, using the piece of wood in one corner to brace it closed. Steeling herself, Maggie thought through what she was about to do. Earlier, while lying on the bed and staring at the ceiling, she'd gone over the plan until it became real and not another one of her fantasies.

Her stomach roiled as she studied the piece of wood holding the door closed. It had been her plan to use it to knock Jack out, grab his gun, and take off. After what happened to Arnie, the thought of striking another man, someone who'd done her no harm, didn't feel right. Yet she had no choice. This was her one chance at freedom. When Brodie returned, her opportunity would be lost and there might never be another. With a shaky hand, she grasped the rough-hewn stick, tightening her fingers around it. Taking a deep breath, letting it out slowly, she pushed the door open a crack, then shrank back at the sound of gunfire.

"Deputy, you gotta come quick. They're holding a man at gunpoint." She could hear what sounded like boots running on gravel, a man panting as if out of breath.

"I can't come now. I gotta—"

"Jack, the men are threatening to kill him," the man rasped out. "You are the new deputy, right?"

A crack between the boards allowed her enough space to peek through, seeing a short man holding a bowler hat in one hand, gesturing down the street with the other.

"Well, yes, I'm the new deputy, but—"

"They say he tried to sneak out of the hotel without paying his bill. Now they're saying they'll kill him if he doesn't pay up."

She could see the indecision on Jack's face as he glanced over his shoulder at the front of the privy.

"We don't have time for you to fiddle around, Jack. Come on." The man took off at a run, gesturing for Jack to follow.

"Hold on. I'm coming." He faced the privy. "Miss King, now you just stay right there and don't go nowhere. I'll be right back. You hear me?"

She sucked in a breath, not quite believing her good fortune. "Yes, I hear you."

"All right then. You just wait for me." He ran after the man, not once glancing back over his shoulder before he dashed around a corner and disappeared.

Still holding the stick in her hand, she pushed the door open, took a good look around, and ran.

"She told me she'd wait, Sheriff. Promised not to leave." Jack sat outside the jail, his face buried in his hands as he waited for Brodie to dismount and walk up the steps.

"Who, Jack?" Brodie fisted his hands on his hips, glaring at the deputy, a sense of dread washing over him.

Jack glanced up. "Miss King. She—"

Brodie didn't wait to hear the rest. Throwing the door open, he dashed to the back, his jaw dropping, first at her empty cell, then at the man who sat on the bed of another.

"Afternoon, Sheriff. Seems you may be missing a prisoner." Sam Covington crossed his arms and leaned against the wall.

"What the hell are you doing in there, Covington?" Brodie didn't look at him, his gaze still fixed on the cell where he'd left Maggie the night before.

"Seems there's been an unfortunate misunderstanding."

"Another one? Appears those misunderstandings seem to follow you around." Trying to contain his anger before he lit into Jack, Brodie focused on Sam. "What happened?"

"I made the poor choice of staying the night upstairs at Lucky's Saloon. When I awoke, my money, watch, and identification were gone."

"So you took off?"

"Of course not." His indignant voice almost had Brodie grinning. "I decided a trip to the bank was needed, as well as another telegram to Pinkerton. Before I could leave, a couple *gentlemen* tossed me outside and threatened to kill me if I didn't produce the money forthwith. When your new deputy showed up, they pressed charges. So here I am. A guest in your jail."

Muttering a curse, Brodie stared at Sam. "Just what I need," he grumbled before turning to find Jack standing in the doorway of the jail. "Get in here and explain to me how one unarmed female got away from you." He'd calmed down some since hearing of her escape. She couldn't get far on foot without funds or a weapon.

Brodie listened as Jack went through his version of what happened—taking her outside, the gunfire, arresting Sam, and realizing Maggie had run off.

"Did you try to find her?"

Jack shook his head. "I locked Covington inside, then went out to fetch her. Couldn't tell which way she went with all the brush and thick leaves." He jumped out of his chair and began to pace. "She told me she'd wait for me to get back, Sheriff."

Brodie pinched the bridge of his nose, sending an incredulous look at Jack. "And you believed her?"

Jack's face fell as he slumped back into the chair. "Maybe I ain't cut out to be a deputy."

Maybe not, Brodie thought, shifting slightly in his chair to spear Jack with a hard look. "You made a mistake, lad. I'm going to guess you won't make the same one again."

Jack shook his head. "No, sir. I learned my lesson good."

Brodie slapped his hands on the desk and stood. "Aye, I believe you probably did." He had an idea while talking with Jack. One he wanted to put into action right away if he was going to start a search for Maggie.

"Now, why would I want to do that, Sheriff?" Sam paced to the front of the cell, a smile tilting up the corners of his mouth.

"Seems you don't have much of a choice. Lucky's is charging you with trying to avoid paying for your room, you have no identification, meaning no one knows exactly who you are, and you have no way to get more funds. Am I correct?" Brodie crossed his arms, resting his back against the wall separating the cells from the front of the jail. He wouldn't admit he'd hoped the ex-Pinkerton man would make a mistake like this.

"You can vouch for me. You have the telegram Allan Pinkerton sent, confirming my status as an agent." Sam's face hardened when he realized the game Brodie was playing.

"As much as I hate to admit it, I can't seem to recall any telegram."

Sam walked to within a breath of the bars, his gaze fixed on Brodie, who'd moved within a foot of him.

"What do you want, MacLaren?"

"You come to work for me as a deputy. I'll pay the money to Lucky's and get them to drop the charges."

"How long?"

"A year."

Sam's brutal curse echoed off the hard walls of the jail. Whirling around, his back to Brodie, and placing fisted hands on his hips, he looked at the ground, shaking his head as he got himself under control. "Don't you believe that's a little excessive given it's for one night's fare in a brothel."

"Nae. I think it's fair. You could spend quite a long time trying to come up with the money to pay it on your own without a way to prove to the bank who you are, having no way to get in touch with Pinkerton."

Sam turned back to face Brodie. "You owe me a chance to reach him."

"Probably." Brodie's smile caught Sam off guard.

He took a couple steps closer to the bars, his face resigned. "I'll give you six months as your deputy, then I leave."

"Done." Brodie reached his hand through the bars, waiting until Sam walked up and grasped it.

"I'll hand it to you, MacLaren. For a small town sheriff, you drive a hard bargain."

"I do what's needed to get the job done." Brodie unlocked the cell.

"And my first job?" Sam walked through the door and into the front.

"Help me find the missing prisoner."

Chapter Seven

Stumbling from one hiding place to another, Maggie dropped down behind a stack of crates in an alley a few blocks from the jail. She'd been careful, dashing between buildings and crossing streets with little activity. Reaching an area where businesses gave way to private homes, she spotted the empty crates behind a carriage house. Glancing around the corner, she saw an impressive three story home with a wraparound porch and beautiful garden. Even her wildest fantasy never had her living in a place so grand.

"Bring the carriage around to the front, Walter."

"Yes, sir, Mr. Fielder. I'll do it right away."

At the sound of voices, Maggie huddled behind the crates, pulling one in front of her, hoping she wasn't spotted.

"Now, now, Sugar. You just let old Walter get this harness around you so we don't keep Mr. Fielder waiting. That's it, girl."

A few minutes later, the carriage appeared, making a sharp turn down the alley, narrowly missing Maggie by no more than a foot. Letting out a relieved breath, she pushed from her place on the hard dirt, doing her best to brush herself off.

"Hey."

The sharp voice startled her. Whirling around, she saw a young man, no more than fifteen or sixteen, standing by the doors of the carriage house.

"What are you doing back there?" He walked toward her, his face twisted into a menacing scowl.

Maggie almost tripped on the hem of her dress as she stepped away from him. "I, uh..." Turning, she ran.

"Stop!"

The command did nothing to slow her down, but the sound of boots pounding on the hard dirt had her heart racing. When the alley ended, she hesitated for a brief moment, long enough for a strong hand to grip her arm and spin her around.

"Got you." The smirk on his face increased her panic.

Drawing back her arm, she fisted her hand, swinging it forward to connect with his jaw. Dropping her arm, the boy staggered backward, wide eyes signaling his shock. This time Maggie didn't hesitate. Racing between two homes, she made a sharp right turn, then another, then a left turn, hoping to lose him. Seeing the door to a root cellar, she pulled hard, surprised when it opened easily. Taking the steps down, she pulled the door closed and huddled in a far corner behind two wooden barrels.

"Help me, Walter. She ran that way." The boy's voice indicated he wasn't far behind, and someone else had joined him.

Praying she'd made the right decision, Maggie brought her knees to her chest, circling them with her arms, then closed her eyes. Alarm spread through her when she heard voices just outside the cellar. Bringing her hands up, she covered her mouth, afraid she'd cry out in fear. Forcing herself to take deep breaths, she dropped her hands and listened.

"No sign of her. I can't believe it, Walter. I had her in my grasp, and..."

"And what, boy?"

"Ah, nothing. Come on. Mr. Fielder is probably standing out front of the house, wondering where we took off to."

The voices receded, but Maggie didn't move. Adjusting to the dark, her gaze landed on a row of shelves. The top one held several old blankets and what appeared to be old clothes. The rest were filled with jars of food, baskets of fresh vegetables and fruit, and sacks of flour. Her stomach rumbled. She hadn't eaten since supper the night before, but even her hunger wasn't enough to dislodge her from the hiding place.

When the cool dampness of the ground seeped through her clothes, she stood, shivering at the chill. Listening for sounds outside, she stepped toward the shelves, picking up a glass jar. Her mouth watered when she held it up to the small beam of light coming from a crack in the door. Peaches.

Gripping the lid, she twisted, unable to budge it. Picking up her skirt, she wrapped it around the top, then tried again. This time it gave way. Setting the lid aside, she drank the juice and ate several bites of the fruit, sighing at the wonderful taste.

Leaning against a wooden barrel, she finished the jar, trying to decide what to do next. The smart choice would be to wait until sundown when she could travel without anyone noticing. She'd even be able to take one or two jars of food with her. The hazard would be if someone from the house visited the root cellar. Rubbing her eyes, she yawned, feeling a wave of exhaustion spread through her. She weighed her options. Sleep and slipping out of town during the night were the easy choice.

Grabbing an old blanket, she shook it out, then laid it on the ground. Stretching out, she curled into a ball, resting her head on her hands. Within minutes, she fell into a deep sleep.

Not a trace of her, Brodie thought as he hunkered over his evening meal. He and Sam had scoured the town, riding up and down every street and alley, between buildings and homes. They'd seen nothing. If only he'd gotten back to Conviction sooner, he could've told her his thoughts, found her a decent attorney, and given her some assurance all would work out. Then he would've done all he could to find the real killer. Instead, he had to hunt her down and bring her back to jail. An escape attempt never sat well with a judge or jury.

"We can start out at dawn, go door-to-door and ask if anyone's seen her." Sam took another bite of beef stew, his mind working over the possibilities of where she might be hiding. "She's scared. Probably didn't take anything with her, except what she had on, and we know she doesn't have a horse. She's still in Conviction—I'd stake my life on it."

Brodie nodded. "And there are a hundred places she could hide."

"Yes, but she'll have to emerge to eat and, uh...do her business. Someone *will* see her and report her to us. Of course, if the young woman steals a horse..."

Brodie mumbled a curse at the thought of her adding to the growing list of foolish actions that could keep her in jail...or worse.

"Aye. We have to find the lass before she does something more senseless."

Sam set down his fork, leaned back in the chair, and crossed his arms. "You mean other than killing her husband?"

"He wasn't her husband and I don't believe she killed him." Brodie leaned forward, lowering his voice so diners at the other tables couldn't hear. "I explained my reasoning. There's no way she could've gotten Arnie outside without leaving a trace. Stoddard had at least a hundred pounds on her. From the amount of dried blood Colin and I saw in the shallow grave, he died outside from the blows to his skull and face."

"And your doctor is certain it couldn't have been from the crack on the back of his head?" Sam picked up his cup of coffee, taking a sip.

"Aye. That's what he says."

Sam studied Brodie's face, seeing more than just a lawman losing a prisoner. The sheriff had more vested in finding Miss King than he wanted to admit, and Sam was pretty certain he understood the reason.

"Maybe Jack and I should look for her while you find a good attorney."

"Nae. I'll be searching for her, same as you."

"I may be overstepping, but in my experience, it's unwise for a lawman to pursue someone they care about. Are you certain you're the right person to bring her back?" When Brodie stiffened in his chair and stared back without responding, Sam continued. "You want a suggestion?"

Brodie didn't respond as his gaze narrowed.

"Well, I'll give it anyway. You stay here and locate a lawyer who can use what you've found to make a case to the judge and jury. When we find her, and we *will* find her, you'll have someone ready to meet with her, hear her story."

Brodie's jaw worked, but he held his tongue. Standing, never breaking eye contact with Sam, he tossed his napkin down and braced his hands on the table, his eyes signaling his determination.

"Nae, Deputy. If anyone brings the lass in, it will be me."

"What the hell happened? Where's Maggie?" Joel Stoddard stood with his hands clenched at his sides, glaring at his older brother, Syd. They'd never gotten along, but their oldest brother, Arnie, had hated them both, tolerating them enough to use their services when needed. Both had left weeks earlier—Syd to investigate San Francisco banks ripe for robbing, and Joel after another bitter fight regarding Maggie. Neither had seen Arnie since.

Syd smirked. "Appears the wench had enough of our oldest brother. The rumor is Maggie's locked up in the Conviction jail."

Joel's eyes widened. "For what?"

"Murdering her *husband*." Syd couldn't keep the grin off his face.

"They think Maggie murdered Arnie? That's not possible." Joel ran a hand through his hair, pacing the cabin.

"See there?" Syd pointed to the dried blood on the floor. "I heard she hit him on the head with her fry pan. Killed him that quick." He snapped his fingers. "The sheriff found Arnie's body in a grave out back."

"How do they know it was her?"

"She admitted it." Syd's laugh sliced through Joel, but he held his temper. It would do him no good to go after his brother. Arnie had been the true villain, and against all definitions of right and wrong, it appeared Maggie might pay the price.

"You heard all this in town?"

"Sure did. Over a game of cards at Buckie's. Doc's got the body in his morgue." Syd lowered himself into a chair and pulled out a cheroot, twirling it between his fingers, then striking a lucifer and lighting the tip of the thin cigar. Inhaling deeply, he let the smoke out in a slow stream. "Guess we got rid of both our burdens, little brother."

Joel stopped pacing long enough to shoot Syd a withering look. "How do you figure that? Maggie never did anything to you or me. That woman was sweet as a spring day, even after everything Arnie did to her."

"Ah hell, Joel. You always had a soft heart when it came to women, especially the King gal. She weren't nothing. Thought she was better than the three of us and didn't hesitate to let us know it."

Joel's irritation grew, anger beginning to take over. "She was an innocent, Syd. Arnie bought her off a man who'd kidnapped her. She did what Arnie demanded in order to survive."

"You feel sorry for her, even after she killed our brother?" Syd leaned forward, resting his hands on his knees, the cheroot dangling between two fingers.

"Hell yes, I feel sorry for her. And I don't believe she killed Arnie. She isn't capable of murder, no matter what he did to her."

"Well then, I guess we have a problem, kid." Syd snubbed out the burning cigar on the floor, blew off the ashes, then slid what remained into his coat pocket.

Joel's eyes narrowed at the change in Syd's voice. "What problem?"

"Someone killed Arnie. If not Maggie, then who?" Syd locked his gaze on Joel, his hand moving to the handle of his gun.

Joel tracked his movements, moving a few steps backward. "You and I were gone. Seems someone else came around, killed Arnie, and scared Maggie off."

"And her confession?"

"I've no doubt if Maggie said she hit him with her fry pan, she did. The woman can't lie worth anything. Maybe that's when she ran. Then someone came looking for Arnie and took advantage of him being knocked out."

"Listen to yourself, Joel. Seems to me you're making excuses for the woman." Syd stood, walked toward the stove, then poured a cup of stale coffee. "He pushed her too far, she grabbed the closest object, and killed him. Period." He took a sip, grimacing at the taste, tossing the rest out the door. "Of course, you could always ride into Conviction and plead her case for her. After all, you *did* get that fancy law degree back east.”

Neither of his brothers had ever let Joel forget how their mother had pushed her youngest son to get an education and make something of himself. By the time Joel finished school hundreds of miles away, their mother had been shot in a botched robbery. He’d practiced law a couple years before the pain and anger over his mother’s death pushed him to ride with his brothers—a decision he’d regretted a thousand times.

Joel’s body stilled. The suggestion wasn’t a bad one, unless you included the fact she might accuse him of being one of her kidnappers. Her anger had never been directed at him, though. She’d saved that for his older brothers who treated her worse than if she were a brothel whore. He could ride to town, visit her in the jail, and offer to be her lawyer. What’s the worst that could happen?

“It’s not a bad idea, Syd.” He almost laughed at the disbelieving look on his brother’s face. “I doubt she has money to hire anyone in Conviction, and according to you, no one else will believe she didn’t do it.”

“That’s the craziest dang thing I’ve ever heard. Now you listen to me, Joel. Leave this be. You’ve got no business stirring things up, especially when she killed our brother. We may not have had the brotherly bond people speak of, but he was still kin and she murdered him." Syd stalked up to Joel, stopping no more than a foot away. "You stay clear of her. You hear me?" He emphasized the last with a stab of his finger.

Joel didn't back away, but his expression sobered. "Sure, Syd. I hear you." *In this family, that doesn't mean a damn thing,* he thought as he strolled out the door toward his horse.

Maggie stirred at the sound of a door creaking and voices.

"I heard you, Mother. Two jars of green beans."

"Also a jar of cherries."

"All right, Mother. Cherries, too."

It took a split second for Maggie to remember where she was...and why. Jumping up, she wrapped the blanket around her and scurried to the other side of the cellar behind the wooden barrels, hunkering low, hoping whoever came down wouldn't spot her. Taking a deep breath, she willed herself to stay quiet and still.

She needn't have worried. Carrying a lantern, a girl of perhaps sixteen dashed down the stairs, grabbed what she needed, and headed back up without glancing around the small space. Relief washed over Maggie—until she heard the slide of a lock. Her heart plummeted. The door hadn't been locked when she rushed into the dark space, and she hadn't noticed one. Now what?

Dropping the blanket, Maggie moved to the stairs and glanced up at the door, her hands shaking as she rested one on the rail. She froze when the first step creaked as she ascended. Waiting, listening, she continued up until she spotted the sliding lock through a crack in the door. The sun had set, the sky pitch black, but she figured it couldn't be too late or the girl wouldn't have come down for supper supplies.

The timing was perfect for her to get out of there.

Placing her hands above her head, she pushed the door up and down, a tiny bit at a time, hoping to dislodge the bolt. It moved a little, then the tip became stuck in place. No matter how many times she jiggled the door, the slide wouldn't budge. If only she had something she could slide through the crack, she might be able to jostle the longer end enough to dislodge the slide and gain her freedom.

Glancing around, she spotted a shelf full of tools. Walking back down, she checked the shelf, picking up one tool after another until she saw a slender file near the back. Perfect. Grabbing it, she turned toward the stairs, then froze at the sound of the girl's voice.

"Are you sure this is the last of it, Mother?"

"Yes, dear. Just another jar of cherries."

Maggie clutched the file as she hurried to pick up the blanket, wrapped it around her, and waited.

Not noticing the change in the position of the lock, the girl opened the door, letting it fall open, and came down the steps carrying the lantern. This time, she didn't rush, her shoulders tensing as if she sensed something different. Holding the lantern higher, she took a slow turn around, then let out a breath and shook her head. Satisfied, she picked up a jar of cherries and left. This time she slammed the door closed, but there was no sound of the sliding lock.

Maggie closed her eyes and prayed the girl didn't realize her lapse, returning to correct her error. Minutes passed, but she continued to stay in her hiding place. After what seemed an eternity, her panic subsided enough for her let go of the blanket. Walking to the shelves, she selected one jar each of peaches and beans, then spotted a treasure. An old war bag had been tossed into a corner.

Wasting no time, she grabbed it and stuffed the jars, along with the file, inside. Reaching above her, she yanked on the pile of clothes, dislodging them so they fell in a heap on the floor. Combing through them, she slipped on an old jacket, then crammed a tattered shirt inside the bag. Satisfied, she gripped the bag in her hand and started up the steps.

Pushing the door open a few inches, she looked around, unable to see much in the dark. She couldn't wait any longer. Slipping outside, she lowered the door, ducked down, and skirted along the side of the house to the back alley. Looking one way, then the other, she straightened, tightened her hold on the bag, lifted her chin, and began walking.

Chapter Eight

"Gentleman." A man of average height with thinning dark hair, a goatee, and slim mustache set his hat on the desk, watching as Brodie finished strapping on his gun belt and stuck out his hand.

"You're here early this morning, Mr. Fielder."

"I heard you hired a new deputy. Two in fact. I thought I'd stop by and introduce myself." He clasped Brodie's hand, then turned toward Sam. "I'm August Fielder and this is my assistant, Walter Higgins."

"Sam Covington, Mr. Fielder, Mr. Higgins. I'm the newer of the two deputies." He shook both men's hands, flashing a wary grin, curious about the man and his business in Conviction.

"Mr. Fielder is one of our most prominent citizens," Brodie said by way of explanation. "He owns a good portion of the land in town, plus some cattle and mining interests."

"Impressive. Do you run any businesses in town, Mr. Fielder?" Sam took on a relaxed pose, although his eyes narrowed as he studied the man.

"I'm an attorney by education, so I do practice law on occasion. Along with the cattle, the mine, and some agricultural endeavors, I don't have much time to run other businesses." Fielder glanced at Walter and chuckled. "Walter is in charge of finding proprietors who wish to lease space in one of my buildings, which includes much of the land around the docks." He glanced between Brodie and Sam, getting the impression they were ready to ride out. "It appears you're ready to leave."

"We are. Seems a certain prisoner slipped through our fingers and we're on a search to bring her back." As one of the men who'd offered Brodie the job, he felt obligated to share what had happened.

"This wouldn't be the woman accused of murdering her husband, would it?"

Brodie nodded. "Yes, Mr. Fielder, it is."

"I hear there were extenuating circumstances regarding how she came to live with the man and how he treated her. Is there any truth to the rumors?" Fielder watched Brodie's expression darken a moment before he masked it.

"It seems Arnie Stoddard forced her to act as his wife, never marrying her—not that she would have accepted. According to her, she was kidnapped from a Denver hotel, then sold to

Stoddard. He brought her to California and kept her tucked away in a cabin outside of town." Brodie hesitated a moment before continuing. "I felt something wasn't right about the way Stoddard died. When Doc confirmed the cause of death, I decided to ride back up to the cabin and take another look." He cleared his throat, seeing the interest on Fielder's face. "I don't think she killed him."

"Unfortunately, the woman may have muddled her case by fleeing. It never looks good when someone accused of a crime escapes."

"Agreed. That's where we're headed now, Mr. Fielder. To find her before she does something else that would worsen her case." Sam picked up his hat, holding it in his hand.

Fielder looked at Brodie. "Does she have an attorney?"

"Nae. And she has no money. I'd appreciate any recommendations you can provide."

Fielder nodded, rubbing his goatee, deep in thought. "Bring her in and then come get me. We'll discuss what you've learned and see if we can come up with a defense plan." He nodded at Brodie and Sam, then started to turn away. "Oh. What does the woman look like?"

Brodie described her deep red hair, clear blue eyes, and creamy skin sprinkled with freckles across her nose.

"Oh my." The three men turned their attention to Walter. "I do believe one of Mr. Fielder's workers had a run-in with this woman yesterday afternoon."

Brodie stepped closer. "Tell me about it."

"He found her behind the carriage house, hiding behind some crates. When he called to her, she ran. I joined him briefly, but we lost her as she ran between buildings."

"Why didn't you say anything to me, Walter?"

"It seemed insignificant, Mr. Fielder. We thought she was just some vagrant looking for a handout or place to sleep. Now I wish we continued to search for her."

"And that was when, Walter?"

"Late afternoon yesterday, Sheriff. We lost her between some homes near Mr. Fielder's house. I would suspect the young woman is long gone by now."

"Why don't you follow us, Sheriff? Walter can show you exactly where they lost sight of her."

Brodie glanced at Sam, who nodded. "Aye. That's exactly what we'll do."

"This was the last place we saw her, but she was already well ahead of us." Walter indicated a path between two houses. "She ran down here, then disappeared."

"Thanks, Walter. Mr. Fielder, Sam and I will go on from here."

Brodie and Sam walked from the street to the alley before turning around and retracing their steps.

"Oh, Sheriff." The sing-song voice came from the front porch of one of the houses. "Sheriff MacLaren, I was just going to send my daughter to get you."

Brodie touched the brim of his hat. "What can I do for you, ma'am?"

The older woman eyed Sam, her brows drawing together. "You must be new."

Sam slipped off his hat, flashing a broad smile. "Yes, ma'am. I've only been on the job two days."

Crossing her arms, she gave him an assessing stare, then returned her attention to Brodie.

"Someone's been stealing from my cellar, Sheriff, and you need to stop them."

Brodie cast a quick glance at Sam, keeping his face neutral. "How long has it been going on?"

"Well, the best I can tell, just last night."

This got their attention. "Show us." Brodie followed her around the house, Sam right behind him.

She pulled the door of the root cellar open. "Go down and see for yourself. There are some jars of food and a jacket missing. Not sure what else. Whoever did this created quite a mess and I want him found."

"Do you believe it's a man?" Sam stepped in front of her, following Brodie down the steps.

"I can't imagine any woman doing it, Deputy. Can you?" She snorted as if it were the most ridiculous question she'd ever heard.

"Well now, I can imagine a lot, ma'am." He turned his back to her, hearing her mutter something to herself. "Have you found anything, MacLaren?"

Brodie knelt behind the barrels where the blanket still lay. Reaching out, he plucked a piece of cotton fabric from a nail and held it up.

"This is from the dress Maggie was wearing."

"She probably stayed down here until nightfall. We can check the alley for tracks, but it will be hard to identify hers from the others I'd expect to find. If I were trying to get away and didn't have a horse, the first place I'd try would be one of the riverboats. How many come and go each day?"

"We get about three a week. They stay overnight, sometimes two nights, then head back to Sacramento. Today's Friday, so there ought to be at least one of them at the docks." Brodie stood and looked around once more before climbing the steps.

"Did you find anything, Sheriff?"

"Aye, ma'am. You had an intruder all right." He held up the scrap of fabric.

Her eyes grew wide. "Why, that looks like dress material."

"Aye, it is. It happens we're searching for a woman who escaped from the jail yesterday morning. This is from the dress she was wearing. Did you hear or see anything last night?"

She shook her head, still surprised the thief had been a woman.

"Well, she'll not be bothering you again. We're going to find her and get her back behind bars." Touching the brim of his hat, he and Sam walked back to their horses.

"I believe a trip to the docks is in order." Sam reined his horse around.

Maggie dropped the quilt from her shoulders, sliding off the lumpy straw mattress and standing to look out the small, dirty window. Everything smelled of mold and mildew, yet she was grateful she'd stumbled onto the abandoned boathouse a good hundred yards from the main docks. The mattress had been thrown into a corner, the quilt wadded up under it.

She'd intended to get as far away from Conviction as possible before dawn. Instead, she'd spotted the riverboat as it pulled into the docks, music and laughter spilling through the open doors and windows. If Maggie could sneak on and find a place to hide, she'd be able to travel all the way downriver to Sacramento.

There'd been too much activity last night, but the boat seemed quiet this morning. The captain had left a small crew when he stepped onto the dock a couple hours earlier. Suspecting he'd return soon, she worked to straighten her hair and brush the dirt from her dress, guessing the efforts were wasted. Taking another look outside, she opened the door, squared her shoulders, and stepped onto the dock.

Friday morning, Maggie thought, continuing toward the boat. The days had run together over the past two years to the point she'd rarely wondered if it were Monday, Thursday, or Sunday. She didn't care. Freedom and a future had been so far out of reach for so long, she'd forgotten how it felt to have choices.

Stepping onto the gangway, she tightened her hold on the war bag, glancing around. Limited crew worked around the boat, no one paying her any attention. Holding her breath, she kept her gaze fixed on a spot straight ahead, finally taking the last step onto the boat.

"May I help you, miss?"

The deep voice startled Maggie. Stumbling forward, she felt strong hands grip her upper arm, steadying her.

"Are you all right?"

Swallowing her fear and embarrassment, she nodded. "I'm fine."

"Are you making the trip to Sacramento?" He had a kind face, wavy gray hair, and a full mustache.

"Yes, I am."

"Well, you're a day early, miss. We're docked for repairs through today. You may board tomorrow after breakfast. We'll leave late morning."

Her heart sank, accepting she'd have to spend another night in the dirty, dank boathouse. "Oh. I must have gotten my days mixed up."

"No problem, miss. It happens all the time."

Turning, she stepped back onto the gangway, her mind racing. She still had half a jar of beans and less than that of peaches, enough to last her until tomorrow. Forgetting where she was, Maggie almost fell off the end of the gangway at the same time she heard a shout from down the street.

"Maggie! Maggie King! Stop right there."

Her chest tightened at the familiar voice. Panicking, she glanced around, her gaze landing on Brodie riding toward her, another man alongside him. Picking up her skirt, she turned and ran the opposite direction, cutting across the street and turning onto another one crowded with people, buggies, and horses.

"You follow her, Sam. I'm going to ride around and cut her off at the other end of the street."

Sam nodded once before reining his horse toward the street she had run down. Turning Hunter around, Brodie rode up the main street of Conviction, several blocks away from the jail. He'd take a shortcut through a less traveled street. If they were lucky, Sam would herd her directly to him. They'd have Maggie back in her cell before she knew what had happened.

Maggie wove between people on the wide boardwalk, her eyes darting around, seeking a place to hide. She found it hard not to run, which would draw more attention to herself. Glancing over her shoulder, she felt a moment of panic seeing the man who'd been riding next to Brodie fix his gaze on her. Clutching the bag tighter, she made a quick decision, dashing into a nearby store and heading to the back.

"May I help you?" A stout woman, her hair pulled into a tight bun on top of her head, began to come around the counter.

Maggie took a breath. "I've never been in here before." She shot a glance behind her, seeing the man rein his horse to a stop out front. Letting her gaze do a quick sweep of the store, she saw a back door, guessing it led to an alley. "May I just look for a moment?"

"Of course, dear. Let me know if you have questions." The woman walked toward the front, her back to Maggie.

Not wasting a moment, she moved to the door, grasping the handle. Praying it wasn't locked, she turned it, relief flooding her when she pushed the door open. Without stopping, she hurried down the steps to the alley and ran. She had no idea where to go or how to escape Brodie and the man with him. All she knew was they wouldn't get her back in that cell. She'd spent her last day as a prisoner, the same as she'd been the last two years.

Reaching the end of the alley, she held back, looking one way and then the other. There was no sign of either man, but she didn't believe they'd given up. The little she knew about Brodie MacLaren told her he wasn't a man who gave up easily. Well, neither did she.

Loud laughter caught her attention. Turning, she saw a group of women round a corner, walking straight toward her. Before she could change her mind, she melded into the group, her eyes focused straight ahead, ignoring the curious stares from several of the women.

All wore fashionable wool dresses and heavy coats, some trimmed in fur, and hats adorned with feathers and ribbons. She glanced down, pulling the tattered coat she'd stolen from the root cellar tight around her, fingers shaking as her heart raced. Thankfully, no one said a word to her as they continued along the boardwalk.

Looking up, her heart stopped when she saw Brodie sitting atop his horse at the end of the street, his gaze locked on her. Whipping her head around, she froze at the sight of the second man coming up the street behind her.

All the fear, pain, and anger she'd experienced over the last two years roared through her. Moving so her back rested against the side of the building, her eyes darted from one side to the other. Both men were now on foot, walking toward her with slow, purposeful steps. Brodie, his face hard, came from one end of the boardwalk, the second man from the other.

"No." The scream came unbidden, a moment before she pushed away from the wall and dashed into the street.

"Maggie, watch out!"

She heard the panic in Brodie's voice an instant before the shouts from onlookers reached her ears. Turning, her eyes widened in horror as a horse reared above her. An ear-piercing scream ripped from her throat as the reality of what was happening flashed before her. Raising both arms, Maggie attempted to protect herself as two powerful hooves descended upon her.

Brodie paced in the waiting area of the doctor's office, unable to rid himself of the sight of Maggie's frightened face as the large horse reared back then came down on top of her. If he'd been a few feet closer, he could have shoved her out of the way. Instead, he'd held back, watching to see which way she ran. His hesitation may have cost Maggie her life.

"It's not your fault, MacLaren." Sam's hand rested on Brodie's shoulder. "It was an accident. Nothing more."

"I could've stopped it."

"No, you couldn't have. She ran right in front of the wagon. The driver did all he could, but there wasn't any stopping the horse." Sam dropped his hand. "It's in the doctor's hands now."

It didn't matter that Sam's intentions were good and his logic correct. Brodie had seen the determination on her face, the resolve to fight until she had no other choices, when he'd spotted her in the group of women. His gaze met hers, and for an instant, he thought she might run to him, trust him to help her. The next moment her eyes flared in a combination of terror and panic, and she ran with no concept of the danger right before her.

She'd acted out of fear of being recaptured and imprisoned for a crime she didn't commit. And she ran because she feared him.

"I'll be right back." Brodie walked outside, ripped his hat off his head, and gazed up at the late morning sky. The sun felt warm, but the chill in the air reminded him November was days away, the promise of extended rains and a drop in temperatures along with it.

Walking to a water barrel outside the clinic, he scooped up a handful of water, splashing it over his face and neck, thinking of Maggie. She'd been kidnapped and abused sexually, emotionally, and physically. When she'd had enough, she ran to Conviction for help. Instead, she gotten a cocky sheriff who performed his own version of abuse on her, even if it wasn't intentional.

"Sheriff MacLaren."

Brodie stuffed his hat back on his head and turned, wincing when he saw a man approaching him at a fast pace. "Harold." Crossing his arms, Brodie waited while Harold caught his breath.

Harold Ivers, owner, editor, and chief columnist for the Conviction Guardian, grabbed a handkerchief and mopped his brow, his breath coming in gasps. It had to be close to sixty degrees, not the kind of weather that would produce sweat...unless you were considerably overweight and seldom did anything more strenuous than fretting over a news story. Slipping the cloth into his back pocket, he stared up at the sheriff, who stood at least ten inches taller than him.

"You wanted to talk to me?" Brodie prompted.

"Yes, I did. I heard you had a jailbreak yesterday." He pulled a pencil and piece of paper out of his pocket. "Now, I've heard you recaptured the woman who murdered her husband. I need the details, Sheriff. We don't want our readers worrying an escaped murderess is still on the loose, right?"

Brodie bit back a curse, his eyes turning to slits. "Just where did you get your information?"

Blinking, Harold took a step back. "Around, Sheriff. You hear a lot of talk when you run a newspaper. Is it true?"

"Nae, Harold. It isn't." Brodie turned to head back into the clinic.

"What part isn't true?"

Brodie stopped, knowing no matter what he said, Harold would twist it to suit his needs and entertain the readers. Most people thought the opening of the Conviction Guardian a couple years before had been a welcome improvement to a growing town. For Brodie, it meant always knowing the ambitious newspaperman would use whatever means he could to add sensationalism to his stories.

"We caught a suspect." He spoke deliberately, his voice clipped. "There has been no trial, and therefore, no conviction. I'd suggest you wait until the jury makes a verdict before you print more than what I've just told you."

"But, Sheriff..."

Harold's voice faded away as Brodie walked into the clinic, closed the door behind him, then let out a frustrated breath.

"How is she?"

Sam leaned against the wall, his arms crossed, as if the woman in the other room wasn't fighting for her life. "She hasn't woken up yet. Doc says that may be good given the injuries to her head, legs, and arms. If she hadn't twisted to the side at the last moment, the horse would've crushed her skull instead of grazing it. You know, Brodie, she may never wake up."

"Aye. I've thought of that. I'd appreciate it if you'd stay a little longer. I need to send a telegram to Denver and get a message to Mr. Fielder. It's time he began to prepare for her trial."

Sam pushed away from the wall. "You're an optimist, MacLaren, which may be good—as long as Fielder doesn't mind spending his time preparing for a trial that may never happen."

Chapter Nine

Circle M Ranch

"Where did that lass go off to now?" Audrey MacLaren mumbled to herself, standing on the front porch, watching the sun begin to set.

"What has you troubled, Ma?" Quinn called out as he reined Warrior toward the house.

"And who says I'm troubled?" She didn't stop staring at the far end of the property Heather had ridden toward that morning.

"Ah. It must be Heather again." Tossing the reins over the post, he took the steps two at a time as his brother, Bram, came out of the barn. "Didn't Caleb ride with her this morning?" Quinn didn't worry about his sister when one of the lads rode with her. If she weren't so stubborn, determined she could best any man on the ranch, he wouldn't worry at all. It was her pride, the need to constantly prove herself that antagonized most of her kin and caused their mother to fret.

"Fletcher and Sean followed her when she rode off without Caleb. That boy's going to wash his hands of her."

Quinn shot a look at Bram, who stifled a chuckle. Although Caleb tried to hide it, everyone knew he had feelings for Heather. Strong ones. No matter how much he denied the attraction, he couldn't keep from staring at her when he thought no one watched.

"You speaking of Caleb?" Bram asked, knowing full well her meaning.

"Aye. She's too obstinate to see the man he's become, and he's too stubborn to push her." Audrey turned toward the front door. "I've supper to finish. If the three aren't back in an hour..." She glanced over her shoulder.

Quinn nodded. "Aye, Ma. Bram and I will go find them."

Bram crossed his arms, staring after his mother as she closed the door. "How long is this to go on?"

"You mean Heather going off, doing whatever she pleases with no thought to the rest of us?" Grabbing Warrior's reins, he walked toward the barn, Bram keeping pace with him. "God forgive me, but there are times I wish she would do what she threatens and find a place at another ranch."

"She's a lass, Quinn. Other than to cook or clean, who'd hire her? Ranchers around here don't want women in the saddle, acting as wranglers." Bram shoved his hands into his pockets as they entered the barn.

"There are plenty of women who work alongside men." Quinn thought of one in particular. Emma Pearce, a good friend of Jinny, Brodie's younger sister. Where Jinny wanted nothing more than to marry and have children, Emma rode alongside her father as a wrangler. Unlike Quinn's sister, Heather, though, Emma also had no problem helping her mother with cooking and cleaning.

"Aye, but they're family, like Heather. Her dream to ride out on her own, get away from the rest of us, is the lass's fantasy."

Quinn pursed his lips, wondering if Bram was right. Her contemptuous ways and arrogant behavior alienated the family, but could be an asset for a rancher in need of help, such as the woman who owned the spread south of them.

"Maybe old Mrs. Evanston will offer her a job. She's been having trouble finding men who want to stay around and take orders from a woman."

"Aye. And Heather has been spending most of her time on our south border, right next to the Evanston ranch." Bram headed outside, his gaze landing on riders. "Fletcher and Sean are coming in."

"Heather?"

"No sign of her, Quinn."

They waited, seeing the huge grins on their cousins' faces. Neither lost their smiles as they dismounted, walking up to Quinn and Bram.

"You won't believe this, lads. Mrs. Evanston offered Heather a job, and she took it." Fletcher chuckled, then saw the surprised looks. "It *is* good news, right?"

"I told her we'd let everyone know." Sean's smile faded at the disbelief on Quinn's and Bram's faces. "It might be best coming from one of you."

Bram clasped Quinn's shoulder. "Ma won't be pleased, but this may be what Heather needs."

Quinn nodded, staring at the house as his mother came outside. "Aye, but Ma won't be happy she made the decision without consulting the family."

"As Brodie did?"

"Aye, Bram." Quinn's voice held a note of sadness and resignation. "The same as Brodie."

"I'll find you right away if you get a reply, Sheriff." Ira Greene leaned on the counter, his mind working. "I know it's none of my business, but besides the sheriff in Denver, you might want to send messages to a couple of the banks."

Brodie wondered if his meager budget allowed for more, then shrugged. "Do you have names of bankers in Denver?"

"Sure do. From what I hear, the town is going through a rough time. Still rebuilding after the fires a couple years ago, but there are at least two banks doing a good business. I'll send your message to both of them."

Brodie cocked his head. "How do you know all this, Ira? Denver's over a thousand miles away."

Ira chuckled, bending down to scoop up a stack of papers. "I get and send telegrams from all over. With the war between the North and South still going on, the number of messages grows all the time. You learn a lot in my business."

"Aye. It seems you do." And he was glad for any information Ira could help obtain about Maggie's family. After two years, he had no idea if they were still anywhere near Denver. At least he had the foresight to get their names from Maggie when they'd returned from the cabin with Colin.

He couldn't get his mind off her lifeless form when he'd carried her to the doctor's office. She hadn't made a sound, opened her eyes, or given any indication of life. If it hadn't been for her shallow breathing, he'd have thought she'd been killed. Trampled by a horse in her panic to get away from him. She'd clung to life, and he wanted nothing more than to believe she would pull through. If Maggie lived, she'd need an attorney.

It was time for him to talk with August Fielder, let him know they'd found Maggie. He'd indicated he might be interested in representing her. If he accepted her case, Brodie needed to tell him all he'd learned at the cabin. She needed the best defense possible.

Brodie had been lost in thought when his head snapped up at the sound of people crying out. A second later, he felt a strange pulsing sensation under his feet. *Earthquake*, he thought, grabbing the railing to steady himself as he watched men and women, panic on their faces, stream outside.

Doctor Jonathon Vickery grabbed both sides of the bed, trying to steady it as a shockwave jolted the building. Maggie hadn't come out of her unconscious state, and the doctor knew the slight rocking wouldn't make any difference. He believed she would eventually wake up, but not from being jostled out of her coma. He was more concerned about his medicines and supplies stored behind closed doors.

"Deputy, are you still out there?"

When the door pushed open, Sam held the doorframe to keep his balance, then let go when the trembling stopped.

"Do you need me, Doc?"

"Not if that's the end—" He stopped when another jolt rocked the building. This time the doors of the medicine cupboard popped open. "Grab those before they fall." He nodded toward the bottles rocking back and forth, ready to tumble to the floor at any moment.

Sam let go of the door, losing his balance, then righted himself to grab two bottles. Bending down, he set them on the floor as a stronger tremor ripped through the building, this third one stronger, lasting longer than the others. He heard a loud crash out front and what sounded like the front door slamming open. Screams filled the air outside, and Sam knew he had to see if he could help.

"Are you all right here, Doctor?"

"If the tremors stop, then yes. I know you need to check on the rest of the town. I'll take good care of Miss King while you're gone." Doc Vickery looked down at Maggie's still form, seeing no change. "Go ahead, Deputy. Come back or send Sheriff MacLaren when you've taken care of everything."

Sam glanced at Maggie, nodding before heading out the door. What he saw stopped him in his tracks. Buildings under construction had come apart, broken wood scattered everywhere. Many of the signs attached above shop entrances lay splintered on the ground. Shattered glass covered the boardwalk. People walked around as if in a trance, some still holding onto posts or rails, fearing another shockwave.

And he had yet to check the other streets, or see Brodie.

Rushing across the street, he put his arm around an older woman who staggered, her hand trying to stop the bleeding from a wound on her head.

"May I help you to the doctor's office?"

She gripped his arm. "Yes, young man. I'd appreciate it."

Looking toward the clinic, Sam saw several people already congregating at the entrance, waiting to see Vickery. *One doctor for all these people*, he thought, escorting the woman through the front door, ignoring those already waiting, then nodding at a man who stood so she could take his seat.

"I'll be back in a moment." Sam knocked on the room where Maggie slept, then poked his head inside. "Doc, there are a number of injuries. What do you want me to do?"

Vickery was already preparing his bag, stuffing it with medicines and bandages.

"Go to Buckie's. Tell them we need tables cleared and the help of the ladies. Most of them will be glad to do whatever is needed." Then he glanced at Sam. "Assuming there are any tables still usable and the ladies aren't panicked."

"What about Miss King?"

"Send one of the ladies back here. All she needs to do is keep watch on the patient, then come for me if she wakes up." Vickery snapped the bag closed. "Tell them I need as much hot water as possible."

"I'll leave right now. Oh, there's an elderly woman out front with a severe head injury."

"Tell her I'll be right out, Sam." Vickery checked Maggie one more time, securing her blankets, then grabbed his coat as Sam knelt in front of the woman.

"Doc will be right out to check on you." He glanced around at the others. There must have been at least twenty people waiting. "The rest of you need to walk down to Buckie's Castle. Doc wants to set up a makeshift hospital there."

Ignoring the grumbling, Sam dashed outside, running toward the saloon. He had a moment of panic seeing the windows blown out, both swinging doors hanging from their hinges, and the large sign on the ground, broken into three pieces. Stepping through the opening, he let out a breath. Other than broken bottles and scattered chairs, the place looked to be in good condition. He stepped to the bar where the dazed bartender stood, hands fisted at his sides.

"The doctor needs the use of the saloon and your ladies to help with the injured. He also needs as much hot water as possible."

The bartender continued to stare, his jaw slack. Sam slammed his fist on the bar, getting the man's attention.

"Did you hear what I said? We need your help. Now. The injured will be here any moment."

"I think they're already here." The bartender's gaze moved to the door where men and women formed a crowd, some with broken arms or legs. "I'll get the tables ready and heat the water. Would you go upstairs and check with the ladies?" With that, the man started to move, signaling to others in the saloon to help.

"I'll go." Gwen, one of the women who'd worked at Buckie's the longest, pushed herself up from her hiding place behind the bar. "I'm sure you have more urgent things to do than round up the girls, Deputy. I'm certain they'll be glad to help."

Touching the brim of his hat, Sam smiled. "Thank you, ma'am. Doc also asked that one of the ladies go to the clinic and watch over an unconscious patient. I need to find the sheriff and see how many more people are injured."

"You tell Brodie that Gwen is helping out here. He'll know not to worry." She winked, then picked up her skirt and dashed up the stairs.

Sam walked up to the bartender who continued to space out the tables, wiping each down. "Thank you." He turned to leave, then stopped at the man's words.

"You can thank Gwen when this is over. She and the MacLaren men go back a ways. She'd do anything for them." A slight grin split his face. "Thought I'd let you know."

Although he didn't care about Gwen's friendship with the MacLarens, Sam was grateful for the information. He walked outside as Vickery came up.

"They're ready for you, Doc. Gwen is getting the girls together."

"Ah, Gwen. Yes, she's a good one." Leaving Sam outside, the doctor stepped through the broken doors to survey the scene. "Everyone take seats where you can. I need to see you in the order of those most critical, and I mean life-threatening or ready to lose an arm or leg." He walked to the bar and set out his supplies, letting the injured decide their own severity. Turning, he offered a reassuring smile to a young boy lying on a table, whimpering, holding an arm bent at an odd angle. A woman, most likely his mother, stood next to him, stroking his forehead.

Doc Vickery leaned over him. "Have you ever had a broken arm or leg, son?"

Gritting his teeth and squeezing his eyes shut to stop the tears, he shook his head. "No, sir."

"Well, I've seen many of them, and we're going to put yours back just like new. All right?"

Although his lower lip trembled, he nodded. "Yes, sir. That would be real good."

When the quake started, Brodie tried to reach the clinic, needing to check on Maggie, make sure she was safe. Cries from down the street had him running in the opposite direction, calming citizens and checking for injured. A rancher stopped long enough to tell him Doc Vickery had set up a makeshift clinic at Buckie's. Brodie wondered if Sam had stayed with Maggie or left to check on the damage and those who'd been hurt. Surely they wouldn't leave her alone.

A strange sense of panic surged through him. Glancing around to confirm he'd done all he could for now, he hurried to the clinic, shouldering his way past small groups of people, most appearing to be in a daze.

"Doc? Sam?" He saw no activity in the front part of the clinic, and no one responded. Slamming open the door to the room where he'd left Maggie, he stopped at the sight of Gwen.

"I wondered when you'd get here, Brodie." She returned her gaze to Maggie.

Staring at her inert form, he stepped to the side of the table, seeing no change from when he'd left.

"She's been like this since I arrived. Before he left for Buckie's, Doc said her breathing is better." Gwen glanced at him. "He's at the saloon, treating those injured in the earthquake."

His gaze didn't waver from Maggie. "Aye. That's why I came back. To make sure someone watched over her."

Gwen had known Brodie several years. Like she'd done for some of the older MacLaren cousins, she'd introduced him to what happened between a man and a woman, and how to treat a lady when in her bed. She knew he'd never courted any of the women in town, had no desire to be tied to one person—not yet anyway. The way he looked at Maggie, though, she wondered if that might soon change.

"I heard she escaped from your jail."

"Aye."

"How did this happen?" Gwen nodded at Maggie, then leaned back in the chair, stretching her arms above her head.

Brodie sighed, his shoulders slumping. "Sam and I had been searching for her all over town. We spotted her at the docks. Unfortunately, Maggie saw us and ran. When we finally found her again, Sam was at one end of the street and I was at the other, trapping her between us. She panicked and ran into the street, right in front of a wagon. The horse reared back and..." He scrubbed a shaky hand down his face, his voice fading.

"If you're thinking her getting hurt is your fault, Brodie, you're wrong. She put herself in the situation by escaping, then running away from you and Sam." Her compassionate but firm voice got his attention. "I heard she killed her husband."

"She admitted to hitting him with a skillet, but I don't think that's what killed him, and neither does Doc Vickery." He took another look at Maggie before turning toward Gwen. "Can you stay a bit longer?"

"As long as you need me to, Brodie."

He nodded. "Thank you, Gwen. I need to go speak with August Fielder."

Her eyes widened. "You think he can help her?"

"I believe he might. Now that we've found her, I need to tell him what I've learned and do my best to convince him to be her attorney."

"I understand he takes few cases and charges a lot to represent someone. If Fielder does agree to help her, can she afford him?"

He shook his head. "Nae. The lass has no money. After he hears what I believe happened, I'm hoping he'll consider doing it anyway."

"I suppose all you can do is ask the man." She pursed her lips, her face neutral. "You go ahead. I'll stay until you or Doc return. And, Brodie, trust me when I say it will all work out."

Chapter Ten

It took Brodie over an hour to go the few blocks from the clinic to Fielder's house. With all the debris in the streets, he'd chosen to walk rather than ride. Everyone stopped him, most scared and confused, having no idea what to do next. He did his best to reassure them, directing the injured to Buckie's, and requesting they stay close to home in case another earthquake struck.

Stepping up to Fielder's front door, he knocked, hoping the man would see him. An older woman wearing a black and white uniform opened the door, letting her gaze wander over him until she saw the badge.

Removing his hat, he took a step forward. "I'm Sheriff MacLaren. Is Mr. Fielder at home?"

"I know who you are, young man." She crossed her arms, not budging from her spot guarding the entrance to the house. "Mr. Fielder went to the Gold Dust Hotel to check for damage. He mentioned something about inspecting the entire town. I believe he hoped to find you."

"How long ago did he leave?"

She glared at him. For a moment, Brodie didn't think she'd answer. "He left not long before you arrived."

"In case I don't find him, please let Mr. Fielder know I need to speak with him. It's urgent."

"As urgent as an earthquake?"

Ignoring the way her voice dripped with sarcasm, Brodie thought about Maggie. The horror on her face when she saw he'd found her, fear taking control as she ran into the path of the horse. "Aye, it is. Thank you, ma'am."

Walking back to the street, he looked around, noting the minimal damage to the homes. As he hurried back to the jail, he checked businesses along the way to make certain no one else needed his help. Thankfully, few buildings had collapsed, most being old shacks located along the docks.

"Brodie, wait up."

He turned to see Stein Tharaldson ride up to him and dismount. Taking a closer look, he saw numerous scrapes and bruises on his friend's face and arms.

"Are you all right?"

"As good as can be expected. The front wall of the feed storage barn is in pieces and one of the lofts collapsed. At least no one was inside when the earthquake hit." Stein settled his hands on his hips, making a slow turn to survey the damage. "Not as bad as it could've been."

"Aye. We were lucky this time."

"I already have my boys working on repairs. Thought I'd ride in to see if you needed any help. Ma said she's available to tend to anyone who's hurt."

Like Stein, his mother had a huge heart, always offering to help those who needed it, whether it be repairing damage to their home or taking care of someone who'd fallen ill.

"Doc Vickery set up a temporary clinic at Buckie's. Let's go talk with him, find out if he needs more help."

"Who's helping him now?" Stein asked as he climbed into the saddle, holding his hand out so Brodie could swing up behind him.

"From what I've heard, some of Buckie's ladies and a few of the local church women."

Stein laughed. "Well, that ought to be a real sight to see."

"Millie, would you come help me calm this young man so I can take care of his leg?" The boy squirmed while Doc Vickery held a bandage to his forehead. He couldn't be more than six or seven, yet he seemed determined not to cry.

"What can I do, Doc?" Millie walked up, placing a reassuring hand on the boy's arm as she smiled down at him.

"Hold this bandage to stop the bleeding while I work on his leg." He leaned toward her to whisper in her ear. "You'll need to hold his arms down tight when I tell you. What I need to do is going to hurt like a, well...it will hurt a lot."

Brodie and Stein walked in, seeing the doctor tending the child, Millie at his side.

"Do you need some help, Doc?" Stein moved closer, nodding at Millie, then looking at the determination on the boy's face.

Doc lowered his voice. "Millie will need help holding him down while I straighten his leg."

Stein moved to the other side of the table to help secure the other leg and arm. "Whenever you're ready, Doc."

Another minute went by as Vickery got ready, then glanced at Millie and Stein, and nodded.

"Now."

The boy's scream pierced the air as tears streamed down his face.

"You're a brave young man, son." Vickery continued to work at a rapid pace, thankful he had Millie and Stein to help him. "We're almost done, then you can show us where you live. All right?" He'd been looking for the boy's mother or father to walk through the door. So far, no one had shown up looking for him.

The boy closed his eyes and nodded.

Brodie's gaze moved from the boy to the other tables, watching women, who couldn't have been more different, work together as if they'd known each other their entire lives. It amazed him how people who'd never think about talking to each other on the street thought nothing of coming together during a calamity.

"Appears you have all the help you need, Doc. If you don't mind, I need to find August Fielder."

"You go ahead, Sheriff." Vickery turned to look over his shoulder. "If you find anyone else who needs help, we have room for more injured."

Brodie clasped a hand on Doc's shoulder. "Thanks."

He crossed the street, walking toward the jail. People were already picking up broken wood, sweeping shattered glass from the boardwalk, and moving smashed signs out of the way. As he stepped up to the jail door, he heard a loud, familiar whistle, his mouth tilting up at the corners.

"Hey, lad. Do you need some help?" Quinn slid off his horse and looked around, his face somber as he surveyed the damage. "Aye, it appears you do. The others are right behind me. They stopped to help move a tree blocking the street."

A moment later, his brother, Fletcher, along with Blaine, Colin, Bram, Camden, and Sean rode up.

"How is the ranch?" Brodie asked as they dismounted.

"We could feel the earthquake, but haven't found any damage so far." Fletcher slapped his brother on the back. "Ma wanted me to make sure you were all right."

"It took *all* of you to do that?" Brodie glanced at each of them, a wave of emotion coursing through him.

"Aye. There was no question about any of us staying behind." Colin stepped beside him. "What can we do?"

"You're sure?"

Colin crossed his arms, cocking a brow. "We wouldn't be here if we weren't."

The others nodded, settling the matter.

"Divide up. Check with as many people as you can to find out what help they need. I'm sure Fielder will call a meeting of the town council so they can decide what aid can be provided."

Brodie drew in a breath, wondering if his father, Ewan, a member of the town council, would ride into town. He hadn't seen him since accepting the job as sheriff.

"If you're wondering about Da, he said he will be riding in today," Fletcher said, as if reading his brother's mind.

Brodie nodded, hoping his father would take time to talk to him. They needed to clear the rift between them. "If you find more injuries, take them to Buckie's. Doc Vickery has a temporary clinic there. I need to find Fielder."

"You go ahead. The lads and I will take care of the rest. We'll meet you back here in two hours." Colin turned to the others. "Quinn, take Bram and start at the far north end of town. Blaine, you and Cam check the streets around the docks. Fletcher, you're with me." Without another word, Colin swung up on Chieftan. "We'll start east and work our way west."

Brodie watched them all ride off, his chest swelling, feeling a sense of pride in his family.

"Sheriff, I hear you've been looking for me."

Brodie turned around to see August Fielder walking toward him. His coat had been discarded, his sleeves rolled up, his pants covered in dirt.

"Yes, sir. Do you have time to go inside?"

"Whatever you need."

To keep herself from dozing off, Gwen paced around the small examination room. Maggie hadn't stirred the entire time, and Gwen became more concerned as each hour passed. Doc Vickery hadn't been able to come back, although he had sent one of the ladies to check on them.

Walking to the front, Gwen righted some chairs, then picked up a broom resting against a wall and began to sweep. The clinic had been lucky, suffering only a couple broken windows. Stepping outside, her eyes widened at the extent of the damage. A new building down the street was now a pile of rubble. She was about to turn to go back inside when a shout stopped her.

"Colin and Fletcher. It's good to see you boys. Are you here to help?"

"Aye, Gwen. What are you doing here?" Colin slipped to the ground, putting his arm around her.

"Did you hear about Maggie King?"

"The woman Brodie arrested?" Colin's brows drew together. "What happened?"

She explained, ending by telling them Maggie's current condition.

Colin mumbled a curse as he and Fetcher followed her inside. "She seems like a nice lass. It doesn't seem right."

He'd barely gotten the words out when a man walked into the clinic, walked up to Gwen, and grabbed her by the arms.

"Where is she?"

Colin stepped between the man and Gwen, Fletcher taking up position behind the stranger, their bodies rigid with anger.

"Let her go. Now." Colin pushed the man back into Fletcher's hands. The younger cousin smiled as he shoved him outside.

"If you have something to say to the lady, you can say it from there." Fletcher crossed his arms, blocking the entrance.

Gwen watched Fletcher from her spot next to Colin. One of the tallest of the MacLaren cousins at six-foot-five, Fletcher had impressively broad shoulders for a man of just eighteen. His caramel brown hair hung down his forehead, his steel gray eyes enhanced with swirls of light green and blue. They were all good-looking men, but she knew Fletcher already attracted women like flies to honey. Her mouth tilted into a slight smile.

Colin walked up next to Fletcher. "Who are you and what's your business here?"

The man glared at both of them, then straightened his shoulders. "I'm Syd Stoddard. The woman in there killed my brother, and I'm going to make sure she pays for it."

"That's great news, Mr. Fielder. I'm certain Maggie...I mean, Miss King will be relieved to have a man of your experience representing her."

Fielder watched Brodie's expression, seeing something in his eyes he couldn't quite define. Ignoring it, he stood. "I think we should go check on her. See if she's come out of her coma."

Crossing the street, they walked toward Doc Vickery's clinic. Brodie noted a man outside, his back to them as he talked to Colin and Fletcher. Brodie saw the hardened smile on his brother's face, knowing the look all too well. Fletch was angry, ready to explode.

"Colin, Fletch, what's going on?" Brodie moved next to the man, letting his gaze wander over him.

"This is Syd Stoddard, *Sheriff.*" Fletcher emphasized the word. "He's Arnie Stoddard's brother."

Brother? Brodie thought, taking a closer look at the man. "Miss King never mentioned Arnie had any kin."

"Miss King? Is that what she told you?" A sneer crossed Syd's face. "She and Arnie were married."

Brodie moved to within inches of Syd's face. "I assume you have proof of that, Mr. Stoddard. If not, the facts point to her being kidnapped and held against her will. Seems to me you would've been part of that."

Syd's face twisted, his body tensing as he stepped away. "I ain't got to prove anything to you. She killed my brother, and I'm here to see that she hangs for it."

"If I may." Fielder moved between the men, facing Syd. "I'm August Fielder and I'll be representing Miss King. You're a man I'd like to speak with, Mr. Stoddard. It seems you may know quite a bit about what happened to your brother."

Syd stuttered, holding up his hands. "All I know is what I heard when I got into town. The bitc...Maggie killed him. Beat him to death is what I heard."

"So you weren't there, Mr. Stoddard?" Fielder watched Syd's eyes flicker, darting between each of them.

"No. I ain't seen Arnie in a couple months. I was coming through town on my way to the cabin when I heard about it."

"I see." Fielder turned toward Brodie. "I'm going in to see if Miss King is able to talk." He moved past Colin and Fletcher, leaving Syd for Brodie to handle.

"I expect you to stick around. I'm sure Mr. Fielder will want to talk to you again, as will the judge." He glared at Syd. "If you step within a hundred feet of Miss King, I'll arrest you...unless you give me reason to do more."

Syd's eyes blazed at the threat. "I don't plan to go anywhere. Fact is, I'll be happy to build the gallows myself." He pushed past Brodie, his pace rapid as he headed up the boardwalk.

"Eejit," Fletcher mumbled, then turned at the sound of a loud moan from inside.

"Maggie." Brodie dashed into the room to find Gwen hovering over her, a soothing hand stroking Maggie's forehead. Fielder leaned against the wall, watching. "She awake?" He glanced at Gwen, then back at Maggie, seeing her eyes try to stay open, then flutter closed.

"What...what happened?" Her voice was thick and rough from lack of use. Her eyes opened to slits as she tried to sit up.

"Stay down, Maggie." Brodie placed a hand on her shoulder, gently guiding her back down. "You were in an accident."

"Brodie?" Her strained whisper sliced through him.

"I'm right here." He bent down close to her ear. "What do you need, lass?"

"Water..."

Gwen poured a glass, holding it to Maggie's lips as Brodie raised her head.

"Just a little now, lass." Brodie swallowed the lump in his throat, noting the cuts, bruises, and swelling on her face. "That's enough." He glanced at Gwen, who took the glass away.

"I hurt all over." She tried to lift her arm, wincing.

"Try to keep still. The doctor will explain everything when he gets back." Brodie straightened as Maggie's eyes drifted shut and her breathing calmed. Glancing behind him, he saw Fielder, Colin, and Fletcher watching him. Feeling his face color, he whipped around. "Don't you two have something to do?"

"Aye, lad, we do." Colin smiled, a knowing look on his face Brodie didn't like.

"We'll be back in a bit." Fletcher took one more look at Maggie, then followed Colin outside.

Fielder cleared his throat as he moved a couple paces forward. "Progress, Sheriff MacLaren. Not enough for me to speak with her yet, but progress all the same. I'll be calling a meeting of the town council for tomorrow and I'd like you to attend."

"I've seen most of the city, and asked some men to check again. They'll let me know what else they find and who needs help."

"Excellent. You can go over it at the meeting. Afterwards, I plan to ride up to the cabin and take a look around for myself. I'll need directions."

"I'll go with you, Mr. Fielder. Seems I find something new each time I walk around the place."

"Very well. I'm sure I don't need to say this, but watch out for Stoddard. He had a look about him I didn't like. There'll be no railroading in this town, and he seems the type of man to incite people to take matters into their own hands."

"I agree. I'll find out where he's staying and have one of my deputies keep track of him."

"Good. I'll see you tomorrow."

Brodie watched Fielder leave before turning back to Maggie.

"If you're going to stay, why don't you pull up a chair? I'll let Doc Vickery know she woke up."

"Thanks, Gwen. I don't know what—"

"Don't thank me, Brodie. I'd have done it for anyone and you know it. And I'd do anything for you and the boys." She smiled, then walked toward the door.

"I know," Brodie whispered as she disappeared out the front door. Grabbing a chair, he sat next to the bed, reaching up to cover Maggie's hand with his. Something about the feel of her skin comforted him in a way he'd never known. Warmth ran through his body, a sense of peace engulfing him. It was as if he belonged here with her. The entire situation confused him.

Ever since she'd arrived in Conviction, his senses had been on alert, his body responding each time he saw or thought of her. He didn't understand any of it. She couldn't be more wrong for him. If he were looking for a woman, which he wasn't, she'd be the last person he'd seek.

She wasn't tall enough and had little meat on her bones. He liked women with curves he could sink his fingers into, women who matched his tall, broad frame. Maggie didn't fit into either category. Besides, within a few weeks, she might find herself on the way to San Quentin. The thought sickened him.

Tightening his grip on her hand, he leaned forward, whispering in her ear.

"We'll get to the truth, Maggie. I promise we will. I'll not let them send you away, lass." He took a shaky breath, his eyes glassy. "Nae. As long as I draw a breath, you'll not be going to prison."

Chapter Eleven

"May I help you?" Walter held the front door of the Fielder house open, sizing up the young man standing before him.

Joel Stoddard tightened the grip on his hat, shifting his weight from one foot to the other. He'd seen his brother, Syd, an hour ago at one of the many saloons in Conviction, learning August Fielder would be defending Maggie. Tensions between the brothers had worsened since their argument at the cabin and didn't improve when Joel announced his intention to meet with the lawyer.

"I'd like to see Mr. Fielder, if he's available."

"May I tell him who's calling?"

"Joel Stoddard."

Walter's eyes widened slightly before he nodded. "Please, come inside." Walter walked away, returning a minute later to usher Joel down the hall.

"Ah, another Stoddard brother." Fielder stood, walking around his desk and extending his hand.

"Mr. Fielder." Joel grasped his hand, then glanced around the large room. Bookcases lined two walls, a fireplace on a third with windows overlooking a beautiful garden. "You have a beautiful home."

Fielder followed Joel's gaze. "Thank you. I'm quite pleased with it. Please, sit down and tell me what I may do for you."

Placing his hat on his lap, Joel leaned forward. "I understand you have agreed to be Maggie's lawyer."

"Yes, that's correct."

"You've had a chance to meet my brother, Syd. I'm certain he gave you his belief she's guilty."

"Yes. Your brother was quite adamant about wanting to see her hang. Do you share his thoughts?"

"That's why I'm here, Mr. Fielder. There isn't much Syd and I agree on. In this instance, we couldn't be further apart. I believe she's innocent, and I'm offering you my help."

Fielder rested his arms on the desk and leaned toward Joel. "I see. And what is it you're offering to do?"

Joel cleared his throat. He'd learned Fielder was the wealthiest citizen in Conviction, head of their town council, an attorney, and owned several businesses. He also knew the imposing man sitting a few feet away took few cases—only those which meant something to him. And no one could remember a time the lawyer had lost.

"I know I don't look like much, Mr. Fielder. My brothers and I came from hard beginnings. Neither Arnie nor Syd ever saw the need for education, neither improving himself by completing school."

"I take it you did."

"Yes, sir. I never wanted to work our farm. Ma sacrificed a great deal to make sure I went as far as I could in school. When I graduated, I walked out with a law degree." He noticed Fielder's gaze flicker, then narrow. "I practiced a couple years before she died and I returned home. What I'm saying is, I believe in Maggie's innocence and I'll do whatever is needed to clear her name and find the real killer." He held Fielder's gaze. "My brother was *not* a good man. He and I had words many times about his treatment of Maggie. Did she hate him? I'm certain she did, although she never said as much. Did she kill him, leaving him rotting in a shallow grave with his face bashed in? Never."

Fielder leaned back in his chair, his elbows on the armrests, steepling his fingers. "Do you have an idea who killed your brother?"

"Yes, sir, I do. And if you'll let me, I'll do my best to prove it."

"Have you ever worked on a murder case, Mr. Stoddard?"

"No, sir. I did attend as many as my schedule permitted while in school and during my two years of practice. I believe I have a good feel of what needs to be done."

"May I ask where you attended law school?"

"Yale, sir."

Standing, Fielder walked to a bookcase and pulled out a thick volume, handing it to Joel.

"This, Mr. Stoddard, is the definitive book on successfully defending someone in a murder trial. I'll expect you to have read it by the time we meet again the day after tomorrow."

Joel's eyes popped wide and his jaw dropped. He stood, holding the book in a shaky hand, extending the other toward Fielder, who took it in a firm grasp.

"Thank you, sir. You won't regret this." Joel turned to leave.

"A good school...Yale. I went there myself."

Joel stopped, glancing over his shoulder to see a grin on Fielder's face.

Brodie's family left town to return to their ranch late the night before, carrying a message requesting Ewan's attendance at a council meeting the next afternoon. Brodie had been up since four in the morning. His first stop had been the clinic to check on Maggie, who didn't wake up during his visit. He sat by her side for an hour, holding her hand, then left for the jail to prepare a list of what would be needed to repair the town. The council meeting had been set for one o'clock, giving him enough time to ride through town and check on Maggie once more.

Leaning back in his chair, he rubbed tired eyes, then stretched his arms above his head. Several times the night before, he'd been tempted to leave his bed, dress, and walk to the clinic to sit by Maggie's side. He couldn't explain his almost compulsive need to see her, and didn't want to examine it too closely. Brodie finally drifted off to sleep well after midnight. When he woke up, the first person he thought of was Maggie, something else he didn't want to scrutinize.

"I thought I'd find you in here." Sam walked in, filled a cup with the several hours old coffee, then sat across from Brodie. "I stopped by the clinic. Maggie is still asleep. Doc said to tell you she had a restless night, but never woke up."

"I don't know how he does it."

"What? Go days without sleep?" Sam sipped his coffee, grimacing at the taste. "I don't know. It may be one reason he asked Gwen if she'd consider leaving Buckie's and working as his assistant."

Brodie's head snapped up from the list he'd been preparing. "Gwen leave Buckie's? She's what makes the saloon so popular."

Chuckling, Sam set the cup down. "I've heard the same more than once. You know, she and I talked about it a few nights before the earthquake hit. She'd never intended to earn her living on her back."

Brodie nodded. He knew her history. How she'd emigrated from Ireland, then followed her lover to San Francisco. After his death, she moved to Conviction. Unable to find a respectable job, she'd taken what was offered—work as one of Buckie's ladies. At first, she'd seen it as degrading and humiliating. Over time, she'd come to accept it, forgetting her dreams of one day finding a husband and raising a family.

"Aye. The lass took the only job she could get and has never been able to leave it. This could be the chance for a new start...if the people of Conviction will accept her as something other than what she's been. Did Gwen accept his offer?" Brodie hoped she had.

"According to Doc, she's considering it." Sam picked up his cup, poured some water into it and sloshed it around, then dumped the liquid into a bucket next to the stove.

"The lass would be daft if she turned it down."

Sam grinned as he opened the door. "We both know she's anything but daft. Gwen will take the job, I'm certain of it. I need to make the rounds of the north section of town, see if any more damage has been discovered. I'll be back by the time you leave for the council meeting."

Brodie glanced up. "Have you seen Jack around?"

"Several times. The young chap seems incapable of sitting still for longer than a few minutes. He's been helping some of the merchants clean up in between making his rounds of the south end of town." Sam closed the door as he stepped onto the boardwalk, letting Brodie digest the comments he'd made about Gwen.

The ex-Pinkerton man hadn't been in Conviction long, yet he seemed to have formed a friendship with her. Brodie knew trusting didn't come easy to Gwen, especially when it involved men. She was close to a couple other ladies at Buckie's, and over the years, her fondness for the MacLarens had turned into them seeing her as an older sister, someone they could confide in and who would never betray their trust. Brodie would do anything he could to help her, and knew his cousins felt the same.

"Sheriff. Hold up."

Brodie glanced behind him, stifling a groan at the sight of Harold Ivers. He'd wondered when the newspaperman would show up again

"I don't have time to talk right now. I'm already running late for a town council meeting." Brodie didn't stop, knowing his refusal wouldn't halt Ivers from following him.

"Very good, Sheriff. I'm on my way there myself."

Brodie relaxed. Maybe Harold would focus his attention on the town's efforts to rebuild after the earthquake instead of trying to dig up more details on Arnie Stoddard's death.

"From what I know, there is one item on the agenda today—helping the townsfolk rebuild. Nothing else." He locked his gaze on Harold. "Am I clear?"

"Of course. The meeting is about the earthquake. Afterwards, though, I'd like a few minutes of your time to ask questions about the woman who murdered Stoddard.”

Brodie’s abrupt stop had Ivers tripping over his own feet. “She’s in custody, but has not had a trial. As I said before, I wouldn’t label her a murderess and neither should you.” He continued walking.

“From what I heard, she confessed—”

“To hitting the man, not murdering him.” As always, Brodie’s patience withered as Harold continued to keep pace with him. “Her attorney will work it out and present the case.”

Harold’s steps faltered. “Attorney? I hadn’t heard anything about her hiring someone.”

“Aye. He took the case yesterday.”

“Who is it?”

“August Fielder.” Brodie felt a surge of satisfaction when the pencil fell through Harold’s fingers, rolling on the boardwalk until it slipped through a crack and disappeared from sight. “Hope you have another pencil, Ivers. You’re going to need it.”

“What do you mean you’re helping Fielder defend Maggie?” Syd’s voice roared above the noise of the saloon crowd, causing many to stop and stare. "Do you want the woman who killed our brother to get away with it?" He threw back the whiskey in his glass, slamming it onto the bar, nodding at the bartender for a refill.

Joel watched his older brother, always wary of what he might do. The wrong word or wrong look could cause a blowup, usually ending with Joel sprawled on the ground with a bloody nose... or worse.

Taking a slow, deliberate sip of his drink, he looked at Syd's reflection in the mirror behind the bar. "If she's innocent, she won't be getting away with anything."

"But she killed him," Syd hissed, gripping his glass tight enough for his knuckles to turn white.

"You don't know that, Syd. Neither of us were there when it happened. It could've been anybody. Maybe someone Arnie swindled tracked him down and got their revenge." Joel leaned closer, lowering his voice. "Do you truly believe Maggie could've done what we heard? Bashed in his face, then buried him?" He shook his head. "No. She would've knocked him out, then gotten as far away as she could before he woke up and exacted his punishment. You and I both know how ruthless his punishment could be."

Syd didn't respond, slipping deeper into his alcohol-induced darkness. Another sign Joel needed to be careful around him.

Joel didn't know why he'd come into Buckie's, except to relax after being awake for over thirty-six hours. The thick book Fielder had given him took every minute of his time since leaving the man's mansion. He'd taken copious notes and reread several chapters in preparation for their meeting later in the afternoon.

No matter what Syd thought, Joel refused to believe Maggie guilty of murder. He also believed the only way to clear her name would be to find the person who did kill Arnie—a monumental task requiring help.

Finishing his drink, Joel set the glass down and cast a wary gaze at Sydney. "You aren't going to do anything foolish, are you?"

The look Syd shot him would cower most men, but not Joel. "What are you thinking I'll do?" He signaled the bartender again. This time Joel shot him a warning glare.

"You may want to ease up on that, Syd."

"My drinking ain't none of your business. But you defending Arnie's killer *is* mine."

Joel's jaw tightened, knowing Syd was capable of doing just about anything when the alcohol took control.

"I'm going to tell you what I don't want you to do, then I'm leaving. Don't take the law into your own hands. Don't incite people to believe Maggie's guilty. And, unless you have some proof otherwise, don't try to stop me. As God is my witness, I'll push back, Syd, and you won't like the Joel you see." Turning, he strode out of Buckie's, leaving his slack-jawed brother behind.

"Excellent meeting, gentlemen. I believe we have a plan in place. With Sheriff MacLaren's leadership, I'm confident the town will be back to normal within weeks. Now, if there is nothing else, we'll adjourn." Fielder stood, turning to the men on either side of him and shaking hands.

"Mr. Fielder, do you have a few minutes to speak with me?" Harold Ivers wasted no time moving forward.

"I believe you heard it all at the meeting, Ivers. There is nothing more I can add." August picked up his hat, intending to leave, when Harold stepped in front of him.

"This is about you defending Miss King."

"I see. And what is it you'd like to know?"

"First, why did you agree to defend a woman so clearly guilty and is without funds?" Harold's intent gaze missed the flash of anger on August's face.

"Mr. Ivers, let me be clear. Miss King's guilt is far from proven. As for her lack of funds, surely you know that is of no concern to you or your readers. Now, if you'll excuse me."

"My understanding is the woman confessed to killing Stoddard."

August's face turned red, the only outward sign of his acute irritation.

"You have your facts wrong, sir. Let me give you some advice. I'd think twice before printing any of the drivel that so easily passes through your lips as truth. The *truth* of Mr. Stoddard's death is still to be determined, and that information will be heard in front of a judge. The woman will not be tried and convicted in your newspaper. Am I clear, Mr. Ivers?"

Shaken by the public rebuke, Harold swallowed the lump in his throat, then stepped back as Fielder walked past.

"You can't stop the truth from coming out, Mr. Fielder."

"It's not the truth I'm worried about. It's the stream of innuendoes and insinuations which concern me. Now, I really must leave. Good day to you, sir."

Brodie didn't move a muscle as he listened to the exchange, wishing he were as adept at handling the pesky newspaperman.

"Brodie."

His head snapped toward the familiar voice. "Da."

Ewan cleared his throat. "You handled yourself well today, lad."

Brodie nodded. "It wasn't hard. The lads helped me talk to people, figure out what needed to be done. All I did was give the report."

"And volunteer to lead the rebuilding."

"Aye, but there's not as much as there could've been. I've gotten telegrams from San Francisco and San Jose. They have much more damage than Conviction. Thanks to everyone working together, much of the destruction is cleaned up, awaiting repairs."

Ewan nodded, proud of his son, realizing how much he'd already grown in his new role. "You've not been to the ranch in a while. Your ma is missing you, lad."

Brodie's stomach twisted at the mild rebuke. He loved his family and missed them, too.

"Is my chair still available for Sunday supper?"

"Aye, although we may need to dust it off." Ewan's sincere grin broke the tension. "First, have supper with me before I ride back."

A warning sounded in Brodie's head. "Is there something wrong at the ranch?"

"Nae. Everyone is fine. We can talk over supper."

"Walk with me to the jail. I need to let my deputies know what happened at the meeting. I'd like you to meet them. Then I need to stop at the clinic to check on someone."

"Ah. Your prisoner?" Ewan's voice held no judgment as he glanced at Brodie.

"Aye. I need to see how she's doing."

"According to your brother, she's someone I should meet."

Brodie groaned, guessing what Fletcher, or any of his cousins, might have said. He'd already stopped in to see her three times since leaving his bed that morning. Each time she seemed more lucid, her eyes more focused, although the wariness remained. She didn't trust him.

They'd spoken little. With Fielder as her lawyer, the fact she wouldn't speak to him didn't bother Brodie. He had confidence in Fielder's abilities.

What he hoped for, found himself lying awake thinking about, was the day he could open the cell and allow Maggie her freedom. Although it was a gamble, knowing he didn't deserve it, Brodie wanted to find a way to convince her to stay in Conviction and give him a chance, give *them* a chance, because what he'd seen in her eyes, felt in her touch, could never be erased. And, with every fiber in his being, Brodie believed Maggie felt the same.

Chapter Twelve

"What do you mean Heather took a job with Mrs. Evanston?" Brodie held his drink suspended partway to his mouth.

"I'm surprised your brother didn't tell you when he was in town yesterday. It's all the family has talked about the last week—besides the topic of you never coming to visit." Ewan quirked a brow at Brodie.

"I'll be there Sunday, Da." Brodie sighed, accepting he'd need to do some groveling for his ma's benefit, even if he was an adult and the decision to take the sheriff job was his to make. Still, the family had always discussed all big changes. "Why did she decide to work for the widow?"

"We don't know. She rode off one morning with Fletcher and Sean to look for strays. As always, she left them behind, taking a trail south to the Evanston ranch. They didn't think much about it until she returned a few hours later and told them she'd agreed to work for Mildred. While we were all at Sunday supper, the lass snuck back and took her clothes. Audrey is still raging."

"What about Caleb?"

"The lad shrugged it off, although I don't believe that's how he feels." Ewan nodded at August Fielder as he and another man he didn't recognize walked into the Gold Dust, taking seats at a table across the room. "If the lass would open her eyes, she'd see all she ever wants is right in front of her at the Circle M."

Brodie's attention focused on Fielder and the man with him. His features looked familiar, yet he felt certain he'd never met the man.

"If you want, I'll ride out to Widow Evanston's to check on her, Da, make sure all is well." He saw the look on his da's face, knowing he understood. "It may be I'll see Heather while I'm there."

Ewan nodded. "Audrey would be grateful." He stopped when their meal arrived, waiting until the woman walked away. "Tell me about Miss King."

Brodie's gaze narrowed at his father. "You saw her. As soon as the doctor says it is all right, I'll move her back to her cell."

Brodie and Ewan had stopped at the clinic after a brief visit at the jail to let Sam and Jack know the decision of the town council. When they'd stepped toward the bed, Brodie sucked in a shaky breath.

The bruising had worsened. Her face, neck, chest, and arms were covered in patches of purple and yellow. Scratches crisscrossed her skin. Doc Vickery had set her left arm, telling Brodie it would be weeks, possibly months before she recovered. His main concern was the gash on her head. They'd left a few minutes later, Maggie never aware of the visit.

"You don't mean to put her back in jail in her condition?" Ewan set his fork down. "The lass needs to be somewhere she can heal, which isn't on one of your uncomfortable beds with a mattress no thicker than a blanket."

Brodie leaned back in his chair, still aware of Fielder across the room. "What would you have me do, Da? She's wanted for murder. Until she stands trial, I have to keep her locked up."

"Then find a place where she has a regular bed and someone to watch over her. Your ma would be furious if she knew your plans for the lass."

Brodie stiffened at the mention of his mother. He thought of the small house the town provided him at the end of the same street as the jail. One bedroom and a main room, including a living area and kitchen. His bedroom at the ranch had been bigger.

"The safest place for her is in the jail where Sam, Jack, or I can watch her. Doc Vickery is across the street if she needs him." He squeezed the bridge of his nose. "Maybe I could ask Gwen to sit with her."

"Gwen? The woman who works at Buckie's?"

Brodie's eyes flared, his mouth tilting up at the corners. His father rarely came to town other than on ranch business or to attend a meeting. Brodie had no idea he knew about Gwen. "Aye. Doc Vickery offered her a job. Do you know Gwen?"

"Do you mean in the same sense the rest of you boys do?"

Chuckling, Brodie held up his hands, palms out, feeling his face flush. "I'd say you don't know what you're talking about, except I'd be lying."

Ewan grinned at his son's obvious embarrassment. "You don't have to admit anything to me, lad. It's the way of things for young men everywhere."

Brodie nodded, his face sobering. "Yes, sir. It's the same woman, and I'd be lucky to have her watching over Maggie."

Ewan rubbed his stubbled chin. In his fifties, he had always been a handsome man, the same as all the MacLaren uncles. As tall and broad as their sons, they'd been a force. The deaths of Colin's father, Angus, and Quinn's father, Gillis, had changed the dynamics, forcing all the cousins to shoulder more of a burden at a younger age.

"In her condition, I suppose there's little chance she could escape. A woman watching over her *will* make a difference."

"Aye, Da. She also needs to be where Mr. Fielder can meet with her."

"August is a good man, and from what I've heard, an exceptional lawyer. He said the two of you will be riding out to the Stoddard place tomorrow."

Brodie nodded. "He wants to see where Stoddard died. I'll show him what I found." He leaned forward, intending to tell Ewan more, when Fielder approached their table with his guest close behind.

"Gentlemen." Fielder inclined his head toward the man beside him. "I'd like you to meet Joel Stoddard."

Brodie shoved his chair back and stood, his body tense. "Another brother? Are you after Miss King's life, too?" He could see the man's convulsive swallow, his face pale.

"Sheriff," Fielder warned.

"I can understand why you'd think that, but I have no desire to see Maggie punished for a crime I don't believe she committed."

The two studied each other, neither noticing Ewan come up beside Brodie.

Fielder stepped forward. "Joel sought me out. The man has a law degree and is offering to help with Miss King's defense. I've invited him to accompany us to the cabin tomorrow. No harm in having another set of eyes looking over the place, especially when the man used to live there."

Brodie had no reason to dislike the man who stood a couple inches shorter than he, with a face his mother, Lorna, would call *angelic*. No stubble, as if he'd never shaved, his clear eyes warm and guileless. As he studied Joel, Brodie found himself wondering how close he and Maggie were, if they ever had feelings for each other. A wave of something Brodie didn't like gripped him, his hands flexing at his sides. Jealousy had never been a sensation he'd experienced. If this were it, he didn't like it. Not one darn bit.

"If it suits the two of you, meet me at the jail after dawn and we'll ride out. When was the last time you saw the cabin, Mr. Stoddard?"

"A few days ago with Sydney. I had returned from being gone a couple months, and Syd had ridden in from San Francisco. We just happened to arrive at the cabin the same day." He shoved his hands into his pockets. "Syd is convinced she's guilty. What I saw at the cabin convinced me otherwise."

Fielder shifted his gaze between the two men. "We'll be there. Afterwards, I plan to meet with Miss King and would appreciate it if Joel was there."

"I'll be there as well." Brodie didn't know why he volunteered, other than needing to learn the extent of the relationship between Joel and Maggie.

"Very well. Now, if you'll excuse me, I still have business to attend to before returning home." Fielder glanced at Ewan. "Next time you're in town, stop by and see me. I'd like to discuss a business idea with you, and Ian, if he's available."

"Of course, August." Ewan's gaze followed the two men as they walked outside, wondering what August wanted to discuss. "The man's mind never rests," he muttered, loud enough for Brodie to hear.

"Aye. He has more energy than two men his age." Brodie returned to his chair as their desserts were served, noticing his father still watching after Fielder. "The man has so many interests, Da, it's hard to tell what's on his mind. My guess is it has something to do with his cattle business."

"Perhaps." Ewan sat down, leaning his arms on the table as his gaze narrowed on Brodie. "Now, tell me about your feelings for Miss King."

Leaning forward, arms resting on his thighs, Brodie sat in a chair next to the bed where Maggie slept. He'd been there since saying goodbye to this father a couple hours earlier, fighting the urge to reach out and take her hand in his.

She'd come out of the coma, but continued to lapse into sleep, sometimes lasting hours. At times, her body jerked in spasms, her breathing short and labored. Other times her face softened, Brodie getting a glimpse of what she would have looked like as a girl of fourteen or fifteen, well before Stoddard had gotten his claws on her. Waves of anger coursed through Brodie's body when he thought of what Arnie had done to her. For an instant, he wondered if Syd or Joel had ever touched her. The thought produced a hard ball of ice in Brodie's stomach.

"If you don't mind, I believe I'll get some rest."

Brodie's head jerked up. So lost in his own thoughts, he'd forgotten about Vickery sitting in a chair across the room. Clearing his throat, he stood.

"You go ahead, Doc. I'll stay as long as you need me."

Vickery took one more look at Maggie, checking her breathing, broken arm, and state of her bruising, then glanced up at Brodie. "I expect her to have a hard night. Gwen will be here before dawn to relieve you."

"Sam told me you offered her a job. That was good of you."

Vickery chuckled. "The offer was more self-serving than you know. I'm desperate for help. Conviction has grown well beyond what one doctor can handle. I've sent for an associate from back east. A man I used to work with for a while during the war. If all goes well, he'll be here within the month, along with his wife and child. Gwen will be helping both of us." Although the air in the room wasn't hot, he swiped an arm across his forehead. "She deserves better than working at Buckie's. It would be different if she chose to stay, enjoyed the life, but she doesn't. We'll be helping each other."

Other than a brief smile and a nod, Brodie had no words to offer.

"I'll see you in the morning. Let Gwen know to come and fetch me if anything happens before I return."

"Goodnight, Doc." He waited until the door closed, then sat back down, taking hold of Maggie's hand. He couldn't hold back a groan at the feel of her skin, wanting nothing more than to wrap his arms around her and whisper she had nothing to worry about. Instead, he pulled the chair up as close as possible and tightened his grip.

"I'd never say this in the light of day, lass, telling you how beautiful you are or how much I'd like to see you free." He reached up with his other hand, brushing strands of hair off her face, feeling the slight warmth of her skin. "You truly are a bonny lass, Maggie King. When this is over, I intend to be here for you in any way you want. You deserve your life back, and I want to be the man to help you discover it."

Brodie's voice cracked. A month ago, he never would've thought his emotions would be tangled up so much with one woman. He'd have laughed at anyone who suggested he'd be tied in knots over a woman accused of murder. It had taken his da all of five minutes to figure out the extent of his feelings for Maggie. Denying it would've achieved nothing. He'd never been a good liar.

"When this is over, we'll take a trip. Maybe on a steamboat down the Feather River to Sacramento. Or go to San Francisco. Would you like that, Maggie? We'd visit the ocean and stay at one of the grand hotels. I'd tuck your arm through mine, letting every man we see know you're taken." Swallowing the lump in his throat, he scrubbed a hand down his face and took a shaky breath. "There are so many places I want to share with you, Maggie. So many..." Yawning, he placed his left arm on the bed, letting his forehead rest against it as he continued to hold her hand. "A few more weeks, lass, and you'll be able to make any choice you want. I hope it will be me..." His voice trailed off as his eyes closed and he drifted off to sleep.

Hearing his deep breathing, Maggie slowly opened her eyes, her chest tightening. Turning, she looked at the locks of thick black hair falling across his face, wishing she could touch it, let her fingers slip through the silky strands. With one arm pinned to her side, her other hand locked with his, all Maggie could do was stare.

Brodie's words couldn't be true, she thought. They'd known each other such a short time, and under horrible circumstances. He was a lawman, she his prisoner. Nothing good could come of relying on his words or wishes. Exhaustion, guilt over the accident, concern for her recovery—anything could have prompted his declarations. In the light of day, he'd reconsider, glad she'd been asleep when he spoke of dreams and promises.

Of course, she wasn't asleep. His deep voice, still marked with a caressing Scottish lilt, had woken her from a particularly vivid dream. An uncommonly peaceful one in which he'd played a prominent role. Maggie's first thought had been how real and close his voice sounded as he spoke with Doc Vickery. She'd kept quiet, believing sleep would claim her again within minutes. Instead, she'd felt the warmth of his hand taking hers. It had taken all her willpower to remain still and allow his words to wash over her. No man had ever spoken to her as if she were important, worth caring about.

Looking at the man as he slept, she let one lone tear escape, creating a trail down her cheek to her jaw. Again, she was powerless to swipe it away. If only his words were true. The girl who still lived within her prayed they were. The beaten woman who controlled her spirit cautioned her to keep a lock on her emotions and accept reality. Dreams were for girls—not Maggie. She'd left that innocence behind a long time ago. For now, the woman in her won.

The trip to the cabin crept by, slowed by thick fog and a light drizzle. Even with Joel acting as their guide, they'd made a wrong turn twice, forcing them to backtrack.

Brodie thought the early start would prove to be in their favor. He'd woken in the doctor's office with a start, reaching for his gun before hearing Maggie's soft breathing and a door open as Doc Vickery walked inside. Brodie had taken one more look at Maggie before leaving to meet Fielder and Stoddard. He'd hoped to be back in town before noon. Now it appeared they'd be on the mountain a good part of the day.

"Up ahead." Joel picked up his pace, heading for a vague outline still shrouded in fog.

"Wonderful, Joel. Now we can get down to business." Fielder dismounted, walking straight inside the cabin, then waited for Brodie. "Explain to me what you and Colin found when you brought Miss King here, then the second time when you came alone."

Brodie went through each visit in detail, leaving nothing out. Fielder stopped him several times to clarify a point or ask a question, then motioned for Brodie to continue. They ended outside next to the all but vanished shallow grave. It hadn't taken long for the elements to erase the spot where Arnie Stoddard had been hastily buried.

"Do you have anything to add, Joel?" Fielder asked, continuing to glance around as he considered what Brodie said.

"No, sir. I believe the sheriff and I have the exact same opinion on what happened and agree Maggie could not have committed the murder. One question remains, though. If not Maggie, then who?"

Fielder looked at Brodie. "Did you find anything to suspect someone else of riding in, killing Stoddard, then riding out?"

"Nothing. Colin and I found numerous hoofprints, which didn't prove anything. Finding Miss King's tracks proved easier since she was on foot."

Fielder paced around the outside one more time before circling back to the front of the cabin and going inside. He spent a few more minutes satisfying himself they'd learned all they could before joining Brodie and Joel next to their horses.

"I must agree with you, gentlemen. Assuming Doc Vickery's right that the blow to the back of the head didn't kill Stoddard, I don't see any way Miss King could have murdered him. I believe she knocked him out, left, then someone else came along and took the opportunity to finish the job, carry him outside, and bury him." Fielder rubbed his chin, then dropped his arm to his side. "I can lay out a good case and hope it's enough to convince a jury of her innocence. The only way to be certain she's found not guilty is to find the person responsible."

Brodie had said the same to himself several times over the last few days. He seldom held doubts about his abilities. Knowing the outcome of Maggie's trial might very well rest on his shoulders, he hoped his skills and experience would be enough. He'd never imagined he'd be facing such a difficult situation within weeks of taking the job as sheriff. And never had he felt such a strong sense of imminent disaster.

Chapter Thirteen

"Syd Stoddard's drunk and letting everyone at Buckie's know how he feels about Miss King getting a trial." Sam slipped his thumbs into the pockets of his vest, staring out the jail's front window, watching the evening crowd grow at the saloon across the street.

Brodie walked up beside him, shaking his head at people who'd even consider the opinion of Stoddard worth their time. "How are they reacting?" Turning from the window, he stalked back to his desk and sat down.

"As you'd expect." Sam turned toward Brodie, leaning his back against the wall and crossing his arms. "Most ignore him, others listen, then go back to what they were doing. A few sympathize. I'm afraid it won't take much to push the rest to his way of thinking."

"It's at least another week before the judge gets here. He could stir up a lot of people by then." Brodie dragged a hand down his face, his mind on Maggie.

"Wasn't he supposed to be here by now?"

"A change in plans. Seems a group of outlaws decided to rob the bank the same day the judge arrived in Yubaville."

Sam chuckled. "Seems there's no end to the number of men who have more grit than brains."

"I don't know if it's grit. My da would call them eejits for having no brains at all. Regardless, the judge must now stay longer in Yubaville. At least it gives Fielder more time to prepare."

"Morning." Jack walked inside, stomping his boots on the wooden floor to loosen the dried dirt, then looked up at Brodie. "We got a situation on the River Belle. You might want to come see."

Smiling, Brodie stood and grabbed his hat. "Did the captain refuse to pay the ladies again?"

The River Belle had become well-known for offering gambling, music, and the services of ladies the captain hand-selected to provide private entertainment for male passengers. Several weeks before, he had a riot on his hands after distributing the wages, shorting the women a significant amount. It had taken Brodie an hour to sort out the mess, obtaining a promise from the captain to either live up to his agreement with the ladies or risk suspension of his docking privileges in Conviction.

"Nope. Seems one of the passengers got into a fight with a few men holding sympathies for the South."

California had sided with the North in the current war. Although thousands of miles from a majority of the conflicts, the state had become a significant contributor of both money and men to the Union. Few in the region openly voiced their support of Lee's army.

"If that's all it is, Jack, arrest the ones who jumped him and get Doc Vickery down there to see to the man." Brodie placed his hat back on the hook and sat down.

"He's not the one who needs the doc, Sheriff."

Sam's mouth quirked up at the corners. "I believe I'd like to see this."

"You and Jack go ahead. I'm heading over to the clinic to check on our prisoner."

Sam and Jack cast quick glances at each other, saying nothing as they walked out.

"How's she doing?" Brodie pulled off his hat, fingering the brim as he watched Vickery lean over Maggie.

The doctor glanced up, his red-rimmed eyes reflecting the long days and nights he'd been working. "Come over here and see for yourself."

Taking the few steps to the edge of the bed, Brodie's eyes met Maggie's for a brief moment before her expression fell and she glanced away. He could understand how much she must hate him. She'd been so close to getting away, leaving her past behind and reclaiming her life. He'd stepped in, causing her massive physical pain, as well as an uncertain future. Brodie knew he had no right to harbor such strong feelings for her, lying awake at night, wondering why he couldn't cut her from his thoughts.

"How long before I can move her to the jail?"

The already stern look on the doctor's face hardened, his mouth drawing into a thin line. "You know my feelings about having her back at the jail."

"You and everyone else feels the same, but I've no choice in the matter. She'll be on trial for murder soon, and she's already tried to escape once. I can't allow her to try again."

"Have you no eyes?"

Brodie startled at the rare moment of anger in the doctor's voice.

"The woman is battered and bruised with a broken arm, swollen legs and ankles, and a gash on her head still causing blinding headaches.

She needs to stay someplace she can be tended to until her wounds heal. Unfortunately, I must keep beds ready for others who need my care. Moving her to the hard cot in the cold jail will do her no good at all."

Letting his gaze rake over her, he stopped to stare at the lone tear traveling down her cheek, her eyes closed tight, still refusing to acknowledge his presence.

"What of Gwen? Has she decided to leave Buckie's?"

Straightening, Vickery grabbed a towel and wiped his hands, a look of exhaustion passing over his face. "Yes. She starts tomorrow, for which I'm quite grateful." Lowering himself into a nearby chair, he sat back. "If you insist on keeping Miss King at the jail, Gwen might have time to stop by or sit with her if no one is there, although I can't make any promises."

"Whatever Gwen could do would be welcome. If you don't mind, I'd like a few minutes alone with Miss King."

Vickery stood, tossing the towel on a nearby table. "Take as long as you need. I'll be in the back."

Waiting until the doctor shut the door behind him, Brodie pulled up a chair, but didn't sit. Instead, he focused on her slender form, the way her body shivered beneath the thin blanket.

Before he could second-guess his actions, Brodie laid a hand on her shoulder, stroking it down her arm to her wrist, then repeating the motion until she began to relax.

"Please, don't."

He almost missed her soft plea.

"I won't hurt you, Maggie."

She shifted toward him, her eyes sparking. "You've already hurt me. I came to you for help, but..." She choked back whatever else she was about to say, trying to turn away before a strong hand held her in place.

"Can't you understand I've no choice?"

She swallowed the tight knot of fear that had become a part of her. The last two years had proven how alone and abandoned she'd become. Joel had helped when he could, but other than his small kindness, she'd received nothing from men except pain and betrayal. No matter what Brodie had said when he thought she'd slept, his words were nothing more than water pitching off a cliff, crashing upon the rocks below.

Shaking her head, she refused to listen, not accepting that choices didn't exist.

"We all have choices, Sheriff. I could've kept running past Conviction until I found a safe place to hide. No one except Joel and Syd knew about me. I could've disappeared, found my way to San Francisco." Pausing, she sucked in a shaky breath. "I hear jobs are plentiful there."

"Aye, if you want to work in a brothel, lass." His words were barely above a whisper. He could see her body tense under the blanket.

"I suppose most people would believe that's all I'm suited for now. There was a time I had dreams, imagining a bright future, falling in love, having children. Now..." Her voice cracked. Clutching the blanket between her fingers, she turned away, closing him off.

"Maggie, lass, you must listen to me." Once again, he settled his hand on her shoulder, hoping she didn't shake him off. When she stayed still, he continued. "Not one of us who's heard your story believes you killed Arnie."

She turned back toward him, her brows knitting together in a frown, waiting for Brodie to continue.

"It's the reason August Fielder took your case. It's the reason Joel Stoddard is helping him."

At this, her eyes widened.

"Joel?"

Brodie's face softened. "Did you know the man has a law degree?"

"Are we speaking of Joel Stoddard, Arnie's brother?"

"Aye. I'm guessing he never told you."

Shaking her head, she pulled the blanket up below her chin, then looked up at him. "You don't believe I killed Arnie?"

"No, lass. I don't."

"Then why put me back in jail?"

He let out a deep sigh, lowering himself into the chair. "As the sheriff, I can't just let you go on what I believe. We have to do this right. Fielder is your best chance. He's doing this because he believes you are innocent. Clearing your name and finding the real killer is what will give you peace. You'll have a future, Maggie. One where you can fall in love and have a family."

A flash of hope crossed her face before she shook her head. "I'm sorry, but I can't let myself believe this nightmare will go away because you believe it will. Unless you already know who killed Arnie."

He didn't answer. Instead, he leaned forward, searching her face. "Who wanted Arnie dead, Maggie? Who hated him enough to kill him?" An almost hysterical laugh answered him.

"Everyone hated Arnie. I can't think of a single person who wouldn't have a reason to kill him."

"All right. It's a start, although quite a broad one. Do you know of anyone who threatened him, spoke of killing him?"

Catching her lower lip between her teeth, she closed her eyes, remembering the day Arnie and Joel had their last fight. Or the day Syd had stormed off to San Francisco on orders from Arnie. Both had spoken of wishing their brother to hell or wishing him dead, although she'd never believed either had been serious. As much as they hated Arnie, each could've ridden out at any time. It wasn't as if some hidden fortune bound them together.

"Neither Joel or Syd would've come back to kill him. It would have been easier for them to leave, get as far away as possible." Inhaling a shaky breath, she remembered two people who'd been to the cabin before his death. "An outlaw named Tom Franks rode in late one night a couple weeks before Arnie died. He said Arnie owed him money from a hotel robbery. Arnie pulled a gun on him and told him to ride out, never come back. A few days later, another man found us. I'm not sure of his name." She thought a moment, her brows drawing together. "There were others, but that was before we moved into the deserted cabin." She looked up at him. "I'm sorry. I don't remember any other names."

"Was it unusual for you to have visitors at the cabin?"

"Other than Joel and Syd, no one ever came to the cabin. Tom was the only one." Maggie closed her eyes. "I'm so tired."

He knew it was selfish, but he didn't want to leave her at the clinic. She needed to be in the jail where he could watch over her, be near her. "Maggie, I want to move you to the jail tonight."

She didn't open her eyes, even as the corners of her mouth tilted up. "Not tonight, Brodie," she breathed out. "I'm too tired."

He stilled at the use of his name. It sounded right coming from her lips. "Say it again, Maggie."

"Hmmm?"

"My name, Maggie. Say it again."

His request was met with silence. Reaching for the blanket, he tightened it around her shoulders, tucking it under her. Leaning back in the chair, he crossed his arms, settling in for a long night, knowing he wouldn't be able to walk out the door and leave her behind.

Sam leaned down, grasping Brodie's shoulder, keeping his voice low. "Wake up, MacLaren." It took another attempt before he jerked awake, his eyes opening to slits.

Sitting up, he rubbed his face with both hands, then shifted his gaze to Maggie, alarm coursing through him as he stood to stare down at her.

"Is she all right?" It wasn't so much a question as a demand.

"From what I can see, the lady is fine." Sam couldn't hide the amusement in his voice. Brodie hadn't mentioned a word about his feelings, but they were clear to anyone who watched and listened.

Brodie whipped around, pinning Sam with a hard glare.

Sam held his hands up, taking a step back. "It's long past sunup, Fielder is at the jail waiting to speak with you, and your new deputy has arrived."

"New deputy?"

"He says you replied to his telegram, asking him to ride out. Nathan Hollis, a captain in the Union Army."

Brodie mumbled a curse at the same time Doc Vickery walked in the back door. He'd forgotten about the man's inquiry and his return message.

"My apologies, gentlemen. I must have overslept." He continued toward the bed, unaware of the tension in the room a moment before. "How is the patient this morning?"

"Still asleep. I don't believe she woke up all night." Brodie walked across the room, grabbing his hat off a hook before taking another glance at Maggie. "I'll be at the jail, Doc. Let me know when she wakes up. I plan to move her over there this morning."

"You know how I feel about that, Sheriff."

"Aye, but I've not changed my mind. The lass will be going back to the jail today." He didn't look at Sam as he walked outside, inhaling a deep breath of the crisp morning air, which turned his thoughts to Thanksgiving.

The previous year, President Lincoln had proclaimed it an official holiday, and the MacLarens had embraced it wholeheartedly, the women preparing a meal meant to feed an army. It had been a wonderful day, as well as the first and only time the entire family had celebrated the holiday. The thought of Colin's father, Angus, and Quinn's father, Gillis, had his stomach clenching. Both had been murdered while Colin, Quinn, and Brodie traveled to fetch Sarah. He knew the grief would take years to heal.

"MacLaren, wait up." Sam came up beside him as Brodie stepped to the jail door. "There's something you need to know about Hollis."

"Not now, Sam. Fielder's already been waiting long enough." Brodie pushed open the door, stopping at the sight of a man sitting in one of the chairs, one leg crossed over the other, his right arm gesturing as if telling a story. Brodie's gaze narrowed on the man's left arm. It had been amputated below the elbow.

"Good morning, Sheriff MacLaren." Fielder extended his hand. "Hollis and I were sharing stories of our time back east. Seems we know a few of the same people."

The initial shock wore off as Brodie walked forward to grasp Fielder's hand, then turned as Hollis stood. "I'm Sheriff MacLaren. Sam tells me you're Nathan Hollis." He gripped the man's hand in his, feeling the strength.

"Yes, sir, I am. It took me a few days longer to arrive than planned. I hope the job is still available."

"I've never seen anything like it, Sheriff." Jack walked up next to Nathan. "When Sam and I got to the River Belle last night, Hollis already had two men on their backs and a third against the wall. And he hadn't even drawn his gun."

"That right, Hollis?" Brodie took a good look at the man, noting his tall frame and wide girth, although he doubted the man had an ounce of fat on him.

Shrugging, his mouth curved into a smile. "They aren't the first to underestimate me."

"I don't doubt it. I assure you, I'll not be that man. We're glad to have you, Nathan."

"If you call me Nate, we have a deal."

"Nate it is then." Brodie reached into his desk, picked up a badge, and tossed it to his newest deputy, then turned toward Jack. "I'd like you to show Nate around Conviction."

"Sure will, Sheriff. You know you can count on me." He turned towards Hollis. "Come on, Captain. Guess we don't need to go by the docks." Jack laughed at his own joke. "You've probably seen as much of it as you want to for a few days."

"Do you have a horse, Nate?" Brodie asked as the men started outside.

"Brought him, along with all I own, on the boat with me."

"Good. Jack, show Nate where he'll be staying."

"The boardinghouse will be our first stop, Sheriff."

Brodie waited until they'd left, then faced Fielder. "I spoke with Miss King last night. She gave me the name of a man who threatened Stoddard."

Sam moved forward. "If you have a name, I can track him down."

Fielder stepped between the two. "A good beginning, gentleman. Now the hard work begins."

Chapter Fourteen

Later that afternoon, Brodie brought Sam and Nate with him to transfer Maggie to the jail. Doc Vickery and Gwen did what they could to get her ready, all the while not hiding their disdain about his decision. To her credit, Maggie said nothing, even wrapping her arms around Brodie's neck as he carried her across the street, Sam on one side of him and Nate on the other.

Maggie's body pressed against his, her face nuzzling his neck as her warm breath washed across his skin, straining his limits. For a brief moment, he considered handing her off to Sam, then quickly pushed it from his mind. The thought of another man holding her so close triggered a jealous reaction he couldn't think about right now. He reminded himself she was a temptation he didn't need, even as his mind screamed she belonged to him.

"The cell is all ready for her." Jack held the door open, stepping aside to let them pass. Poking his head outside, he saw few people had turned their way, an indication the town had already lost interest in Maggie as they worked to rebuild the town.

Brodie kicked the cell door open, sliding Maggie from his arms and onto the bed. "I'm sorry, lass." His mumbled apology seemed a poor excuse for his decision to move her into the cold, bleak space.

She didn't immediately release her arms from around his neck, her wide blue eyes staring into his. Desire swelled when he saw the heat he felt reflected back at him. Her porcelain skin had paled even more during her recovery, enhancing the freckles scattered across her nose and cheeks. He wanted to kiss each one, then capture her lips with his. Before he could finish the thought, her arms dropped to her sides and she shifted her gaze away.

"You can leave now. I'll be fine." Her flat voice squeezed his heart, carving a deep hole in his chest.

Straightening, he noticed Sam and Nate retreating to the front of the jail, giving them privacy.

"Can I get you anything?"

The flash of cold, steely eyes gave him his answer before she spoke.

"No. I'd prefer to be alone, Sheriff." Grabbing a blanket with her right hand, she leaned against the wall, doing her best to spread it across her legs, sending Brodie a warning look when he leaned down to help. "I can do this."

The words were sharp and full of pain—pain he believed wasn't all physical.

Squatting next to the bed, he picked up her hand, threading his fingers through hers, waiting for her to look at him. When she didn't, he let out a deep sigh.

"I told Fielder about Tom Franks. Sam is already trying to track him down."

She glanced at him for a brief moment before turning away, but not before he saw hope rise and then fade from her face. "You won't find him."

He cocked his head to the side. "And why is that, lass?"

She licked her lips, a nervous gesture he'd come to recognize. "Arnie always said Tom was more ghost than man. Arnie said he could disappear into the wind without a trace left behind."

"I'll let Sam know. He likes nothing more than a challenge." Brodie's eyes crinkled at the thought. He knew Sam had already sent word to Allan Pinkerton, welcoming any help the man could provide. According to Sam, he believed there was a special place in Hell for men who took advantage of women, such as Arnie Stoddard. Pinkerton had replied within an hour, confirming he'd do what he could to locate Franks.

"I know you're trying to help me, and I'm grateful. It's just..."

"What, Maggie?" Brodie gripped her hand tighter, his eyes searching hers.

She shook her head and looked away, unable to hold his gaze any longer.

"If you're thinking it's hopeless, you'd be wrong, lass."

"MacLaren. You'd better come out and listen to this." Sam stood a few feet from the cell, his gaze switching between Brodie and their joined hands.

He let go of Maggie's hand and stood. "Get some rest. If you need anything, call for me or one of the deputies."

She nodded, her expression one of crushing hopelessness. He wished he had more to offer, some type of promise all would be fine. As much as Brodie believed she'd make it through this and Fielder would secure her freedom, he couldn't swear to it.

Locking the cell, he walked to the front and stepped outside, hearing Syd Stoddard's now familiar voice. At least twenty men stood outside Buckie's Castle, listening to him rant about his brother's murder and the woman being held in jail.

"She don't need no trial." Syd's booming voice rang out up and down the street, causing people to stop and stare. "There's only one person who wanted Arnie dead." He pointed toward the jail. "That person is sitting in the jail, waiting for a judge who won't be in town for weeks. You know who is paying for men to watch her and feed her? The good people of Conviction, that's who."

A low rumbling spread through the crowd, although no one made a move toward the jail.

"There ain't no need for a trial."

"What are you saying, Syd? We can't just storm in there and hang a woman." An older man Brodie recognized as a hand at one of the local ranches stepped forward. "If you have proof she did it, tell the sheriff."

Brodie, Sam, and Nate spread out, moving closer to the crowd. Glancing over his shoulder, Brodie saw Jack standing in the jail doorway, his hand resting on the butt of his gun. He remembered the evening he'd taken Jack outside to see a demonstration of his shooting skills. Given what he'd seen, he would've placed money on Jack taking care of the crowd in front of them all by himself.

Syd ignored the cowhand's attempt at reason. "She and my brother lived alone in an old cabin up in the hills. She admitted to hitting him over the head and leaving him for dead. I don't need no more proof than that."

A few in the crowd nodded, some looking at Brodie and his deputies. Still, no one moved toward the jail.

Brodie had heard enough. "Mr. Stoddard. I'm going to ask you to stop trying to tempt these fine people into doing something they'll regret."

"They ain't going to regret hanging a murderer."

Brodie stepped next to Stoddard and faced the crowd. "The woman in there is going to get a fair trial. You all know August Fielder." He watched as most nodded. "You know he doesn't take on many cases. He's convinced she's innocent and has agreed to defend her. I don't know about you, but I have to take his actions into consideration."

"That don't mean anything."

A shot rang out before Syd could continue, the bullet hitting the ground inches from Brodie's feet. Shouts and screams followed as people scattered, most heading for cover inside the saloon.

Brodie pulled his gun as he, Sam, and Nate dashed back toward the jail. "You two see anyone?"

"No." Sam held his gun in front of him, scanning the windows above the saloon.

"It came from up there." Nate pointed to the building next to Buckie's.

"The bank?" Brodie asked.

"I'm certain of it."

"I believe Nate's right, Sheriff." Jack glanced at Brodie from his position a few feet away. "The shot hit the ground just behind you."

"As far as I know, the upstairs is used for storage. I'd better go check it out."

"Not alone, MacLaren." Sam moved alongside him as Brodie stepped onto the street.

"Nate, stay here with Jack. Make sure no one gets to Maggie."

"Yes, sir." Nate backed into the jail, followed by Jack, then closed the door.

"One cartridge. Fits what we heard." Sam bent down, picking up the only evidence someone had fired from the window a foot away. "But why shoot at you? It wasn't that hard a shot." He glanced out the window to the street below. "Anyone with a little experience could have hit you from here."

"A warning. Maybe it wasn't meant to hit either Stoddard or me. Perhaps it was intended to disperse the crowd."

"Someone tired of hearing Stoddard. If I'd have thought of it, I might have done the same."

Sam grinned as he turned away from the window, hooking his thumbs in his gun belt.

"You've an odd sense of humor, lad."

"You've no idea, MacLaren."

They took one more look around the almost empty room above the bank before leaving for the jail. Brodie didn't break stride as he walked inside and headed for Maggie's cell.

"She's doing fine," Jack called, but Brodie didn't hear him.

Unlocking the cell, he took quiet steps to the bed, hearing Maggie's deep breathing. For the first time in over an hour, he relaxed, letting out the breath he'd been holding. He tried not to make noise as he sat beside her, resting his hand on her shoulder. Brodie didn't know how it happened, how his life had become so connected to hers. Being near her, touching her, had become as important to him as air, food, and water.

Moving his hand, he fingered a strand of her deep mahogany locks. Gwen had washed Maggie's hair, brushing until it shone, letting it fall in soft curls around her shoulders. She'd offered to braid it for Maggie before Brodie carried her to the jail. Maggie had refused, saying she liked the feel of it against her skin. He agreed, stroking her head.

"Brodie..." Her sleepy voice drew him closer.

"I'm here, lass."

"Don't leave me."

"I'll stay here all night if you want me to." He cupped her face with his hand, stroking a finger down her cheek.

Turning, she kissed his palm, then placed her own hand over his. "I wish my life were different."

Clearing the lump in his throat, which had formed the instant her lips touched his skin, Brodie leaned closer, his face inches from hers, his voice husky. "Different in what way, lass?"

She kept her eyes closed, as if opening them would break the spell and erase her courage. "If I were someone else, maybe you could like me."

"Ah, lass. I already like you. If you knew how much, it would likely scare you." He cringed as the declaration he'd made a few nights before flashed through his mind. Brodie still didn't understand what had inspired him to make the confession. At least she'd been asleep and would never know how much of a fool he'd made of himself, or how much he wanted her.

Opening her eyes, she saw the sincerity in his, again wishing they'd met under different circumstances. Something about Brodie MacLaren made Maggie believe he could be her guiding light—a pathway back to the person she used to be.

No matter how she pushed him away, trying to bury her feelings and control her fear of trusting a man, she'd developed a strong affection for the rugged lawman. Her rational mind told her most men were not like Arnie. Her father and grandfather were wonderful. Doc Vickery, August Fielder, Brodie's deputies, and Brodie had treated her well, often with kindness. Even Joel Stoddard had been her protector, taking his own harsh punishment from Arnie for his efforts.

She wanted...needed, to find her way back. If Fielder could prove her innocence, maybe she could still have her dream, find a man like Brodie, fall in love, marry, and have children. If only...

"Maggie? Are you all right, lass?"

Closing her eyes to clear her rambling thoughts, she nodded. "Yes. I'm fine. A little tired."

"Then you should rest." Brodie tugged at the blanket.

"You'll stay?" Her voice trembled, as if she feared he'd go back on his word.

He stroked his knuckles down her cheek, feeling an instantaneous pull toward the woman he wanted with an intensity that scared him.

"I said I would, lass. All night if you want me to."

"Thank you." She leaned into his touch, glancing up, her heart pounding at the intensity in his moss green eyes.

Knowing he shouldn't, yet unable to stop, he leaned down, brushing his lips across hers. The light touch wasn't nearly enough. He settled his mouth over hers, taking what she offered for a few brief moments before pulling back, his breath ragged and voice rough.

"Have you eaten?" He stood, needing to put distance between them, if only for a few minutes.

Maggie shook her head, fighting to keep her eyes open. "I'm not hungry. Only tired." She turned onto her side, facing him.

Nodding, he let out a slow breath before sitting back down and resting his hand on her shoulder.

"Sleep, lass. I'll be here when you wake up."

Even as her mind shut down, she nodded, willing herself to believe his words were true.

Brodie kept his promise, staying until Maggie woke before dawn. He helped her outside, escorted her back, then left to fetch breakfast for both of them. Sam, Nate, and Jack stopped in, but he sent them on their way. With Maggie the lone occupant of the jail, their services could be put to better use helping to repair earthquake damage, or keeping peace along the docks.

Over the last few months, attacks, robberies, and vandalism had increased along the waterfront. As Conviction grew, so did the attraction for gamblers, outlaws, and those seeking an easy dollar. With them came another level of scoundrel—drunks, pickpockets, and men who molested women and children. Brodie knew the need for more lawmen grew with each passing week. He already had three deputies, with approval to hire three more.

Scribbling a quick telegram, he stood, walking to the back to let Maggie know he'd be gone for a few minutes.

"I need to send a telegram. Do you need anything before I go?"

She sat on her bed, huddled in a corner, reading a book Gwen had given her. Glancing up, her mouth curved into a smile. Brodie's heart constricted as his eyes lit up.

"The telegraph office is open on Sunday?"

"It's Sunday?" Brodie had lost all track of time. Worse, he'd promised his da he'd be at the ranch for supper.

Soft laughter filled the cell. "Yesterday, Gwen told me it was Saturday, so..."

He didn't want to leave. After last night, all he wanted was to stay by her side, protect her, make her feel safe and cared for. But he had an obligation to the family who'd always stuck by him. A family he loved.

"I must find Sam or one of the others to stay with you." Brodie dragged a hand through his hair, wishing he could take Maggie with him.

"Why? Where do you have to go?" Her smile vanished as she set the book aside and leaned forward, wishing it didn't hurt so much to stand or walk.

He explained the promise to his family. "I'll be back before sundown. The deputies will be here if you need anything."

"Of course. It's important to keep promises to family."

He unlocked the cell and walked to the bed, holding out his hand. "Sam and I are still trying to find your family, Maggie. Maybe you'll see them again soon."

She shook her head and pulled back. "No. I don't want them to see me like this. It's better if they believe I'm dead rather than know what happened."

His gaze narrowed at her. The joy he'd seen a few moments before had vanished, replaced with fear. "Your family will understand."

"No, they won't." Her insistence stunned him. "My father would never understand." She glanced up at him, her eyes blazing. "Never."

He sat down on the bed, wrapping an arm around her shoulders, drawing her close. "Shhh, lass. We won't talk of it now." He reached over, picked up the book, and handed it to her.

"I don't feel much like reading anymore." She pulled away, scooting back against the wall, letting his arm fall from her shoulders. "You should be going if you want to see your family."

Brodie sighed. "Aye. I can't disappoint Ma again. Da would never forgive me."

"Then go. Send one of the deputies to stay with me." She opened her book in an attempt to shut him out.

"Ah, Maggie. You're going to be the death of me, lass." He bent down, placing a finger under her chin and lifting her face to him for a brief kiss. Straightening, he saw the surprise on her face and chuckled. "I suppose that wasn't wise."

"No, Sheriff. It probably wasn't." This time her smile was genuine, lighting her face, giving him something to think about while he spent time with his family.

"I'll be back soon, Maggie. Try not to get into trouble while I'm gone."

She snickered, then buried herself back in the book, holding the moment close to her heart.

Chapter Fifteen

"You came." Lorna dashed down the porch steps, wrapping her arms around her oldest child.

"I told Da I'd be here." He hugged her tighter, realizing how much he'd missed seeing his ma each day.

Pulling back, she swiped away a tear and smiled. "It's been so long, I thought you might forget."

"From now on, I'll plan to be here every Sunday, maybe ride back with everyone after church."

Smiling, she slipped her arm through his. "Come inside and say hello to your brothers and sisters, then you can find your cousins." Lorna knew her son well. The fact he'd taken a job in town didn't change his need to spend time with the men who were his closest friends.

"Brodie!" Jinny stood up from the piano and ran to him, jumping into his arms. At nineteen, she was a year older than Fletcher and four years younger than Brodie. "It's about time you came to see us." Planting a kiss on his cheek, she loosened her arms and let him set her down.

"Where are the wee ones?" Brodie glanced around, listening more than looking for his youngest sister, Kenzie, and nine-year-old twin brothers, Clint and Banner.

Jinny laughed, thinking how much the twins had grown in just the last few weeks. "Kenzie's begun riding with Fletcher whenever Ma allows it."

"At ten?"

"Ach...you forgot her last birthday." Lorna came up behind him. "She turned eleven late last month."

Brodie grimaced. No one ever missed a family birthday. "I won't miss another."

"Well, then, the twins will turn ten in early December. Jinny and I will make a list of all birthdays so you don't forget." Taking a look around, she crossed her arms. "I still have cooking to finish before everyone arrives. Now would be a good time to find the lads. Ewan should be with them at the big barn." She patted his cheek. "It's good to have you home."

He leaned down to place a kiss on his mother's cheek. "Love you, Ma."

"You can't ride him like that." Quinn sat on the fence with several others, laughing as he watched his brother, Bram, try to break a two-year-old colt.

"I can ride him anyway I want." Bram glared at Quinn, even as his face broke into a smile. "I've already ridden him without a saddle, so this should be easy."

Brodie smiled, hearing the chorus of laughter following Bram's boast. Few on the ranch could outride Bram or were more proficient at breaking horses to saddle. Still, you could never count on anything when dealing with a skittish animal. No one saw him as he stepped around the barn and to the corral, then leaned against a post.

"Big talk, little brother. We'll be seeing how long you can stay on him." Quinn flashed a grin, even as his body tensed. As much fun as they had mocking each other, everyone stayed on alert while working around the stock. Quinn nodded at Colin, who stood on the other side of the corral, both ready to dash inside if anything went wrong.

"All right, you beautiful beast. It's time to acknowledge who's boss." Bram stroked the colt's neck while Fletcher held firm to the bridle. Bending, he picked up a thin blanket, placing it over the horse's back, continuing to stroke the colt's neck while whispering words of encouragement. After a few minutes, he bent again, picking up the lightest saddle they owned and setting it on top of the blanket, cinching it. The colt danced around, moving its hind legs back and forth while Fletcher kept a secure, yet gentle grip on the reins.

Continuing to whisper in a calm, reassuring voice, Bram let the colt settle down, getting used to the extra weight on his back. Everyone stayed silent as several more minutes passed. Finally, Bram nodded to Fletcher, taking the reins from his hand.

In one swift motion, Bram swung into the saddle, his full concentration on the animal. The colt dashed forward, then bucked, turning to his right, then left, trying to rid himself of the unaccustomed load. Bram shifted his weight, clamping his legs around the horse, and held on as he talked to the animal.

Those watching remained quiet, not getting caught up in the usual commotion associated with breaking a horse. Instead, they'd shout encouragement, telling him to hang on and not let the beast get the better of him.

Their words floated through his mind, keeping him centered on the task. He'd been bucked off many times, ending up with nothing more than bruises and scratches. Bram had no intention of being carried out of the pasture today.

Time ticked by, the colt beginning to tire, then stopping in the middle of the field, snorting, stomping his hooves into the dirt. Bram sat still, staying alert. In the past, he'd been lulled into thinking the fight was over, only to be unprepared for a last effort by the horse to buck him off. He'd ended up on the ground, his pride wounded more than this body. The same wouldn't happen today.

Amongst cheers from his family, Bram kicked the colt with the heel of his boot, guiding him in a wide circle around the pasture.

"You owe me a day of chores." Fletcher laughed at the incredulous look on his cousin's face.

"Actually, you owe *both* of us a day of chores." Sean stood next to the fence, grinning.

"Ach. You lads weren't serious, were you?" Quinn jumped down from the fence, crossing his arms.

"I'm afraid we were." Sean clasped him on the shoulder. "If it's too much for an old man like you, we could adjust the bet."

"Are you calling me an old man?" Quinn swatted Sean's hand away. "I can outwork both of you lads any day."

"I'd have to agree with the old man part." Brodie walked up, surprised no one had noticed him watching.

"Brodie. When did you get here?" Fletcher gave his brother a quick hug. "Have you seen Ma?"

"Aye. I value my life too much not to see her first." He glanced past them at Bram, who still guided the colt around the pasture. "He was born to work with horses."

"The lad has a magic touch." Quinn leaned against the fence. "He, Sean, and Fletcher have been talking to Ewan and Ian about expanding the horse breeding business. They believe we can do more than just supply horses to the army."

"Is that so, Fletch?" Brodie glanced at his brother. Fletcher had a special skill at breeding horses, developing strong animals sought after by private buyers and the military. Sean, though, had a gift for healing. Few knew of his dream to attend veterinary school in Edinburgh, Scotland. Sean hadn't even mentioned it to his father, Ian.

"Da and Ian are considering it. Quinn, Colin, and Blaine agree with us and have spoken with them. It would help if you could make time to speak with them, too."

"You know I'll do what I can, Fletch. If you're finished here, ride back to the house with me and tell me what I need to do."

Jack paced back and forth in front of the desk, wishing he could be out with Sam and Nate instead of keeping watch on a woman who could barely walk. Maggie had spoken little since he took over for Sam an hour before, only asking for more water. She'd even refused lunch.

Deciding he needed to get some fresh air, even to just sit out front and watch the activity, he checked on Maggie once more.

"I'm going outside, Miss King. Yell if you need anything."

She looked up from her book and nodded. "Do you know when Sheriff MacLaren will return?"

"No, ma'am, I don't. He's having supper with his family. That's all I know."

"Do you know much about the MacLarens, Deputy?" Maggie cringed, wishing she'd kept her curiosity to herself.

"Mostly just what people say. They have one of the largest ranches around. I don't rightly know how many MacLarens there are, but close to thirty. My understanding is they came over from Scotland ten, maybe fifteen, years ago, then joined a wagon train for California." Jack stopped a moment, stroking his chin. "I do know

236

Colin's and Quinn's fathers were murdered a few months ago."

"I'm sorry to hear that. I've met both of them. They seem decent."

"More than decent is what I've heard. Brodie's father, Ewan, is on the town council and is good friends with August Fielder."

She sat forward. "My lawyer?"

"Yes, ma'am. 'Course, I think most people in Conviction would like to call both men their friends. You know how people are." Jack shoved his hands into his pockets. "Well, guess I'll go outside a spell, get some fresh air." He grimaced, realizing what he'd said. "I don't mean—"

"It's all right, Deputy. I know what you mean." Maggie wished she had the same freedom to leave. Given the opportunity, she'd try to escape again. Leaning back against the wall, her thoughts shifted to Brodie. No matter how this worked out, she'd be leaving Conviction. If found guilty, it would be a short trip to the prison at San Quentin. If innocent, there'd be no other choice except to leave. Leaving wouldn't bother her at all. Saying goodbye to Brodie MacLaren wouldn't be as easy.

She watched as Jack turned and walked toward the front. Maggie picked up her book, hearing him close the door at the same time an explosion shook the walls of the jail, followed by a second a little further away.

Tossing the blanket aside, she stood, hobbling to the cell doors to grip the bars, her hands shaking. "Deputy!" Her voice cracked as a third explosion caused the floor to buckle. She yelled again, getting no answer. Before she had a chance to scream for help, the back door of the jail burst open. She blinked, then her eyes widened, recognizing the man standing in the doorway, a gun pointing at her.

"Syd..." Her stomach plummeted at the sight of the man she hated almost as much as she did Arnie. "What are you doing here?"

"I guess that would be obvious, missy. I've come to get you out of here." Syd shifted to look outside. "Seems there's been some damage done to a few stores. Guess that means the deputies will be busy a while."

"You're the one who caused the explosions?" She let go of the bars and stumbled backward.

"Well now, missy, you know I have special skills in blowing things up. Usually it's a bank safe. It's been a while, though, so I made an exception today. I needed the practice, if you understand me."

Maggie shook her head, retreating to the back wall of her cell. "Why would you do such a thing? People could've been killed."

"You questioning my ability?" He moved toward her cell, aimed the gun at the lock, and fired. Pulling the cell door open, he motioned with the gun. "You're coming with me."

Her eyes darted around the cell, looking for something she could use to fend him off.

"Don't be thinking you can escape from me, missy. From what I've heard, you ain't in no condition to run." He stalked forward, grabbed Maggie's arm, and yanked her to him. "Now, you and me are going to walk right out the back, get on my horse, and leave town before anyone knows you're missing."

She tried to pull free, but he slammed her against the wall, lowering his face to within inches of hers.

"We can do this nice 'n easy, or I can knock you out and carry you to my horse. Your decision, missy."

She turned her head away, gagging at the sour smell of whiskey on his breath. "I told you before not to call me that."

Syd laughed, tightening his hold as he dragged her from the cell and out the back door. "You always did have too much sass."

Dragging her feet didn't help as he shoved her out the back and toward his horse. With a groan, Syd picked her up, tossed her behind the saddle, then climbed up in front of her. Taking his rope, he slid it around her, then him, securing it to the saddle horn.

"Don't you do anything foolish."

Before she could answer, Syd kicked the horse, taking off at a fast pace down the dirt alley behind the jail. Turning toward the river, he dodged horses, people, and wagons before making a sharp turn to disappear into the woods and out of town.

"You be sure to come back next Sunday, Brodie." Lorna hugged her son, then stepped away, letting Jinny give her brother a hug.

"If you can't make it on Sunday, at least come back for Thanksgiving." Jinny gave him a kiss on the cheek.

"I'll not be missing Thanksgiving, lass. You can count on it." He glanced down at his sister, Kenzie. "Don't be giving Fletcher too much grief when you help round up the steers. He has enough trouble keeping his mind on work."

Kenzie giggled, hugging Brodie around his waist. "He's lucky to have me. No one else wants to ride with him."

Brodie glanced behind her at Fletcher, who stood with his arms crossed, a grin on his face.

"Do you really have to go?" Banner stepped up to him, Clint by his twin's side.

"I'm afraid I do, laddie. But I'll be back as soon as I can."

Banner sighed, holding out his hand. "All right." Brodie clasped his hand, pulling Banner, then Clint into a hug. "Both of you are growing too fast." He rested his hands on their shoulders, kneeling down to talk to them in private. "Now, laddies, Ma needs your help. I know she has Jinny, Fletcher, and Kenzie, but she needs you to do your part. Do you understand?"

"You sound like Pa," Banner grumbled.

Brodie laughed as he stood back up and walked down the porch steps to take Hunter's reins. "I'll see all of you soon."

"Hold up, lad."

Brodie glanced behind him to see his father, Ewan, walking toward him from the barn. "I thought you and Uncle Ian were still at the neighbor's."

"Widow Evanston listened to our thoughts, then booted us out. We did get to see Heather for a little while. She seems happy, although I believe the lass is starting to miss us." Ewan glanced at his wife, a look of affection Brodie had grown used to seeing crossing his face. "Your ma is happy you came today."

"And you?"

"Ach, Brodie. I see you when I ride into town. And I'll be doing that more, so you need to get used to it." Ewan stretched out his hand, which Brodie accepted.

"Aye. I believe I can handle seeing you more often, Da."

Brodie reined Hunter around, waved to his family, and took off for town. It had been good seeing his family, spending time with them, learning what he'd missed. With such a big family, he could spend days before getting caught up on everyone. Right now, as he rode the trail back to Conviction, what he wanted most was to get back to the jail and make sure Maggie was all right.

Chapter Sixteen

Brodie heard two explosions a mile before reaching the outskirts of town. Giving Hunter a quick command, he moved the horse into a gallop. His heart pounded as he thought of what the blasts meant and what he might find. The third explosion ripped through the air as he hit the eastern border of the main street. He barely slowed down as he jumped to the ground in front of the jail and burst through the door.

Seeing no one, he dashed to the back, coming to a halt when he saw the empty cell, Maggie nowhere in sight.

Drawing his gun, turning in a circle, he spotted the open back door and dashed outside. He ran to the alley, looked one way and then the other, seeing stunned people moving about in a daze, as if absorbing what had occurred. Holstering his gun, Brodie hurried back into the jail and out the front door, almost barreling into Jack.

"What the hell happened?" He grabbed Jack by the shoulders.

"Explosions, Sheriff. Three of them. Lots of damage, but no injuries so far. Sam is checking the damage at the docks. Nate is at Lucky's Saloon."

"And the third blast?" Brodie dropped his hold on Jack and spun around, trying to locate Maggie.

"The park two blocks over." Jack stepped away, taking a good look at Brodie, seeing more than concern over the explosions.

"And no injuries. How can that be?"

"Don't know, Sheriff. Guess we'll have to ask the man who set them—if we ever find him."

Brodie glared at his deputy. "We'll find the sonofabitch who did this, Jack. You can put money on it. He's probably the one who took Maggie."

Jack's mouth dropped open. "Miss King? She's not in the jail?" He didn't wait for Brodie to answer before he whirled around and raced to the back, his eyes bulging at the empty cell. "Dadgum. You think someone set the explosions so they could get her out?"

"Aye. But who, and what did they use?"

"Black powder and liquid nitroglycerine." Sam walked into the jail, mumbling a curse when he saw Maggie nowhere around. "She get out?"

"Taken is my guess." Brodie shifted toward Sam. "Black powder I can understand, but nitroglycerine? I thought it was outlawed when a crate exploded at the Wells Fargo building in San Francisco."

Sam offered a bland expression. "MacLaren, we are speaking about outlaws here. Someone who set off three blasts and may have taken Maggie. How do you *think* they got it?"

Brodie pinched the bridge of his nose. "We need to find her."

"And we will. Nate should come with us. His tracking skills could be useful." Sam pulled out his revolver, checking the cylinder, then grabbed another box of ammunition.

"Jack, I need you to stay here." Brodie checked his Colt revolver, then pulled a second gun from a hidden drawer in the desk.

"Sure, Sheriff. What about the explosions?"

"We find Maggie and we'll find who's responsible for setting them. I'd appreciate it if you'd let Mr. Fielder know what we're doing." Brodie slipped both arms into his jacket, then turned toward Sam. "Let's find Nate, then go after the spineless varmint who took Maggie."

"Where are you taking me?" They'd ridden for less than an hour. Maggie's body ached, her broken arm throbbed, and she didn't recognize the trail.

Syd either didn't hear the question or chose to ignore her.

"Syd, where are we going?"

"You are an annoying wench, aren't you?" He made a sudden turn onto a narrow animal trail, then glanced behind him.

"I'm no wench." Maggie gripped the saddle's cantle tighter, her anger rising, accompanied by a renewed sense of panic.

His bark of laughter sickened her. "You cooked, cleaned, and refused to marry Arnie. In my mind, that makes you a wench. But you won't have to worry about that for long."

Her body tensed. "What do you mean?"

"You'll find out soon enough, missy."

A cold ball of fear lodged in her stomach, the same sickening sensation she felt each time Arnie entered the cabin. She hated how the Stoddard brothers had changed her, made her believe she was worthless for anything except providing services to Arnie.

Glancing around, she memorized the path, noticing the location of the sun and an occasional large boulder or dead tree. Looking down, she spotted his knife in a sheath on his belt, and made a decision. No matter the risk, she'd take the knife and use it to gain her freedom.

"There are fresh tracks on a trail up ahead. From what I can tell, it's one horse carrying two people." Nate reined up alongside Brodie and Sam. They'd scoured the trails along the river, finding nothing until Nate rode ahead, disappearing into the thick brush.

"Do you know where the trail goes, MacLaren?"

Brodie shook his head. "Never noticed it before, Sam. If it continues up into those hills, they could be headed for one of the abandoned mines."

They rode in silence for several minutes, each keeping watch on their surroundings. Sam shifted in his saddle, looking over his shoulder at Brodie.

"You understand there's a chance Miss King and whomever broke her out are in this together. This may not be a kidnapping."

"Aye, Sam. The thought had crossed my mind." He didn't want to believe it, and couldn't think of anyone who'd risk their neck by helping her escape. Except...

Sam took a cheroot from his vest pocket, fingering it, but not lighting the thin cigar. "Seems the one person sympathetic to her is Joel Stoddard."

"According to Fielder, he's working almost twenty-four hours a day to come up with a defense to clear her. It's hard to believe he'd break her out after spending no time with her. Fielder's been the one talking to Maggie, with Joel keeping his distance."

"Then who else?" Sam continued to twirl the cheroot as he thought of who else could've helped Maggie escape.

"There's no one. Other than Joel, she has no one." Brodie tried to control the growing knot of dread building in his chest. "It's either someone who believes she killed Arnie Stoddard and wants her to pay for it, or the real killer." He mumbled a curse when a flash of understanding whipped through him. "Syd Stoddard," he ground out, looking at Sam and Nate.

"That would be my guess." Sam slipped the cigar back into his pocket. "We'd better get moving."

At first she'd thought Syd planned to take her to the cabin. The longer they rode through the thick brush and tall trees, though, it became clear they were nowhere near the dilapidated shack Arnie called their home. After a grueling and painful ride, Syd guided the horse into a clearing and toward a cutout in the hillside. Ahead were three entrances into the mountain. Her stomach twisted when she realized they were part of the abandoned mine tunnels Arnie, Syd, and Joel had spoken of more than once. *A good place to hide secrets,* she remembered Arnie saying.

Syd reined up in front of the closest mine, loosened the rope securing him to Maggie, swung his leg over the horse's neck, and slid down. "This is it, missy."

"What is this place?" She didn't move, her legs clamping around the horse's girth.

"This is where you'll be staying for a good, long time." Laughing at his own joke, he reached up, grabbing her around the waist and yanking her to the ground. Shoving her in front of him, he headed toward the entrance. Boards, hastily nailed in a crisscross pattern, sealed the front, a bleak warning of what lay ahead.

"You're not going to leave me in there, are you?" She tried to dig in her heels, slow her progress. His hand tightened around her right arm, digging in, bruising her through the blouse and thin coat she wore.

"Believe me. You ain't going to mind." Syd shoved her forward, chuckling when she tripped and fell to the ground. "Don't move." Pulling his knife from its sheath, he used it to loosen several of the boards. Throwing them into a pile, he stilled at the warning rattle a few feet away. Laying the knife aside, he reached for her, his gaze darting around.

Maggie's gaze never left the discarded knife as she let him pull her up, her skirt brushing against the spot the weapon had been carelessly left. Her broken left arm throbbed as she tried to straighten it enough to grasp the knife without him seeing. Without warning, he dropped his hold on her right arm, drew his gun, and fired.

"Dang rattlers." He fired again, then holstered the gun and walked to where the dead snake twitched. Bending over, he picked it up behind the head, tossing it several feet away, never noticing Maggie as she grabbed the knife, hiding it within the folds of her skirt. Grabbing her arm again, he pushed her toward the mine. "In you go, missy."

Maggie almost lost her grip on the knife as he shoved her inside. Taking a couple staggering steps, she looked around, letting her eyes adjust to the darkness.

"Keep moving." Syd nudged her from behind, pushing her through a narrow passage and into another tunnel. "Hold up." Striking a lucifer, he picked up a lantern and lit it. "Keep going." They continued for another thirty or forty feet before the tunnel opened into what appeared to be a natural cavern.

Maggie looked around and then up. The opening had to be at least fifteen feet high and the same in diameter. Discarded tools, strips of leather, and a pile of old blankets lay strewn around the floor. Before her gaze moved away, she gasped, spotting what appeared to be the heel of a boot sticking out of one edge of a blanket.

"Over there." He nodded toward another tunnel at the other side of the opening.

Maggie approached the narrow entrance, which was no more than two feet wide and five feet high. Fear gripped her as she looked toward the pitch black interior and froze.

"No. I won't go in there."

"You'll be going in there all right." Syd pulled out his gun, nudging the barrel into her back.

Swinging around, Maggie glared at him. "No. I'm not going any further. If you're going to kill me, do it here." She'd shifted the knife from her left to right hand, gripping it tight within the folds of her skirt.

Syd studied her a moment, coming to a conclusion. Gripping her arm, he pulled her toward the pile of blankets and threw her on top of them, crushing her already broken left arm. Her scream of pain faded when she slipped off the blankets, drawing them down to expose a decomposing body. She recognized the clothes, the ravaged face. *Tom Franks*. Another scream, soul deep and powerful, ripped from her throat, echoing in the small space as the horror before her sunk in.

"Did you hear that?" Brodie reined Hunter to a stop and looked around.

"It sounded like—"

Sam clamped his mouth shut as another scream echoed across the meadow separating the dense trees from the hillside dotted with deserted mines.

Nate reacted first, spurring his horse toward an opening where several boards had been pulled away. "It had to have come from in here."

All three dismounted, drawing their guns and stepping into the darkness. Stopping inside,

Brodie blinked several times, letting his eyes adjust as he listened. He moved toward a tunnel several feet away when he heard the sound of male voices. Nodding for Sam and Nate to follow, he stepped into the narrow space, following the voices and small splatter of light.

"Put the gun down, Syd."

"Not a chance, kid. I'm not taking a chance the woman who killed Arnie is found innocent. You and I both know she's not."

"Maggie *is* innocent."

Brodie continued forward, careful to stay as silent as possible. He recognized the second voice as belonging to Joel Stoddard. Stopping a few feet before the entrance to a large cavern, he flattened himself against a wall, signaling to Sam and Nate to do the same.

"You've always defended her, but you're wrong this time. No matter what anyone says, she killed Arnie and buried his body. All I'm looking for is justice. You need to step away from her, or I swear I'll shoot you both."

Brodie risked a glance into the opening, seeing Maggie shifting her gaze between the brothers, her eyes going wide. "It was you, Syd. *You* killed Arnie."

"The hell I did."

"You hated him. Maybe more than I did." Maggie rose, shifting the knife in her right hand, preparing to throw it. "And you killed Tom Franks."

"I didn't kill anyone, missy. Arnie got rid of Tom. I just helped him move the body in here." Syd smirked, turning toward Joel. "I'm telling you, this woman is the one who murdered our brother. She deserves what she gets."

"Brother or not, I can't let you hurt her." Joel raised his gun, pointing it at Syd's chest, preparing to fire. "Maggie is innocent."

"You don't know that." Syd's voice rose as he advanced a few feet toward Joel.

"I *do* know." A pained expression clouded Joel's face as his gaze met Maggie's. "I killed Arnie."

Maggie gasped at the confession, taking a couple steps backward.

Syd's jaw dropped. "You?" he growled, his eyes widening as he took another step forward.

Joel swung his gun, knocking his brother to his knees. Syd grasped the back of his head and moaned, a murderous scowl on his face.

"I found Arnie. Blood was everywhere, but he was alive. I helped him to a chair...grabbed a rag to help stop the bleeding. The longer he sat, the more his rage took over. He vowed to find Maggie, punish her, then make certain she never had a chance to come after him again." Joel's eyes glazed over as he recalled the hate in Arnie's voice and heard what he planned for Maggie. "He would've killed her. I couldn't let him do it."

"So you murdered him?"

Maggie heard the deadly menace in Syd's voice and stepped closer, ready to use the knife if needed. Joel had risked everything to protect her from Arnie. She could do no less for him.

"I did it to save Maggie."

Before she could blink, Syd fired. Joel staggered backward, clutching his chest.

The scream ripping from Maggie's throat seemed to come from someone else as she lunged forward, the knife plunging into Syd at the same time Joel's gun fired, more of a reaction than a purposeful shot. Regardless, the combination of the two wounds stopped Syd, his body crumbling to the ground.

Maggie's panicked gaze moved from Syd's lifeless form to Joel, now on his knees, his face contorted in pain. She didn't hear Brodie speaking her name, or register Sam and Nate rushing to help Joel. Her heart pounded hard and furious in her chest, feeling as if it were about to explode. She glanced down, the blood on her hand and skirt sickening her. An involuntary sob wracked her body, her terrified gaze landing on Brodie as his arms locked around her.

"I have you, lass. You're safe now." He continued to whisper reassurances, feeling Maggie's body relax in his embrace. He watched Sam and Nate work to keep Joel alive, knowing the effort would prove futile. Even if Doc Vickery were in the room with them, the odds were slim of the lad surviving.

"Is he…"

Brodie looked into Maggie's red-rimmed eyes, knowing what she asked. He looked at Sam, who shook his head. "Joel's gone, sweetheart. I'm sorry."

Gripping his shirt, she sobbed, her tears soaking through the fabric. She cried for Joel and the way he protected her, for the brutal years with Arnie, for the girl she used to be, and for the loss of her family.

"You'll be all right now, Maggie. No one else will ever hurt you." Brodie's heart squeezed for the woman in his arms. She'd been proven innocent, but the cost had been high. Closing his eyes, he thought of the future, praying that when Maggie healed, she'd find a place in her life for him.

Chapter Seventeen

"She's a most fortunate woman to have made it back alive." August Fielder sat at his desk, his voice resigned. "I can't say I'm surprised at what Joel did. The boy loved her, even if he never spoke of it."

Brodie sat across the desk, fingering the brim of his hat. It had been obvious to anyone how much Maggie meant to Joel.

"And how is Miss King doing? I heard you moved her out to your ranch."

"Aye. My parents offered to have her stay at their house. She didn't have anywhere else to go, so..." He'd suggested she stay at his house, knowing no matter how much he wanted her there, it wasn't the best choice. It hadn't come as a surprise when she refused. Her acceptance of his parents' offer had been a relief. "They brought the wagon into town yesterday and took her back with them."

"I suppose you'll be spending a little more time at the ranch then?"

"Not much more. I'll follow them back after church, maybe ride out once or twice a week for supper. It depends on what is going on in town."

Brodie had no intention of leaving his job. It didn't mean he wouldn't do all he could to spend time with Maggie while she healed.

"I must say you've done an admirable job hiring deputies." Fielder stood, walking to a small cabinet and pulling out a bottle of whiskey. Without asking, he poured two shots, handing one to Brodie. "And you've exceeded my expectations during your short time as sheriff." He tilted his glass toward Brodie, then took a sip.

"Thank you, Mr. Fielder. It hasn't been dull."

"No, I suppose not." Fielder studied Brodie, wrestling with something.

"Was there anything else?"

"I don't know if you've heard, but Pinkerton believes he's close to locating Maggie's family."

Brodie choked on the last of his whiskey. "No, sir. I hadn't heard."

"Sam mentioned it to me when I saw him in town last night. Seems they left Denver not long after Maggie's kidnapping. Mr. King tried to find her, even hired an investigator. When they couldn't find a trace, they decided to head back east. Pinkerton believes they are in Texas. It's good news, don't you think?"

"Uh, yes. Good news."

"Of course, nothing is certain. It may be a false lead. I never count on anything these days."

"Right." Brodie's voice was flat. He knew his thoughts were selfish, but he couldn't stop himself from wishing her parents weren't found, at least not until he'd had time to plead his case to Maggie, convince her to stay in Conviction.

"Sam should know more soon."

Brodie set down his empty glass and stood. "I'm certain he'll let me know as soon as he learns anything else."

"Do you plan to tell Miss King?"

"Not yet. I don't want to give her false hope. She needs to put all her effort into recovering."

"Give her my best, Sheriff. Perhaps I'll see the two of you in town soon."

Brodie left, thinking of Fielder's last statement, wondering if his feelings for Maggie were obvious. He planned to ride straight to the ranch, have supper, and see if she felt up to a walk. If Pinkerton was on the trail of the King family, he couldn't afford to waste any more time.

"The lass is a wonderful young woman, Brodie." Lorna patted her son's arm, followed by a conspiratorial smile. "She likes you, lad."

He shot a look at his mother, then shook his head. "Did *Maggie* tell you this, or are you just wishing it were true?"

"Oh, you can tell when a lass likes a lad. Maggie couldn't stop looking at you throughout supper."

"That's all?" Brodie had hoped she might have confessed her feelings to his mother. He'd never courted a woman before and needed whatever help he could get.

"And she's been asking questions about you." Lorna stopped when she heard Maggie walk down the hall with Jinny. The two had taken to each other right away. "There you two are."

Maggie glanced at Brodie, her face reddening when he smiled at her. "Jinny let me borrow her heavy coat."

"And a bonnet." Jinny pointed to the beautiful bonnet made of deep blue wool and lined in silk.

"Not just any bonnet," Maggie replied, looking at Brodie. "Did you know your sister made this?"

A warm smile, almost wistful, flashed across his face. "Aye, I do know. In fact, I went with her to the mercantile when she picked out the fabric." Although he'd watched her all through supper, the sight of her walking toward him, unmasked joy on her face, made his heart skip. "Are you ready?" He held out his arm, waiting until she slipped hers through it.

"I am. We shouldn't be gone long." Maggie didn't know why she felt the need to give Lorna an explanation. Maybe because she hadn't seen her own mother in a long time, and the sight of the older woman smiling and nodding her approval gave Maggie a warm feeling, almost as if she were home.

Without another word, Brodie escorted her onto the porch and down the steps. "I'm sure Jinny has already given you a tour."

She looked up at him and laughed. "Jinny, and Fletcher, and Kenzie, and the twins. I feel as if I should be showing *you* around."

"They've been dragging you around with your injured leg?" He frowned, believing he needed to speak to his family about pushing Maggie too fast.

"My leg feels much better now that I have a real bed." She winced at the look on his face. "I'm sorry, Brodie. I know you did all you could to make me comfortable. I also know it was your job, no matter how much I hated being locked up."

His features softened. "It's over, Maggie. All we can do now is look to the future." Brodie guided her into the barn and toward a stall in the back. As they approached, she leaned across him, trying to get a better look. "No peeking, sweetheart."

A chill went through her at his use of the endearment. "What am I not supposed to see?"

"This is the surprise Fletcher mentioned at supper."

"Do you mean the one he only told you about?"

Brodie chuckled as they stopped at the stall. "Aye. That is the one." He leaned down and placed a kiss on her forehead. Unlatching the gate, he pulled it open, letting her see the treasure inside. "Don't go any closer."

She looked at the small animal standing next to its mother, then at Brodie. "Oh my. She's beautiful."

"Beautiful, aye, but it's a *he*."

"A colt?"

"Born right before supper. That's why Fletcher and Kenzie were late." Brodie draped an arm around her shoulders, pulling her close. "This one will be part of our horse breeding program. Bram was here when he was born. Fletcher, Sean, and Bram are the most involved in the horse part of the ranch. Most everyone else works with the cattle."

"And if you were still living at the ranch, what would you be doing?"

He sighed. Over the years, he'd wondered the same, never coming up with a good answer. "I don't know. Ranching and farming have sustained the MacLarens for generations. Every family member did their part, worked the land, doing whatever was needed." Dropping his arm from around Maggie's shoulders, he guided her backward, then closed the gate. "I never seemed to fit. The land never drew me like it did everyone else. The sense I had another calling, a different path, always plagued me."

"Did you ever tell your parents?"

"Nae. They wouldn't have understood. Colin, Quinn, and Blaine knew. I doubt any of them were surprised when I took the job as sheriff. Except..." He walked away

"Except?"

"Those three are as much brothers to me as Fletcher, Clint, and Banner. We discussed everything. If we struggled with a decision and couldn't talk to our parents, we talked it out with each other. We were always there for one another."

She walked up next to him, touching his arm. "The relationships you describe sound wonderful."

"Aye, they are, except I didn't talk to any of them about my decision to accept the job as sheriff. I didn't realize what a terrible mistake that was until the night I made the announcement to the family. Disappointing them was ten times worse than upsetting Da and Ma."

She cocked her head, her mouth tilting up at the corners. "They seem fine now."

"We've come to an understanding. Still, we haven't quite reached the level of trust we had before I left the ranch." Brodie lifted his hand, caressing her cheek with his knuckles. "Were you close to your family?"

Maggie's eyes narrowed and her brows drew together. "It wasn't the same as with your cousins. I'm the oldest. My brothers came along several years later, and Mother, well...she never truly recovered." She glanced toward the house, then back at Brodie. "They are twins, like Banner and Clint. Their birth took every bit of energy she had."

"So you became more of a mother than a sister."

Maggie nodded. "They became my responsibility from the week they were born until I was taken from the hotel room. I don't know how Mother handled it afterwards."

Brodie stepped toward her, gently gripping her shoulders. "What about friends? Did you ever have time for fun?"

She thought a moment, remembering one friend. "Before the boys were born, there was one girl. We'd play at school and after church. She moved not long after the twins were born. Afterwards, I never had time to make new friends. Then Papa sold the farm, deciding we were moving to Colorado. You know the rest."

He couldn't imagine the life Maggie described. The MacLaren clan was huge, at one time consisting of five brothers, including his father. The youngest split from the family, eventually taking his family across the ocean. Although he died during a raid on his ranch, his young sons moved to live with relatives in Fire Mountain, Arizona. The remaining four brothers lived near each other in Scotland, creating their own settlement with little need for outsiders. Brodie had grown up with more love than he could describe and a family that increased in size each year. Unlike Maggie, he'd never felt alone or isolated.

"Are you thinking of looking for your family?" He hadn't meant to ask.

"I don't know what I'm going to do. Being free of Arnie gives me so many more choices than I've ever had. I love my parents. I also worry about my mother and wonder how she's been able to cope with the boys." She sighed, leaning into Brodie, glad for the comfort he provided. "Although it's selfish, I'm not ready to act as their mother again."

He drew her tighter into his embrace, stroking her hair with his hand. "You aren't selfish, Maggie. Perhaps it's time you took time for yourself and decided what you want."

I want you, she thought, burrowing her face into the fabric of his shirt, inhaling his unique scent. Keeping her arms locked around his waist, she leaned back and looked into eyes smoldering with need.

"Maggie..." Brodie breathed out.

"Will you kiss me?"

The corners of his eyes crinkled as he lowered his head. "Aye, lass. For as long as you'll let me."

The fear and revulsion she felt when she thought of Arnie vanished as Brodie settled his mouth on hers. The way he held her, his soft caresses, and the passion burning through her could never compare to what she'd experienced in the past. Tightening her hold around his neck, she leaned into him, loving the feel of her body against his.

The hunger in his kisses created a torrent of heat. He crushed her against his hard chest, sending a sharp stab of desire pulsing through her, setting her aflame. Feeling herself give into the passion his touch created, she returned his kisses with a desire that stunned her.

His hands splayed across her back, holding her firm as they moved lower to settle on her hips. Sighing into his mouth, Maggie didn't allow herself to think, wanting only to respond to the heat building between them.

His lips brushed against hers one more time before he raised his head, gazing into her eyes, placing a gentle kiss on her forehead.

A smile crossed his face as he tucked her against his chest, resting his chin on her head, his voice deep and ragged. "We'd better stop, lass. If we continue, I cannot promise I'll be able to stop."

"And what if I don't want you to stop?"

He drew back, moved his hands to her shoulders and studied her face, seeing the same passion he felt. "This is not the time or place, lass. You've had much happen in the last weeks and I won't be the man to take advantage of it." When she opened her mouth to speak, he touched a finger to her lips. "Don't doubt how much I want you, but our first time will not be on the floor of the barn, yards away from my family. You're important to me, much more than you know, and I mean to take my time with you." He could see a slight tinge of red creep up her face and knew she understood. Brushing a gentle kiss against her lips, he took her hand in his, feeling another stab of sensations rip through his body. "We'd best go back inside."

Walking up the steps to the porch, Brodie stopped, turning her to face him. "I mean to court you, Maggie King. You need to know the man I am and trust you'll never go through what you did with Stoddard. Those days are over, lass. Do you understand?"

Reaching up, she stroked her fingers down his face, feeling a burst of warmth and sparks of hope. "There's no other man I want courting me...no other man I want." She flashed him a brilliant smile an instant before going up on her toes and giving him a quick kiss on the lips.

He had no response, his chest tightening at her words. "I'll be back on Thursday afternoon to take you to supper in town."

She caught her bottom lip between her teeth, her eyes gleaming. "I'll be waiting."

Chapter Eighteen

The days had started to turn chilly as the Thanksgiving holiday approached. Many still did not celebrate it, at least not with the passion of the MacLaren family.

Brodie had invited his deputies to join him on the ranch for Thanksgiving supper. Sam and Nick had accepted. Jack preferred to stay in town, saying he'd send word if he needed them.

Almost three weeks had passed since Maggie had come to stay at the ranch, over two since they'd been courting. Quiet suppers, picnics, and unhurried rides took up their time. Brodie rode out the day before the celebration, ostensibly to help his cousins, but everyone knew his visit was to see Maggie.

"One more, then you can go see your woman." Quinn settled the last fence post into the ground, tamped dirt around it, and waited as Colin, Blaine, and Brodie set the rails. They'd expanded the pasture next to the barn. Brodie had to admit it felt good to work alongside his cousins again.

"She isn't my woman. Not yet anyway."

"Ach. If you believe that, you don't deserve her." Quinn brushed his hands down his pants, laughing when Brodie gave him a modest shove. "Why don't you just marry the lass and end your suffering?"

Brodie's mouth curved into a wry grin, knowing what Quinn referred to. "Maggie's worth the wait. Someday you'll figure out not all lasses are made just for bedding."

Colin and Blaine roared with laughter at the snarl on Quinn's face.

"I don't think that's all they're good for. I happen to like women. Besides, I've not bedded as many as you think."

"Quinn, your whole purpose in life is to see how many women will succumb to your charms." Blaine slapped him on the back. "Although it confounds me what they see in you when they've a choice of a fine male specimen like me."

Brodie looked at Colin, both shaking their heads as Colin rested an arm across Brodie's shoulders. "Lads, it's obvious the two best men are taken and have laid claim to the two best women."

"So true. At least about the women." Blaine picked up the shovel, looking up to see Caleb riding up to join them.

"Need more help?" A grin split his face, seeing the work had been completed.

"Nae. Your timing is perfect. We're done." Quinn glanced behind him and frowned. "I thought you were going to get Heather, convince her to join us for Thanksgiving tomorrow."

Dismounting, Caleb stroked his horse's neck, a scowl replacing his grin. "Quinn, your sister is as stubborn as they come. She's agreed to stay for supper at the Evanston ranch, help the widow cook for the rest of the men."

Quinn's jaw dropped open. "Heather, cook?"

"That's the excuse she gave me for not coming home." Caleb grabbed a handful of rocks from the ground, leaned against the fence, and starting throwing them across the pasture. "I think there's more to it, but she refused to say anything else."

The four cousins glanced at each other, no one knowing how to respond. They might know what to say, how to pull him out of his frustration if Caleb ever admitted his feelings for Heather. Instead, he'd kept them to himself, never inviting comments and never sharing.

Caleb tossed the last of the rocks a few feet away, brushing the dirt off his hands before looking at the four men. "I'm done with her." Grabbing the reins of his horse, he strode away, disappearing into the barn.

"What do you think he means?" Blaine stood next to Colin, his gaze still on the empty space where Caleb had been standing.

"I believe the man has wasted enough time on a woman who isn't interested."

Quinn stepped up beside them. "Heather's daft if she thinks she'll find better."

"It's a shame." Brodie clasped Quinn on the shoulder. "I was looking forward to the lad becoming a legal part of the MacLaren clan. Guess not everyone can be so fortunate."

"This looks wonderful, Ma." Colin looked at the platters of meat, bowls of vegetables and potatoes, and baskets of bread spread out on the table.

Kyla nodded, her mind on her husband, Angus, who'd been murdered, along with Quinn's father, Gillis, a few months before. Angus had been the one to embrace the holiday when President Lincoln signed the proclamation, encouraging the family to support it as well.

"Well, I hope there's enough. Go find the rest of the family and tell them to come inside." Kyla disappeared into the kitchen to help Lorna,

Audrey, and Gail finish the rest of the preparations.

"I'll go with you, Colin. Your mother and aunts are almost finished with the food." Sarah took off her apron and hung it on a chair, then grabbed her husband's hand. "I think they're all out at the corral, watching Bram break another horse."

"Except for Brodie and Maggie. I believe he took her for a ride toward Boundary River."

Sarah sent Colin a meaningful smile. "Ah, then they may not make it back in time for supper."

"I think you may be wrong, sweetheart." He nodded toward two riders coming toward them. "She sure recuperated fast."

"Maggie doesn't talk about it, but I believe she lives for Brodie's visits."

"Aye, lass. As I lived to fetch you back here." Colin leaned down, placing a lingering kiss on Sarah's lips.

"Appears we've interrupted something, Maggie." Brodie slid down from Hunter, took the reins to Maggie's horse and helped her to the ground, his hands lingering longer than normal on her waist. He wanted to wrap his arms around her and have the freedom to kiss her the way Colin kissed Sarah, but it was too soon to show such affection in front of his family.

Besides, it might embarrass Maggie, something he'd never intentionally do.

"With her being pregnant, she requires more attention," Colin joked, tightening his arm around Sarah's waist.

She pushed away, slapping him on the arm. "Ach, Colin MacLaren. You'd best behave or you'll find yourself sleeping with your horse."

Maggie slid close to Brodie, wrapping her hand in his. "Theirs is a special love."

"Has Sarah told you their story?" Brodie squeezed her hand, then let go as the others walked toward them.

"Some of it. She promised to tell me the rest before I leave."

Brodie's heart stopped at the thought of her no longer living at the ranch. "Leave? Where are you going?"

The shock in his voice had her turning toward him, placing a hand on his chest. "I'll have to leave someday, Brodie. I can't stay with your family forever."

"And why not?"

Maggie couldn't contain a burst of laughter. "Because I'm a grown woman who needs to support herself. Although, I'm not quite sure what I'll do." Her face darkened when she thought of her lack of skills, other than cooking and cleaning. "Perhaps the Gold Dust Hotel will hire me."

Brodie grabbed her by the elbow, turning her away from the family and leading her to the side of the house. Looking around, certain no one had followed, he leaned in close.

"What are you talking about?" His voice was calm and filled with anger. "You'll not be cleaning rooms, picking up after drunks, and being ordered about by those who think they're better than you. I'll not have it." Dropping her arm, he placed fisted hands on his hips and paced a few yards away.

When he turned around, his stomach plummeted at the look on Maggie's face. Walking toward her, he held his arms in front of him, palms out, but she cut off whatever he'd intended to say.

"You may think you have the right to tell me what to do with my life, Brodie MacLaren, but you don't. We've made no promises, and I've certainly not given you the authority to lord over me. My life is mine and I mean to live it the way I want." Her words were fierce, voice hard, even as her eyes watered. Swiping at tears, she swiveled away from him, wrapping her arms around her waist.

A minute passed, then another, before large hands settled on her waist and drew her back to the solid wall of his chest.

Leaning down, Brodie placed a kiss on her neck, then sighed when she tensed.

"I'm sorry, Maggie. It's just..." His voice stalled. He didn't know what else to say. Declaring his love for her could scare Maggie away, a circumstance he couldn't imagine. Even the possibility of not having her in his life sent an odd ripple of terror through his body.

"What, Brodie?" She turned in his arms, placing her palms on his chest.

He swallowed the lump building in his throat, knowing the time had come to be honest about his intentions.

"You must know how I feel about—"

"Are you two going to stand over there all afternoon, or are you going to join us for supper?" Jinny stood with her hands on her hips, a smile on her face.

Brodie cursed his luck, turning to face his sister, shielding Maggie so no one could see the line of tears still evident on her cheeks. "We're coming."

"Good, because Ma is about ready to give your food away."

He waited until Jinny disappeared, then inhaled a deep breath, taking Maggie's hand in his. "I promise, we will finish this conversation, lass."

Sam hadn't been in Conviction long, but he joined the cousins in sharing his own stories about Brodie. Each tale built on the last, everyone laughing as Brodie's faced reddened. Sitting beside Maggie, he reached over, taking her hand in his as she shifted a little closer.

"Are any of these stories true?"

"None of them." He reached for the bowl of potatoes, casting a look around the table that dared anyone to dispute him.

"Ach, Brodie. You know that isn't true. At least one of them is close." Quinn stuffed another forkful of turkey into his mouth, a cocky grin on his face as he chewed.

Brodie's mother listened to the conversation, glad for a chance to get to know Sam and Nate.

"Are you enjoying your time in Conviction, Mr. Covington?"

Sam set down his glass. "I'm not sure the word *enjoy* can be used in the same sentence as Conviction, Mrs. MacLaren." Nate nodded next to him. "Since I arrived, Miss King fell under the hooves of an angry horse, there's been an earthquake, explosions resulting in Miss King's kidnapping, and the killing of two brothers. I may be wrong, but it seems a good amount of mischief goes on in your small town."

Brodie's sister, Jinny, sat on the other side of Sam, watching the way his features changed as he spoke. He'd dressed for the occasion, wearing black slacks and jacket, a red and gold brocade vest, white shirt, and thin black tie. In Jinny's mind, the outfit made him look like a gambler more than a lawman. Either way, she thought him the most attractive man she'd ever met.

"Mischief, indeed," Lorna answered, glancing at her sons, Brodie and Fletcher. Unlike her oldest, she knew Fletcher had no intention of leaving the ranch, preferring to concentrate on the horse breeding business with Bram and Sean. "I can't recall a time since we moved here where Conviction has had so much trouble in such a short time."

"Aye, Ma. Perhaps our son has attracted a certain amount of tomfoolery." Ewan settled a hand over his wife's, cocking his brow at Brodie.

Sam listened to the continuing banter, not unaware of the beautiful young woman next to him. Blonde and fair-skinned with deep blue eyes, he noticed her the moment he'd stepped foot into the house, her welcoming smile touching him in a way he couldn't describe. Then he'd learned her brother was his boss. At first, he'd been pleased she'd taken a seat beside him. As supper progressed, the increased attraction made it difficult to concentrate on his food or the conversation.

To his relief, and disappointment, Jinny seemed oblivious to his attraction or discomfort, which he accepted was for the best. He had no interest in striking up a relationship with any woman, especially one tied to Conviction whose brother was the sheriff, and who probably sat on the wrong side of twenty. At twenty-five, he had a good deal of life to live, having no intention of tying himself to one woman. Although if his interests were otherwise and she wasn't related to Brodie, he might feel a good deal different.

"Mr. Hollis, do you plan to stay in Conviction?" Sarah's sister, Geneen MacGregor, glanced across the table at the deputy sitting next to Sam.

Nate had said little during supper, preferring to listen to the continuous conversation. By the looks the MacLarens sent him, he knew Brodie had failed to say anything about the loss of his left arm. He'd always felt fortunate to have the amputation occur below the elbow, giving him more ability to perform most daily functions, as well as defend himself. It didn't take Nate long to learn a well-placed elbow worked as well as a punch to the jaw.

"I do plan to stay a while, Miss MacGregor." He nodded at Brodie. "The town is growing and it's obvious the sheriff can use whatever good men he can find."

"Aye, Nate. I can use a couple more good men. Fielder has given his approval, so if you know of someone..." Brodie's voice trailed off, his body going still when he felt Maggie's hand rest on his leg. "Uh...other men who are interested..." He choked the rest out, noticing the knowing smirk on Quinn's face.

"Jinny and Geneen, would the two of you help us with dessert?" Kyla pushed back from the table. She didn't know about the other women, but she hadn't failed to notice the looks the two women gave Sam and Nate.

"Of course, Aunt Kyla." Jinny began to rise, then waited as Sam stood, pulling out her chair. "Thank you, Mr. Covington." She could feel her face heat, hoping it hadn't turned to crimson.

"My pleasure, Miss MacLaren."

Those around the table sat in silence for a moment before Blaine took pity on Jinny and steered everyone's attention to another topic, one that let his cousin escape the questioning eyes of her family.

After supper, Sam and Nate rode back to town, leaving Brodie to stay another night at the ranch. He left early the day after Thanksgiving, never having another chance to get Maggie alone. Although he'd ridden back after church the following Sunday, staying until dark, they'd had little time to talk.

The women kept Maggie busy with plans for Christmas and a tea party they wanted to give for Sarah in January to celebrate her being with child. The men discussed plans for the horse breeding program, as well as a new partnership the MacLarens were entering into with August Fielder.

It had come to the attorney's attention that one of the holders of an original Mexican land grant, Juan Estrada, had built up substantial debt during the protracted period of defending the grant per the California Land Act. He'd won his right to the grant, but took on a financial burden which now forced him to sell. August, along with Ewan and Ian MacLaren, arranged to buy a major portion of the grant. They would purchase sixty thousand acres, giving Estrada enough money to pay his debts and remain the owner of ten thousand acres. Although a fourth of his original grant, it would allow him and his family to continue their tradition of ranching, debt-free. In addition, other grant owners were now reaching out to Fielder and the MacLarens to discuss a similar deal.

The MacLarens were taking on considerable responsibility and doubling their current holdings, making them the second largest landholder in the area. In addition, they'd be managing the grant owned by Fielder. Without putting too much pressure on him, each of the men in the family made it clear they wanted Brodie to return to the ranch.

It had been a tense discussion. At least his father, Ewan, had stayed silent most of the time, not wanting to put pressure on his son. After several hours, Brodie had agreed to think about returning, with the caveat he wouldn't make a decision until after the first of the year.

By sundown, Brodie had spent less than thirty minutes close to Maggie, most of the time including at least one other MacLaren. The visit had been frustrating, as well as disappointing.

"I'm sorry we've had no time alone." They sat together on the front porch swing, holding hands while keeping a somewhat respectable distance.

"It wasn't your fault, Brodie. The women kept me as busy as the men kept you. I don't suppose you'd be able to ride back out Tuesday for supper. It's my turn to cook, and well..."

He squeezed her hand. "Of course I'll be here...under two conditions."

Maggie's eyes flew open. "What are they?"

"One, you walk with me to the barn tonight to get Hunter, and two, you promise you'll make time for us to talk after supper on Tuesday."

She let out a breath. Those were conditions she could give him. "All right."

Taking her hand, he led her into the barn.

Chapter Nineteen

In the weeks since Thanksgiving, the weather had turned from chilly to frosty. For at least nine months of the year, nearby Boundary Mountain sat covered in snow at the higher elevations. Between mid-December and February, the storms hit the Circle M Ranch in sporadic bursts. Their first storm came early this year, blanketing the ranch in a foot of snow weeks before Christmas.

"It's none of my business, Brodie, but when are you going to ask Miss King to marry you?" Sam stood next to him in Buckie's Castle, turning the glass of whiskey in his hand, trying to keep his thoughts off of Jinny MacLaren.

"Aye, Covington. It's not your business."

Sam chuckled, noticing the narrowed eyes and disgruntled expression on Brodie's face. "Most of the town knows you bought a wedding band." He sipped the whiskey as Brodie turned toward him.

"Most of the town?"

"Well, perhaps not everyone. You are a MacLaren, however, and there appears to be a good deal of interest in each member of your family. And since you *are* the sheriff…" He didn't continue, getting perverse pleasure at watching Brodie draw a hand down his face.

"The lass is skittish."

"You've already bought the ring. I'm assuming you plan to offer marriage whether she is skittish or not."

Brodie sucked in a deep breath, then downed the amber liquid in his glass. Setting it down, he looked at the clock behind the bar, his stomach churning. Waking up that morning, he'd spent the day building up his courage, ready to see if he and Maggie had a future. Plans had already been made for him to ride out to the ranch and spend the evening with her and his family. As the day progressed, his courage diminished until he'd accepted Sam's invitation to meet him at Buckie's for a drink.

The love he felt for her increased each moment they spent together. Brodie had never been like some men who never planned to marry. Someday, he knew he'd meet the right woman and fall in love. At twenty-two, Brodie never expected it would happen so soon. He figured he had years ahead of him to enjoy his bachelor status, settle into his job, and pick the right woman. Then he'd met Maggie.

"Go ahead. Nate, Jack, and I have the town covered."

Brodie nodded, sparing Sam a slight glance before he walked outside, heading toward the livery, never slowing his stride. In his heart, Brodie knew Maggie loved him and would agree to marry. Yet a sense of foreboding gripped him as he swung into the saddle and turned Hunter toward the ranch.

"There's no need for you to help us clean up tonight, Maggie. I know you and Brodie want to spend some time together."

"Thank you, Mrs. MacLaren." Maggie looked at Brodie. "If you're sure you don't mind."

"I have Jinny and Kenzie to help. Plus, the other boys always do their share."

Brodie stood, holding his hand out to Maggie. "Thanks, Ma."

Lorna and Ewan watched their oldest son and Maggie walk toward the study. "I believe he has something on his mind, Lorna." He wrapped an arm around his wife's waist.

"Aye. I believe you're right. I hope the next time we see them they'll be wearing smiles." She leaned her head back on Ewan's shoulder and sighed. She'd seen Kyla go through losing her oldest son to marriage. The difference was, Colin and Sarah lived at the ranch. Without Maggie to visit, she didn't know how often they'd see Brodie if they married. Of course, she and Ewan could both be wrong and Brodie's mind might be on something different than his obvious love for Maggie.

Brodie closed the door behind him, escorting Maggie to the leather sofa he'd sat in so many times since they'd arrived in California. This time, he didn't sit. Instead, he watched as Maggie settled at one end, then paced to the window, looking out at the heavy snow, trying to calm his racing heart.

He pushed aside the sounds of Banner and Clint arguing in another room, concentrating on what he wanted to say. The thought of Maggie turning him down created a hard ball of ice in his stomach. It felt about as large as the snowman he stared at through the window, the one the younger MacLarens had built after chores. Shoving hands into his pockets, he took in an unsteady breath.

"Brodie? Are you all right?"

The concern in Maggie's voice caused his mouth to go dry. He knew the time had come.

He could hear the sound of her dress rustling, footsteps moving toward him. All the plans he'd made, the words he wanted to say, fell from his mind, his concentration failing. Feeling fingers touch his back, Brodie turned, taking her hands in his.

"I'm all right, Maggie." His voice shook, his smile not quite reaching his eyes.

"Are you sure? You don't act like everything is all right."

"No? How am I acting?" He continued staring into her eyes, her voice comforting as he began to gather his thoughts.

She bit her bottom lip, her gaze falling to the floor, then back up to lock on him. "Unhappy, like something is bothering you. Is it me, Brodie? Have I done something wrong?"

Brodie's eyes widened, registering alarm. "No, Maggie. You could never do anything wrong."

Laughing, she squeezed his hands. "I know that's not true." Sobering, she moved her hands up to rest on his chest. "Tell me what's bothering you."

An image of his cousins flashed through his mind. Colin, Blaine, and Quinn standing outside, watching, laughing at how he'd lost his courage over a woman. Determined to get past his fear, he turned Maggie toward the sofa, sitting down beside her, not letting go of her hand.

"We've spent a good deal of time together, lass. You must know how I feel about you."

Her expression softened, although her eyes flashed with amusement. "I can't read your mind, Brodie. Why don't you tell me how you feel?"

He stifled a groan, wondering how this had become so hard. "Well..." He cleared his throat, staying silent.

"Do you like me, Brodie?"

Her question seemed to shock him. "You know I do."

She nodded. "Do you enjoy spending time with me?"

"I could spend every minute of every day with you, lass."

Again, she nodded. "Do you go to sleep at night thinking of me, waking with me in your thoughts?"

"Every night and every morning."

"And touching me...do you enjoy touching me?"

This time the groan escaped his lips. "Aye, lass. I do enjoying touching you." With each answer, his voice became more strained. "I can't imagine a life where I can't reach out and hold you, be with you whenever I want."

Catching her lower lip between her teeth, she nodded again, taking his other hand. "I'm glad because I feel the same about you. I love you, Brodie, and I'm afraid there is nothing I can do about it."

Without thought, he slid to the floor in front of her, knowing his eyes revealed everything he felt for this woman. "I love you, Maggie. I've loved you when I shouldn't have and love you more with each passing day. I want us to build a life together in Conviction." He drew in a breath to clear his head. "Marry me, Maggie King. Be my wife."

It was then he noticed the bright smile and tears streaking down her face, her head nodding almost imperceptibly as she looked into his eyes.

"Yes, Brodie MacLaren. I will marry you, build a family, and wrap my whole life around yours."

Standing, he picked her up, twirling her in a circle as he let out an ear-splitting shout.

In an adjacent room, Lorna looked into her husband's eyes and swiped away a tear of her own. "I believe she said yes."

The next two weeks passed in a blur as everyone prepared for a Christmas wedding. Lorna and the aunts worked on the dress, while the oldest daughters planned the food. A few people from town were invited, including Sam, Nate, Jack, and August Fielder.

The original layer of snow had melted, only to be replaced by almost two feet from a freak storm which moved through the week after Brodie had proposed. He'd ridden back to the ranch once, then was forced to stay away. Between a surge in drunken brawls, petty crime, and problems due to the unusual weather conditions, travel to the ranch had become impossible.

Whenever Brodie became frustrated with his inability to see or touch Maggie, he remembered the look on her face when she'd accepted his proposal. They may be separated, but she was safe with his family. He knew as far as they were concerned, Maggie was already a part of the MacLaren clan.

"MacLaren, you need to come with me. There are some visitors who made it up the river and are staying at the Gold Dust." Sam took off his hat, shaking off the melting snow, and stomped his feet. "I wish it would either snow enough to stay or let the current cover melt."

"Ira Greene at the telegraph office says the weather hasn't been so abnormal in this area for at least twenty years."

"Just my luck." Sam scrubbed a hand down his damp face, shaking the moisture to the floor.

"About these people at the hotel…" Brodie stood to grab his hat and jacket. A few hours before, he'd released the last of the miscreants who'd been sleeping off their drunken binge. The weather seemed to be warming enough that he knew he'd be able to ride to the ranch the following day.

When Sam's expression grew serious, Brodie knew he wouldn't like what his deputy had to say.

"It's a family, Brodie. Their last name is King and they're looking for their daughter, Marguerite."

Brodie sat at the largest table available in the dining room of the hotel, tapping his fingers as he waited. An untouched cup of coffee grew colder as the minutes ticked by. He'd sent a message to the King family, asking to speak with them. The hotel clerk had returned moments later, asking him to wait. After fifteen minutes, he was about ready to leave when a man of average height with a slight paunch and thinning brown hair approached him. Behind him walked a woman about the man's age and two boys. Brodie assumed they were Maggie's brothers.

"Sheriff MacLaren." The man extended his hand. "We're sorry to keep you waiting. It took us a while to get warm after our long journey. I'm George King, and this is my wife, Felicia. The boys are Robert and Jonathon."

He shook King's hand, nodding toward the other three. "Please, sit down. Now, how I can help you?"

"I don't quite know where to start, except we heard about a young woman in Conviction who might be our missing daughter. The clerk here at the hotel said you know about a Marguerite King."

Clearing his throat, Brodie couldn't suppress the surge of doubt pooling around him. The same apprehensive feeling he'd fought since after Thanksgiving. The doubt which had almost stopped him from proposing to Maggie.

"I do know a Marguerite King, sir. Nineteen years old and goes by Maggie, correct?"

"Yes, yes. That's her." George turned to his wife, seeing her face already buried in her hands. "Is she still here?"

"Not in town, but yes, Maggie is still in the area."

George grabbed his wife's hand. "She's here, Felicia. Our Maggie is here." He shifted back to Brodie. "Where is she? Can you take us to her?"

It had taken a great deal of negotiating before King had agreed to wait until the following morning to start for the ranch. Brodie had chosen not to mention his relationship to Maggie.

Even though the weather had cleared, it still took over twice as long to reach the ranch. They'd turned the last corner when Brodie spotted movement on his family's front porch. As they got closer, he recognized Jinny and Kenzie. A moment later, another figure came outside, turning toward him. Even from this far out, he could hear Maggie's shout.

"Brodie!" Running down the steps, she raced toward him as fast as she could in the heavy boots. Careful not to trip, she kept her head down, not looking up until she came within ten yards of Hunter. "Brodie, you made it." Her face lit up a moment before she noticed the wagon behind him and who sat on the seat.

"Maggie." Her father dropped the lines and jumped to the ground.

"Papa?" She glanced at Brodie, then back at her father, uncertain of what to do.

"Yes, Maggie. We found you." George wrapped her in a hug, then turned, helping his wife off the wagon and into their daughter's arms.

"Oh, Maggie. You don't know how we've worried about you, wondered if you were all right. I can't believe we've found you after all this time." Felicia dropped her arms and stepped away, taking a good look at her daughter. "You've changed."

"Yes, Mama, I have." She hadn't expected her parents to come for her. Over the years, she'd convinced herself they'd forgotten all about her.

"It doesn't matter. You'll have plenty of time to tell us everything on the way home." Her father's words were soft as he stepped between Maggie and her mother.

"Home?" Maggie breathed out.

"Of course, angel. You're coming back to Texas with us." Her father spoke as if they'd all agreed.

"Oh, Maggie. We've all missed you so much. The last two years have been a nightmare for all of us." Tears filled her mother's eyes. "There were days I thought we'd never see you again. All we want is to have you back home, safe with us."

"Mama, I don't know if I'm ready to go back. There are people here. I've begun to build a life—"

"Of course you've made friends, Maggie, but your place is with us...with your mother and brothers." Her father reached out, cupping her face with his palm. "Now that we've found you, we can't bear the thought of not having you with us any longer."

Brodie's heart constricted at the plea in her father's voice. They'd lost a daughter, thinking they'd never find her again. He wanted Maggie to do what was best for her, what would make her happy. Still, she had agreed to marry him and he loved her.

"Hold on, Mr. King." Dismounting, he placed a hand on George's shoulder. "Maggie has been through quite a bit. More than you can ever imagine. Why don't we go up to the house? I'll introduce you to my family and we'll talk."

"We appreciate the offer, and you are the sheriff, but you've got no say in the decisions of my family. Maggie will be coming home with us."

Brodie kept himself in control, his voice calm as he came between King and Maggie. "Maggie is nineteen now, an adult, and capable of making her own decisions. She is your daughter and can choose to go with you, but you'll need to give her time to decide."

"You forget your place, Sheriff MacLaren, and what our family has suffered these past two years. Yes, she's my daughter. The baby I helped bring into the world and the girl standing before me now. The same girl who will be leaving with her family."

"I'm afraid I can't just let you take her, Mr. King. If Maggie goes, she leaves because she wants to, not because she feels forced."

King crossed his arms, setting his feet shoulder-width apart. "And who are you to tell me how to handle my family?"

Brodie glanced at Maggie, stepped closer, wrapping an arm around her shoulders. "Maggie has agreed to marry me, Mr. King. I'm your future son-in-law."

Chapter Twenty

"Mr. and Mrs. King, these are my parents, Ewan and Lorna MacLaren."

Ewan stepped forward, extending his hand. "Mr. King, it's a pleasure." He waited, seeing George's face cloud. After a moment, Maggie's father clasped Ewan's hand.

"Mr. MacLaren."

"Please, come inside. My wife has coffee, unless you're ready for something a little stronger."

George's face relaxed. "It's a little early for whiskey, but under the circumstances, I think I may have a small amount."

"Mrs. King, why don't you and Maggie visit with me in the kitchen?" Lorna took Felicia's elbow, gently guiding her toward the kitchen.

Brodie placed his hands on Maggie's shoulders, turning her to face him. "It will all work out, lass. I'm going to join Da and your father in the study." He brushed a kiss across her forehead, then closed the door behind him.

Maggie felt adrift, her world turned upside down by the appearance of a family she'd expected never to see again. The same family who might not accept her when they learned of all she'd been through. Beneath his friendly exterior, George King was a tough man, hardened by a life filled with setbacks and lost dreams. He ruled with a firm hand, having a soft heart for his wife. He did all he could to give Felicia whatever she wanted. If she wanted Maggie to return home, he expected his daughter to comply without argument and with grace.

Glancing at the closed study door, she walked toward the kitchen, hearing muffled voices. Jinny had sent Kenzie and Maggie's brothers to the barn to find Banner and Clint, then joined Lorna and Felicia in the kitchen. When Maggie stepped through the doorway, she saw the distress on her mother's face.

Felicia turned toward her daughter, her eyes filled with pain. "Mrs. MacLaren says you plan to marry on Christmas. Is this true?"

"Yes, Mama. I love Brodie and plan to stay in Conviction with him."

"Surely you know you must come back home with us. Your father will never allow you to marry a man he doesn't know." She walked up to Maggie, resting a hand on her arm. "I don't know what happened the last two years, and I'm sure you've been through much you aren't ready to discuss. I also know you don't have to rush into a marriage because you believe you have no other options.”

Jinny gasped, her eyes widening at the insult not only to Brodie, but to all the MacLarens. Lorna simply crossed her arms, narrowing her gaze at Felicia, knowing there would be a time to speak her piece.

“Mother, I’ll not have you insulting this wonderful family who took me in, helped me when I had no other place to go. Besides, there is much about the MacLarens, and Brodie, you don’t know.”

Felicia’s face reddened a little as her body stiffened. “I meant no insult, Mrs. MacLaren. Please understand. It’s been two years since we lost Maggie. I can’t bear the thought of traveling back to San Antonio without her.”

Maggie’s anger rose. She’d seen her mother often use guilt to get what she wanted. It’s how Maggie became more of a mother than a sister to her brothers. When Felicia had fallen ill, she used guilt to pressure her husband and daughter to take on her responsibilities so she could recover. Three years later, she would still lie in bed most of each day. As much as Maggie loved her mother, she also knew her to be lazy. A woman who’d take advantage of others to make her own life easier.

"I know this must be very hard for you, Mrs. King. I know if I lost Jinny, or any of my children, I'd never want to let them out of my sight again. However, Maggie is an adult now, able to make her own decisions." Lorna poured a cup of coffee, handing it to Felicia. "Please, let's sit down. This doesn't need to be sorted out right now."

Taking a chair next to her mother, Maggie struggled with what to do. She loved her family and did want to spend time with them. As stern as her father was, he'd always taken care of everyone, asking little for himself. She believed if it were up to him, he'd let Maggie stay, welcome Brodie into the family. Because of her mother's wishes, her father would fight with all he had to see Maggie return home with them, no matter the misery it caused her.

She took a sip of coffee and glanced at Jinny, whose gaze searched hers. They'd become close over the last weeks. Maggie couldn't imagine never seeing her, or any of the MacLarens, again. And Brodie. She loved him. The thought of leaving, knowing he'd find someone else to marry and share his life with, tore at her heart. Setting down the cup, she stood.

"I need some air."

"I'll come—"

"No, Mama. You stay here with Mrs. MacLaren. I won't be gone long." Maggie left the room, grabbed her heavy coat, and walked onto the porch. Taking in a deep breath, she crossed her arms and headed toward the corral, watching the young colt scamper around in the mud.

"Your mother means well."

Maggie turned, glad to see Jinny by her side. "I know, but what am I to do?"

Jinny stepped onto the bottom rail of the fence, resting her arms on the top rail to focus on the colt. "I've always loved seeing how our foals grow and change. At first, they are so dependent on their mothers. Needing attention, making sure they aren't left behind. As they get older, they naturally separate, become the horse they're meant to be. Some stay at the ranch. Others are sold, separated from their mothers forever. Yet all survive to make their own way in life. If only being human were so simple." She glanced at Maggie, a soft sadness in her eyes.

"Yes. If only." Maggie looked around the pasture. She'd yet to experience the ranch in the spring when the grass would return as bright green tufts. Sarah would have her baby in late spring, and Maggie would miss it. Miss watching Brodie argue with his cousins, wrestle with his brothers. If she left, she'd miss it all.

"What will you do?"

"I don't know, Jinny. My family has gone through so much. I just don't know if I can handle their disappointment if I stay."

"And Brodie?"

"I do love him. So much more than I can ever describe. I know how much he'll hate me if I leave."

"Brodie will never hate you, Maggie. The lad is daft over you." Jinny jumped to the ground. "I love my brother and know how much you leaving will hurt him. At the same time, you must do what's right for *you*. If you decide to leave, you must tell him soon. Don't let him wonder, hoping you'll stay." She touched Maggie's arm. "I will miss you a great deal if you leave, but I'll understand. The MacLarens are nothing without our family. It's what makes us strong. Keeps us going from one day to the next. Family is what sustains all of us."

Jinny walked back to the house, leaving Maggie alone with a decision which would make some happy while hurting others. She wanted to scream. Hadn't she already been through enough? There'd be no decision to make if she and Brodie were already married. She'd promise to visit her parents when she could, watching them ride home without her. One week separated her from an easy decision and one filled with heartache.

There simply was no good choice.

Kyla offered to have Maggie's family stay at her house overnight. Maggie chose to stay in the room she'd been using at Ewan and Lorna's. After some not very subtle remarks by Mr. King, Brodie had decided to bunk with Quinn.

Although it had almost killed him, he'd made the decision to wait until their marriage to consummate the union. She'd already been through too much, learning about what happened between men and women from a man who cared nothing for her. Brodie meant to show her how different real love was from what Arnie had taken from her.

After breakfast the following morning, he took Maggie's hand, guiding her to the barn and the saddled horses.

"Isn't it too cold to ride?"

"We won't go far. Enough to get away so we can talk without others around."

Maggie knew he meant her parents, who'd been pushing her to leave with them when they rode out that afternoon. She'd let their comments pass without responding, but her lack of an answer wouldn't hold them off for long. They were ready to leave and had every intention of taking her with them.

They didn't ride far, stopping near Boundary River, the banks now overflowing with melting snow. Helping Maggie down, Brodie took her hand and guided her a few feet away.

"What do you want to do, lass? If you want to leave, I'll not say a word. I know this is not easy for you."

"I don't know what to do, Brodie. I've never felt so confused." She turned away to watch the rolling river. Most of the early snow had melted. From listening to Kyla, she knew the rains would be coming, perhaps more snow. For now, the sky was clear. "All I could think about when I lived at the cabin with Arnie was getting away. When you arrested me, all I wanted was to escape. When you asked me to marry you, I didn't hesitate. Each time, I knew what I wanted. Why is it so hard now?"

"Because you love your family and you love me. You're in a difficult position where you think you must choose. Most women don't have such a hard decision. They fall in love, marry, and follow their husband to a new life. Being kidnapped, held as a captive, has changed everything." He stepped up behind her, resting his hands on her waist. "It isn't fair, but you have a choice to make. What's important to you, Maggie? What life do you want?"

An agonizing groan escaped as she buried her face in her hands. "I don't know. I just don't know what to do."

Brodie's heart stopped. He'd been so certain she'd choose him, letting her parents travel back to their life in San Antonio without her. He'd lain awake most of the night, envisioning this time together, thinking she'd wrap her arms around his neck and tell him she'd never leave. The reality of her inner conflict slapped him in the face. If she loved him enough, she'd stay, no matter her love for her parents. The fact she couldn't decide told him all he needed to know.

Lifting his hands to her shoulders, he turned her around to face him. Touching his lips to her cheek, he rested his forehead against hers, taking in her scent, knowing this might be the last time. Leaning back, his gaze captured hers. The pain he saw made his next words easier.

"I can see it plain in your eyes, lass. You aren't sure what to do." Brodie's heart began to crack when he accepted what he had to say. "No matter how much I love you, Maggie, I can't marry a woman with doubts. I want someone who's as committed to me as I am to her. Marriage is hard enough. There's no reason to take the step if doubts plague us from the start. The fact you can't make a choice tells me all I need to know." He saw her eyes tear, her bottom lip tremble, but knew this was right. He couldn't promise his life to Maggie, then wake up one morning to find her gone. "You need to go back to San Antonio with your family."

"No, Brodie. Don't send me away. Not like this." She wrapped her arms around her waist, trying to control the pain ripping through her. "What will I do without you?"

Stroking his knuckles down her cheek, he studied her face. "Ah, lass. You've always been much stronger than you know. I can't imagine any other woman living through what you did without becoming bitter and cynical." Letting his hand stroke up and down her arm, he searched for a calm he knew to be beyond his grasp. "Your family needs you."

"Don't *you* need me?" Her voice broke, tears spilling down her face as the certainty she'd lost Brodie became reality.

"I need you like the air I breathe. You're everything to me, Maggie." Stepping back, he shoved his hands into his pockets so as not to reach out and grab her. "The struggle you're going through, the way you can't make a decision, is tearing me apart. Not choosing me is the same as making a choice for your family. I understand that now and so should you. You may not want to believe it, but someday you'll know this is right."

She reached for him, her hand pausing, then dropping to her side when he took a step away.

"So you're letting me go?" Her voice broke. She might never see him again. All her dreams, their plans, tossed aside because of her inability to hurt her family with what she truly wanted.

Brodie nodded, his face a mask as he worked to hide the pain already laying claim to him. "You have to go. I'll no longer stand in the way." He walked away, unable to bear the hurt in her eyes. Grabbing their horses' reins, he helped Maggie into her saddle, then swung up into his and led them away before he weakened and changed his mind.

Chapter Twenty-One

Maggie stared out the window, every muscle hurting, her clothes covered in dirt after two weeks on the trail. She refused to look into the mirror stored in her mother's reticule, knowing what she'd see—a face streaked with grime, eyes deadened by a shattered heart.

The stagecoach traveling south from San Francisco stopped for no more than twenty minutes at each post, allowing the passengers little time to take care of their needs. Over the last two weeks, her stomach had become accustomed to small amounts of poor food and she'd accepted the lack of privacy. They'd been fortunate. As a family of five, they seldom had to share the coach with other passengers.

"Drink some water."

Maggie glanced down, shaking her head at the water pouch in her mother's hand. "Not yet. I'll wait until we stop." She gripped her reticule tighter, thinking of the money that had been slipped into it, along with a brief note. She discovered it when they'd been waiting for the stage leaving San Francisco, having no doubt who wrote it.

Her chest constricted, remembering the message and the man who wrote it. She'd ruined her chance at happiness, making Brodie believe he wasn't important enough to choose him over her family. The truth had been quite the opposite.

The long days and nights on the trail had given her time to accept the reason for her hesitancy—guilt. Both her parents were experts at using it, and once again, she'd fallen under its spell. Maggie now spent every waking minute figuring out how best to leave her family and find her way back to Brodie.

"Maggie, listen to your mother and take some water." Her father's hard voice drew her attention, the glower twisting her stomach.

"I'm not thirsty, Father. Unless you plan to force it down my throat, I'd prefer you leave me to my own thoughts." Turning her gaze back out the window, she felt not a pinch of remorse at her churlish response. He'd pushed and tormented her since the moment they'd left the Circle M, taking away the small amount of freedom she'd obtained by living with the MacLarens.

She'd given up trying to explain to either parent her love for Brodie. They still saw her as a girl, unable to make her own decisions, certainly not capable of falling in love and choosing a husband. Their condescension and undisguised belief they were better than the MacLarens pushed her further away, making her decision to leave an easy one.

"Marguerite, you will not speak—"

Maggie was saved from another rebuke by the driver's shout, notifying them of the next stop. The first off the stage, she didn't look at her parents as she ran toward the closest building, noting the sign above the entry. *Elk Horn Station.* It seemed to be in better shape than the other stops. As long as they could help her, she didn't care if the building was falling down.

"Excuse me. I'd like to see how much it would cost to take the next stage back to San Francisco."

The clerk turned, cocking his head, his mouth twisting into a grin. "You just arrived and now you want to go back?"

"Yes, sir. I'd like to take the next stage north." Glancing over her shoulder, her stomach clenched at the sight of her parents walking toward the building.

"Well, if you're sure. It should be coming in any minute." He quoted a price, Maggie rushing to pull the money from her reticule and hand it over. Once he took it and wrote her name down, she let out a ragged sigh of relief. "Just wait outside."

She walked past her parents, nodding, saying nothing. Once outside, Maggie signaled the driver, requesting her bag be handed down. His brows lifted as he gave it to her.

"Get what you need, then hand it back. We're leaving in a few minutes."

"I'm not continuing. I'm taking the next stage north." Gripping her bag in one hand and reticule in the other, she took a seat on the dusty bench outside the building and waited for the expected outburst when her parents learned of her decision.

Conviction

"We've come to take you out of this dungeon, lad. You can't stay cooped up in the jail all the time." Colin stood in front of the desk, hands on his hips as he watched Brodie shift in his chair. Quinn and Blaine leaned against the wall a few feet away, arms crossed.

"I don't live here, Colin. You can find me at the Gold Dust for meals and at my place at night. It's not as if I'm hiding out."

"It's been almost five weeks since Maggie left. You made the right decision sending her away. It's up to her now to decide if she made a mistake in leaving."

Brodie tossed down the bullet he'd been twirling between his fingers and leaned back. "What I know is she's on her way to San Antonio and not coming back. If Maggie wanted me, a life here in Conviction, she never would've left. It's over and I'm dealing with it the best I can." It hurt to think of her, say her name out loud, but he wouldn't let the men standing before him know it.

"Your best is pathetic." Quinn pushed away from the wall and stalked forward. "And trust me, you never know what a woman is going to do until she does it."

Brodie tilted his head back and looked at the ceiling. Letting out a sigh, he stood. "It seems I'll get no peace until you lads get me drunk. Fine. We'll go to Buckie's and you can do your best."

"Cards, whiskey, and women. Like old times, lads." Quinn clasped Brodie on the back as they crossed the darkened street, hearing the tinny piano music spilling from the saloon. "Except for Colin. I'm afraid you'll have to settle for the first two."

"It's no problem for me, knowing Sarah is waiting at home."

Brodie didn't respond. Before Christmas, he'd thought his life would involve a wife and a future, including children. The thought he'd lost it all still stung. Still, he had no interest in any woman other than Maggie. Cards and whiskey didn't appeal to him, either, but fighting the three of them would cause nothing but grief.

Pushing the door of Buckie's open, Brodie began to see how spending the night blotting out the memory of what he'd lost might be what he needed. Perhaps Colin, Quinn, and Blaine were right. Spotting Nate at the end of the bar, he nodded. Cards and whiskey might be the perfect cure for his broken spirit.

Taking the driver's hand and stepping onto the street, Maggie looked around, taking a deep breath. She'd made it back to Conviction. It had taken her two weeks to return to San Francisco and almost a week to take the stage to Sacramento before arriving home. *Home*, she thought, a smile curving the corners of her mouth.

Even though most of her time in Conviction had been spent behind bars, Maggie chose to remember her time with the MacLarens, the care she'd received from Doc Vickery, the kindness of August Fielder, and her love for Brodie.

The thought of him had her glancing down at the dress she'd worn for most of the five weeks she'd been gone. Maggie couldn't think of a time she'd felt so dirty. She'd counted out her remaining money during the trip from Sacramento, hoping she had enough for a bath, supper, and a room. A good night's sleep in a regular bed would clear her head. Tomorrow, she'd find Brodie and hope he'd allow her to apologize. She didn't try to fool herself into believing he'd take her back. The pain on his face when he'd told her to leave said more than any words could. She'd hurt him, ruining any chance they had for happiness. Leaving with her family had cost her too much.

Her father had almost picked her up and thrown her back into their stage when Maggie announced her decision to return to Conviction. It had taken all her fortitude to stand firm and refuse to be intimidated or swayed by guilt. Thankfully, the decision had been made for them when the driver heading south shouted he was leaving with or without the Kings. A moment later, the stage going north arrived. She'd given her family quick hugs, tossed her bag to the driver, took a seat, and looked straight ahead. The relief when their stage left had been considerable.

Now, she stood in Conviction, feeling better than she had in weeks. Picking up her bag, she didn't even glance in the direction of the jail, focusing on the Gold Dust Hotel down the street. She stopped at the entrance. A few doors down stood Buckie's Castle, already busy in the early evening. Listening to the tinny piano, she thought of her dwindling funds. Soon, she'd need to find work. For now, she'd rejoice in her freedom and the knowledge of whatever her future held, it would be her choice, and hers alone.

Brodie held his cards in one hand, his other arm wrapped around a saloon girl sitting on his lap. He'd lost count of the whiskeys he'd consumed.

"Keep your mind off the girl, MacLaren, and play your cards." A local cowboy sat across the table, along with one of his friends. They'd known the MacLarens for years, often joining them for cards and drinks.

Brodie didn't respond, studying his cards through an alcoholic fog, a crooked grin on his face.

"Here you are, lads." Laying his cards down, he laughed at the collective groans around the table before scooping up his winnings. "Another round for these fine men." He gestured around the table, then gave the girl a kiss before shifting her off his lap, pointing her toward the bar.

"I've never seen such luck." Colin stretched both arms above his head, glancing at Blaine, noting the mellow look on Brodie's face. It had been a good idea to get him out of the jail and his self-imposed exile. Unlike Quinn, who lived to drink and have a good time, Brodie had never been one to imbibe in excess. A few games of cards and two or three drinks defined a big night out for him. He'd gone well past those amounts already.

"Appears the lad has moved past his thoughts of Maggie, at least for a time. Each day will get better." Blaine crossed his arms, leaning back in his chair.

Colin studied his brother and laughed. "You're saying this from experience?"

"Nae. From listening to you before you fetched Sarah. You may not recall, but you could be an uncivil eejit over the years you two were apart." Blaine accepted the glass from the barmaid. "You're a little more human now."

Colin took his glass and tilted it toward Blaine. "Aye. I remember those times all too well." He took a sip, then set the glass down, watching Brodie rock in his chair, struggling to keep his eyes open. "The lad may have reached his limit."

"Shall we get him out of here?" Blaine stood, ready to carry Brodie outside.

"Nae. We'll take him upstairs. I've a room reserved for him." Quinn stood over Brodie, who'd slumped down in his chair.

Colin frowned, shaking his head. "Brodie won't like it, Quinn. He's no interest in spending the night in bed with one of the girls."

"Look at him. He won't wake up before the sun rises. We'll be saving ourselves a long trip down the street, and I've already paid for the room and a girl who's agreed to sleep with him, knowing he's too far gone to touch. I think the lass is quite disappointed, even if she *is* making a good sum."

Colin rubbed the back of his neck. "All right, but you'd better be prepared for his reaction the next time he sees you."

The three of them struggled to get Brodie up the stairs and down the hall. Kicking the door open, Quinn led the way into the room, stopping by the bed.

"All right, Brodie. Down you go."

The girl standing next to the bed frowned. "Are you sure he wouldn't want me to—"

"Nae," all three men said at once.

"It would be best to leave him be, lass." Colin smiled at her. "He won't wake up until morning. We'd be grateful if you'd check on him a couple times and make certain he isn't bothered."

She nodded, clearly unhappy about staying out of Brodie's bed. "Well, if that's all you want. Seems like a waste of good money to me."

Blaine chuckled. "Maybe next time, lass. For tonight, the sheriff needs his rest."

Taking one last look at his still form, the three left, hopeful that when he woke up, it would be to embrace a new start.

"Why, Miss King. You're downstairs early." The clerk smiled at her as she stopped in front of the counter.

"I smelled the bacon and couldn't wait any longer." In truth, she'd been awake most of the night, unable to sleep for thoughts of Brodie. "Is it too early to eat?"

"Not at all." He motioned for her to follow him into the dining room, giving her a seat by the window.

Thirty minutes later, she'd finished her meal. The seat by the window allowed her an unobstructed view of the jail down the street. She'd seen Sam, Nate, and Jack enter, then leave, guessing Brodie had arrived earlier.

Walking outside, she stood on the boardwalk, straightened her shoulders, and took a deep breath. *No sense waiting any longer*, she thought, taking a step forward.

Chapter Twenty-Two

A warm bath, breakfast, and half-dressed woman greeted Brodie when he opened his eyes. Blinking a few times to try and clear the gritty feeling, he rubbed them, then sat up. The bath appealed to him. The food and woman? Not at all.

"Good morning, Sheriff. Did you sleep well?"

Swinging his legs to the floor, he drew the covers over his naked body. He didn't remember climbing the stairs, getting undressed, or the woman.

"Who, uh…"

"Colin, Quinn, and Blaine brought you upstairs. I undressed you."

"Did we, uh…"

"No," she sighed. "I had strict orders to leave you alone. Now that you're awake…" Her suggestive voice drifted off.

"Sorry, lass. I'm in no shape." *And have no interest*, he thought, rubbing his temples. "I'll use the bath, though."

"All right. If you change your mind, I'll be downstairs."

His head throbbed as he walked to the tub and lowered his abused body into the warm water. Tilting his head back, he closed his eyes, soaking until the bath began to cool. Picking up the sponge, Brodie made quick work of washing himself. Drying off, he dressed, picked up his hat, and made his way down the stairs.

Even though he hadn't eaten and his head still pounded, he felt better than he had in weeks, realizing he hadn't thought of Maggie since the night before. Maybe his cousins were right. He needed to get back to the man he was before meeting her, before he'd made the mistake of falling in love and putting his hopes on a woman he barely knew.

Brodie nodded to the woman who'd been in the room as he settled his hat on his head and pushed the swinging doors open. He didn't pay attention as he stepped outside, not noticing the woman walking past, knocking her off balance. Reaching out, he grabbed her elbow.

"I'm sorry, ma'..." His voice trailed off and his eyes widened as he took a good look at the woman. His breath hitched at the same time his chest constricted. "Maggie?"

Taking a step back, she licked her lips. "Hello, Brodie."

"What are you doing—"

"Brodie, you forgot something." The saloon doors pushed open, the woman from the room standing before them holding his badge in her hand. She looked Maggie up and down, then turned her focus back to Brodie, her voice low and sultry. "I thought you'd need this." She fluttered her eyes at the same time her fingers drew a path down his arm.

Snatching the badge from her hand, Brodie sent a warning look at the woman. "Thank you."

"Come back whenever you've the time, Sheriff."

Brodie took her elbow, turning her toward the saloon, guiding her through the doors. Turning back to Maggie, he narrowed his gaze, his jaw set.

"What are you doing here?"

She stumbled back, his gruff tone startling her. Staring up at him, she froze at the unforgiving look on his face. Her gaze passed between him and the saloon doors, her heart stopping as the reason he'd been inside became clear. All the courage she'd built up over breakfast vanished.

Guessing the direction of her thoughts, Brodie stepped closer, his face softening.

"It isn't what you're thinking, Maggie." Studying her face, he saw confusion...and something else. "We'll find a place to talk. Seems we both have some explaining to do."

She cleared her throat and nodded. "Private?"

"Aye, lass. Somewhere you can explain why you're here and not on your way to San Antonio."

Escorting her down the street, searching for a place they could talk without interruption, Brodie tried to calm his jumbled thoughts.

He'd let her go, watched her ride off with her parents. The last weeks had been the worst of his life. Then his cousins had come to his rescue, forcing him to begin the process of putting Maggie behind him—until he'd walked out of the saloon and collided with the object of his suffering.

Before he realized it, they stood in front of his house, his hand on the small of Maggie's back. Opening the door, he stepped aside, indicating for her to enter.

"Where are we?" Her voice shook as she looked around the small space.

"This is where I live. Sit down while I see to a fire." Slipping out of his coat, he started the wood stove, then lit the lanterns.

Catching her bottom lip between her teeth, Maggie glanced around, choosing to stand. She'd wondered where he lived when he wasn't at the ranch. Although small, she saw it was clean and orderly. A well-used sofa sat against one wall, a table and two chairs were between the living room and kitchen. She guessed the doorway a few feet away led to a bedroom.

Brodie finished, then turned toward Maggie, seeing her still standing. Sighing, he walked up to her. "Maggie, sit down. Please."

She shook her head, meeting his gaze. "This was a mistake. I shouldn't have come back to Conviction. You made it clear how you felt about me before I left. And from what I saw at the saloon, you've already put me behind you."

"What you saw at the saloon didn't involve a woman. It involved too much whiskey and a night in a bed upstairs...*alone*." He paced a few feet closer. "Now, what do you mean about making a mistake in coming back? How long have you been in Conviction?"

Putting thoughts of the saloon girl behind her, Maggie lifted her chin, refusing to doubt her decision to return. "I arrived on the stage last night after parting from my family at Elk Horn Station."

Brodie's face hardened as anger rolled through him. "Do you have any idea how dangerous it is for a single woman to travel alone? What were you thinking, leaving them to return here?" He paced a few feet away, then turned back around. "Answer me. Why did you put yourself in such danger?"

Her body shook, her lower lip trembling at the harsh tone. She didn't know what to think of his reaction. It hadn't occurred to her he'd be angry at her return. What did he care about the danger to her? It had pained him, but he'd let her go, encouraged her to leave. From what she'd heard, taking the stage through hostile Apache country in Arizona and continuing to San Antonio would have been much more dangerous than the trip from Elk Horn to Conviction.

When he didn't get a reply, Brodie stalked up to her, lifting her chin with a finger.

"Maggie, lass, why did you return?"

Her eyes fixed on his, searching for any sign of the love she'd left behind. Swallowing the lump in her throat, she decided it would not be good to lie.

"Because I love you."

Her quiet response ripped through his heart. "Ah, Maggie." Wrapping his arms around her, he crushed her to his chest. "I've missed you, lass." He could hear her quiet sobs, feel tears soaking through his shirt. Stroking a hand down her hair, he leaned back, kissing her forehead.

"I didn't want to leave you, Brodie."

"And I didn't want you to go. I thought it was best for you."

She shook her head, rubbing away the tears. "It wasn't."

Letting out a shaky breath, he chuckled. "I can see that."

Leaning down, he settled his mouth over hers. Feeling her arms wrap around his neck, he drew her closer, deepening the kiss before pulling back, his gaze locking with hers.

"So you're staying?"

"If you still want me."

"Maggie, I've loved you since I first saw you. If you ever leave again, I don't think I'd live through it."

Her mouth tipped up at the corners, her eyes sparkling. "I surely wouldn't want to put your life in danger."

"If you stay, I have one condition."

She sighed. "More conditions, Brodie?"

He grinned. "I think this one is simple."

"All right. What is it?"

"Marry me."

Epilogue

Two weeks later...

"I'm glad she came back. I wasn't looking forward to going with you to San Antonio to fetch her." Quinn grinned at Brodie, who stood alongside Colin and Blaine, watching the family celebrate.

It had taken little time to finish the wedding preparations started before Maggie left. Once the family learned she had returned, everyone pitched in, finalizing the details within days.

"I wouldn't have asked."

Colin settled a hand on Brodie's shoulder. "We wouldn't have let you ride out alone. It was a gamble you took, lad. Letting her leave, pretending you didn't want her."

Brodie sucked in a deep breath. "Aye. A gamble which could've gone either way. If she hadn't returned, I'd have been forced to go after her."

"I'm a little disappointed she did come back." Blaine's voice had no inflection.

"Excuse me?" Brodie lifted a brow.

"I've always wanted to see Texas. Now I may never get out there." Blaine sipped the punch

Quinn had spiked with whiskey. "Ach. How much did you put in here, Quinn?"

"Enough." Quinn tapped the pocket of his jacket, indicating the hidden flask. "Remember, tonight will be Brodie's first time."

"With Maggie," Brodie added.

"Aye. It's been so long for you, I thought you might appreciate some additional courage."

Colin and Blaine laughed at the disbelieving look on Brodie's face.

"We all know you could never go more than a week, Quinn. Are there any women who've caught your attention you *haven't* bedded?" Colin shared a look with Quinn.

Quinn's gaze moved around the room, landing on Emma Pearce. Few people who weren't part of the family had been invited to witness the ceremony. The Pearce family was one of them. If one woman existed who could keep his attention, make him want to settle down and forget all others, he knew Emma was the one. He'd never acted on his feelings, never even discussed them with the men who stood next to him.

"I will say, if I thought she'd be interested, I'd stake a claim on Emma Pearce. She is one bonny lass."

Quinn choked on his drink, stopping himself from reaching out and wrapping his hand around Blaine's throat to set him straight. As if Blaine's comment wasn't enough, he glanced up to see Sam Covington walk up to her. Emma smiled at something he said, then responded, causing him to rear his head back with a roar of laughter. As Quinn watched, his anger flared. He'd never thought he could feel jealousy. Emma's reaction to Sam proved him wrong.

Brodie drank the last of his punch, setting the glass on a nearby table. "It's time I joined my bride, lads."

Moving across the room, his gaze locked with Maggie's. His wife. Everything he'd ever wanted in a woman, and her love for him shown in her eyes. Taking her hand, he pulled her away from the crowd around the table of food, walking her down the hall. Ducking behind the stairs, he took her in his arms.

"I can't wait much longer." He lowered his mouth to hers, feeling the heat rip through him the instant their lips touched. Pulling her close, aligning their bodies, Brodie's control faltered as his need for her grew. The sound of footsteps, someone clearing his throat, had him setting her away.

"It may be time for you to say your goodbyes, lad."

Brodie glanced down at Maggie, seeing her face redden as Ewan approached. Wrapping an arm around her waist, he pulled her close.

"Aye, Da. I need to get the wagon."

"Already done. Fletcher, Bram, and Sean have it out front."

Maggie glanced from Brodie to her father-in-law. "I thought we were staying here. Where are we going?"

Ewan clasped Brodie on the shoulder. "Come outside when you're ready."

As his father walked away, Brodie turned to Maggie. "There are four cabins not far away. We built one for each family to live in when we first arrived at Circle M. The family fixed one up for us to use."

She flashed him a bright smile. "It sounds wonderful. When do we leave?"

Brodie chuckled. "If you're ready, we'll start our life together right now."

Maggie drew her fingers down his face, placing a finger across his lips. "Right now is perfect for me, Brodie MacLaren." She moved her finger, placing a kiss to his lips. "I love you. You'll always be perfect for me."

Thank you for taking the time to read Brodie's Gamble. If you enjoyed it, please consider telling your friends or posting a short review. Word of mouth is an author's best friend and much appreciated.

Please join my reader's group to be notified of my New Releases at: http://www.shirleendavies.com/contact-me.html

I care about quality, so if you find something in error, please contact me via email at shirleen@shirleendavies.com

About the Author

Shirleen Davies writes romance—historical, contemporary, and romantic suspense. She grew up in Southern California, attended Oregon State University, and has degrees from San Diego State University and the University of Maryland. During the day she provides consulting services to small and mid-sized businesses. But her real passion is writing emotionally charged stories of flawed people who find redemption through love and acceptance. She now lives with her husband in a beautiful town in northern Arizona.

I love to hear from my readers.

Email me: shirleen@shirleendavies.com
Visit my website: http://www.shirleendavies.com
Check out my books:
http://www.shirleendavies.com/books.html
Comment on my blog:
http://www.shirleendavies.com/blog.html
Follow me on Amazon:
http://www.amazon.com/Shirleen-Davies/e/B00DW9LUSW

Other ways to connect with me:

Facebook Fan Page:
https://www.facebook.com/ShirleenDaviesAuthor
Twitter: http://twitter.com/shirleendavies
Google+: http://www.gplusid.com/shirleendavies
Pinterest:
http://www.pinterest.com/shirleendavies
Tsu: http://www.tsu.co/shirleendavies

Books by Shirleen Davies

Historical Western Romance Series
MacLarens of Fire Mountain

Tougher than the Rest, Book One
Faster than the Rest, Book Two
Harder than the Rest, Book Three
Stronger than the Rest, Book Four
Deadlier than the Rest, Book Five
Wilder than the Rest, Book Six

Redemption Mountain

Redemption's Edge, Book One
Wildfire Creek, Book Two
Sunrise Ridge, Book Three
Dixie Moon, Book Four
Survivor Pass, Book Five

MacLarens of Boundary Mountain

Colin's Quest, Book One,
Brodie's Gamble, Book Two

<u>*Contemporary Romance Series*</u>

MacLarens of Fire Mountain

Second Summer, Book One
Hard Landing, Book Two
One More Day, Book Three
All Your Nights, Book Four
Always Love You, Book Five
Hearts Don't Lie, Book Six
No Getting Over You, Book Seven
'Til the Sun Comes Up, Book Eight, Releasing 2016

Peregrine Bay

Reclaiming Love, Book One, A Novella
Our Kind of Love, Book Two

Tougher than the Rest – Book One
MacLarens of Fire Mountain Historical Western Romance Series

"A passionate, fast-paced story set in the untamed western frontier by an exciting new voice in historical romance."

Niall MacLaren is the oldest of four brothers, and the undisputed leader of the family. A widower, and single father, his focus is on building the MacLaren ranch into the largest and most successful in northern Arizona. He is serious about two things—his responsibility to the family and his future marriage to the wealthy, well-connected widow who will secure his place in the territory's destiny.

Katherine is determined to live the life she's dreamed about. With a job waiting for her in the growing town of Los Angeles, California, the young teacher from Philadelphia begins a journey across the United States with only a couple of trunks and her spinster companion. Life is perfect for this adventurous, beautiful young woman, until an accident throws her into the arms of the one man who can destroy it all.

Fighting his growing attraction and strong desire for the beautiful stranger, Niall is more determined than ever to push emotions aside to focus on his goals of wealth and political gain. But looking into the clear, blue eyes of the woman who could ruin everything, Niall discovers he will have to harden his heart and be tougher than he's ever been in his life…Tougher than the Rest.

Faster than the Rest – Book Two
MacLarens of Fire Mountain Historical Western Romance Series

"Headstrong, brash, confident, and complex, the MacLarens of Fire Mountain will captivate you with strong characters set in the wild and rugged western frontier."

Handsome, ruthless, young U.S. Marshal Jamie MacLaren had lost everything—his parents, his family connections, and his childhood sweetheart—but now he's back in Fire Mountain and ready for another chance. Just as he successfully reconnects with his family and starts to rebuild his life, he gets the unexpected and unwanted assignment of rescuing the woman who broke his heart.

Beautiful, wealthy Victoria Wicklin chose money and power over love, but is now fighting for her life—or is she? Who has she become in the seven years since she left Fire Mountain to take up her life in San Francisco? Is she really as innocent as she says?

Marshal MacLaren struggles to learn the truth and do his job, but the past and present lead him in different directions as his heart and brain wage battle. Is Victoria a victim or a villain? Is life offering him another chance, or just another heartbreak?

As Jamie and Victoria struggle to uncover past secrets and come to grips with their shared passion, another danger arises. A life-altering danger that is out of their control and threatens to destroy any chance for a shared future.

Harder than the Rest – Book Three
MacLarens of Fire Mountain Historical Western Romance Series

"They are men you want on your side. Hard, confident, and loyal, the MacLarens of Fire Mountain will seize your attention from the first page."

Will MacLaren is a hardened, plain-speaking bounty hunter. His life centers on finding men guilty of horrendous crimes and making sure justice is done. There is no place in his world for the carefree attitude he carried years before when a tragic event destroyed his dreams.

Amanda is the daughter of a successful Colorado rancher. Determined and proud, she works hard to prove she is as capable as any man and worthy to be her father's heir. When a stranger arrives, her independent nature collides with the strong pull toward the handsome ranch hand. But is he what he seems and could his secrets endanger her as well as her family?

The last thing Will needs is to feel passion for another woman. But Amanda elicits feelings he thought were long buried. Can Will's desire for her change him? Or will the vengeance he seeks against the one man he wants to destroy—a dangerous opponent without a conscious—continue to control his life?

Stronger than the Rest – Book Four
MacLarens of Fire Mountain Historical Western Romance Series

"Smart, tough, and capable, the MacLarens protect their own no matter the odds. Set against America's rugged frontier, the stories of the men from Fire Mountain are complex, fast-paced, and a

Drew MacLaren is focused and strong. He has achieved all of his goals except one—to return to the MacLaren ranch and build the best horse breeding program in the west. His successful career as an attorney is about to give way to his ranching roots when a bullet changes everything.

Tess Taylor is the quiet, serious daughter of a Colorado ranch family with dreams of her own. Her shy nature keeps her from developing friendships outside of her close-knit family until Drew enters her life. Their relationship grows. Then a bullet, meant for another, leaves him paralyzed and determined to distance himself from the one woman he's come to love.

Convinced he is no longer the man Tess needs, Drew focuses on regaining the use of his legs and recapturing a life he thought lost. But danger of another kind threatens those he cares about—including Tess—forcing him to rethink his future.

Can Drew overcome the barriers that stand between him, the safety of his friends and family, and a life with the woman he loves? To do it all, he has to be strong. Stronger than the Rest.

Deadlier than the Rest – Book Five
MacLarens of Fire Mountain Historical Western Romance Series

"A passionate, heartwarming story of the iconic MacLarens of Fire Mountain. This captivating historical western romance grabs your attention from the start with an engrossing story encompassing two romances set against the rugged backdrop of the burgeoning western frontier."

Connor MacLaren's search has already stolen eight years of his life. Now he is close to finding what he seeks—Meggie, his missing sister. His quest leads him to the growing city of Salt Lake and an encounter with the most captivating woman he has ever met.

Grace is the third wife of a Mormon farmer, forced into a life far different from what she'd have chosen. Her independent spirit longs for choices governed only by her own heart and mind. To achieve her dreams, she must hide behind secrets and half-truths, even as her heart pulls her towards the ruggedly handsome Connor.

Known as cool and uncompromising, Connor MacLaren lives by a few, firm rules that have served him well and kept him alive. However, danger stalks Connor, even to the front range of the beautiful Wasatch Mountains, threatening those he cares about and impacting his ability to find his sister.

Can Connor protect himself from those who seek his death? Will his eight-year search lead him to his sister while unlocking the secrets he knows are held tight within Grace, the woman who has captured his heart?

Read this heartening story of duty, honor, passion, and love in book five of the MacLarens of Fire Mountain series.

Wilder than the Rest – Book Six
MacLarens of Fire Mountain Historical Western Romance Series

"A captivating historical western romance set in the burgeoning and treacherous city of San Francisco. Go along for the ride in this gripping story

that seizes your attention from the very first page."

"If you're a reader who wants to discover an entire family of characters you can fall in love with, this is the series for you." – Authors to Watch

Pierce is a rough man, but happy in his new life as a Special Agent. Tasked with defending the rights of the federal government, Pierce is a cunning gunslinger always ready to tackle the next job. That is, until he finds out that his new job involves Mollie Jamison.

Mollie can be a lot to handle. Headstrong and independent, Mollie has chosen a life of danger and intrigue guaranteed to prove her liquor-loving father wrong. She will make something of herself, and no one, not even arrogant Pierce MacLaren, will stand in her way.

A secret mission brings them together, but will their attraction to each other prove deadly in their hunt for justice? The payoff for success is high, much higher than any assignment either has taken before. But will the damage to their hearts and souls be too much to bear? Can Pierce and Mollie find a way to overcome their misgivings and work together as one?

Second Summer – Book One
**MacLarens of Fire Mountain
Contemporary Romance Series**

"In this passionate Contemporary Romance, author Shirleen Davies introduces her readers to the modern day MacLarens starting with Heath MacLaren, the head of the family."

The Chairman of both the MacLaren Cattle Co. and MacLaren Land Development, Heath MacLaren is a success professionally—his personal life is another matter.

Following a divorce after a long, loveless marriage, Heath spends his time with women who are beautiful and passionate, yet unable to provide what he longs for . . .

Heath has never experienced love even though he witnesses it every day between his younger brother, Jace, and wife, Caroline. He wants what they have, yet spends his time with women too young to understand what drives him and too focused on themselves to be true companions.

It's been two years since Annie's husband died, leaving her to build a new life. He was her soul

*mate and confidante. She has no desire to find
a replacement, yet longs for male friendship.*

Annie's closest friend in Fire Mountain, Caroline
MacLaren, is determined to see Annie come out
of her shell after almost two years of mourning.
A chance meeting with Heath turns into an offer
to be a part of the MacLaren Foundation Board
and an opportunity for a life outside her home
sanctuary which has also become her prison. The
platonic friendship that builds between Annie
and Heath points to a future where each may
rely on the other without the bonds a romance
would entail.

*However, without consciously seeking it, each
yearns for more . . .*

The MacLaren Development Company is
booming with Heath at the helm. His meetings
at a partner company with the young, beautiful
marketing director, who makes no secret of her
desire for him, are a temptation. But is she the
type of woman he truly wants?

Annie's acceptance of the deep, yet passionless,
friendship with Heath sustains her, lulling her to
believe it is all she needs. At least until Heath
drops a bombshell, forcing Annie to realize that

what she took for friendship is actually a deep, lasting love. One she doesn't want to lose.

Each must decide to settle—or fight for it all.

Hard Landing – Book Two
MacLarens of Fire Mountain
Contemporary Romance Series

Trey MacLaren is a confident, poised Navy pilot. He's focused, loyal, ethical, and a natural leader. He is also on his way to what he hopes will be a lasting relationship and marriage with fellow pilot, Jesse Evans.

Jesse has always been driven. Her graduation from the Naval Academy and acceptance into the pilot training program are all she thought she wanted—until she discovered love with Trey MacLaren

Trey and Jesse's lives are filled with fast flying, friends, and the demands of their military careers. Lives each has settled into with a passion. At least until the day Trey receives a letter that could change his and Jesse's lives forever.

It's been over two years since Trey has seen the woman in Pensacola. Her unexpected letter

crosses with the intriguing, and much too handsome, Cam Sinclair. But Lainey's plans are set. An opportunity to buy a flourishing preschool in northern Arizona is her chance to make a fresh start, and nothing, not even her fierce attraction to Cam Sinclair, will impede her plans.

As Lainey begins to settle into her new life, an unexpected danger arises —threats from an unknown assailant—someone who doesn't believe she belongs in Fire Mountain. The more Lainey begins to love her new home, the greater the danger becomes. Can she accept the help and protection Cam offers while ignoring her consuming desire for him?

Even if Lainey accepts her attraction to Cam, will he ever be able to come to terms with his own driving ambition and allow himself to consider a different life than the one he's always pictured? A life with the one woman who offers more than he'd ever hoped to find?

All Your Nights – Book Four
MacLarens of Fire Mountain
Contemporary Romance Series

"Romance, adventure, cowboys, suspense—everything you want in a contemporary western romance novel."

Kade Taylor likes living on the edge. As an undercover agent for the DEA and a former Special Ops team member, his current assignment seems tame—keep tabs on a bookish Ph.D. candidate the agency believes is connected to a ruthless drug cartel.

Brooke Sinclair is weeks away from obtaining her goal of a doctoral degree. She spends time finalizing her presentation and relaxing with another student who seems to want nothing more than her friendship. That's fine with Brooke. Her last serious relationship ended in a broken engagement.

Her future is set, safe and peaceful, just as she's always planned—until Agent Taylor informs her she's under suspicion for illegal drug activities.

Kade and his DEA team obtain evidence which exonerates Brooke while placing her in danger from those who sought to use her. As Kade races to take down the drug cartel while protecting Brooke, he must also find common ground with the former suspect—a woman he desires with increasing intensity.

At odds with her better judgment, Brooke finds the more time she spends with Kade, the more she's attracted to the complex, multi-faceted agent. But Kade holds secrets he knows Brooke will never understand or accept.

Can Kade keep Brooke safe while coming to terms with his past, or will he stay silent, ruining any future with the woman his heart can't let go?

Always Love You– Book Five
MacLarens of Fire Mountain
Contemporary Romance Series

"Romance, adventure, motorcycles, cowboys, suspense—everything you want in a contemporary western romance novel."

Eric Sinclair loves his bachelor status. His work at MacLaren Enterprises leaves him with plenty of time to ride his horse as well as his Harley...and date beautiful women without a thought to commitment.

Amber Anderson is the new person at MacLaren Enterprises. Her passion for marketing landed her what she believes to be the perfect job—until she steps into her first meeting to find the man she left, but still loves, sitting at the management table—his disdain for her clear.

Eric won't allow the past to taint his professional behavior, nor will he repeat his mistakes with Amber, even though love for her pulses through him as strong as ever.

As they strive to mold a working relationship, unexpected danger confronts those close to them, pitting the MacLarens and Sinclairs against an evil who stalks one member but threatens them all.

Eric can't get the memories of their passionate past out of his mind, while Amber wrestles with feelings she thought long buried. Will they be able to put the past behind them to reclaim the love lost years before?

Hearts Don't Lie– Book Six
MacLarens of Fire Mountain
Contemporary Romance Series

Mitch MacLaren has reasons for avoiding relationships, and in his opinion, they're pretty darn good. As the new president of RTC Bucking Bulls, difficult challenges occur daily. He certainly doesn't need another one in the form of a fiery, blue-eyed, redhead.

Dana Ballard's new job forces her to work with the one MacLaren who can't seem to get over himself and lighten up. Their verbal sparring is second nature and entertaining until the night of Mitch's departure when he surprises her with a dare she doesn't refuse.

With his assignment in Fire Mountain over, Mitch is free to return to Montana and run the business his father helped start. The glitch in his enthusiasm has to do with one irreversible mistake—the dare Dana didn't ignore. Now, for reasons that confound him, he just can't let it go.

Working together is a circumstance neither wants, but both must accept. As their attraction grows, so do the accidents and strange illnesses of the animals RTC depends on to stay in business. Mitch's total focus should be on finding the reasons and people behind the incidents. Instead, he finds himself torn between his unwanted desire for Dana and the business which is his life.

In his mind, a simple proposition can solve one problem. Will Dana make the smart move and walk away? Or take the gamble and expose her heart?

No Getting Over You– Book Seven
MacLarens of Fire Mountain
Contemporary Romance Series

Cassie MacLaren has come a long way since being dumped by her long-time boyfriend, a man she believed to be her future. Successful in her job at MacLaren Enterprises, dreaming of one day leading one of the divisions, she's moved on to start a new relationship, having little time to dwell on past mistakes.

Matt Garner loves his job as rodeo representative for Double Ace Bucking Stock. Busy days and constant travel leave no time for anything more than the occasional short-term relationship—which is just the way he likes it. He's come to accept the regret of leaving the woman he loved for the pro rodeo circuit.

The future is set for both, until a chance meeting ignites long buried emotions neither is willing to face.

Forced to work together, their attraction grows, even as multiple arson fires threaten Cassie's new home of Cold Creek, Colorado. Although Cassie believes the danger from the fires is remote, she knows the danger Matt poses to her heart is real.

While fighting his renewed feelings for Cassie, Matt focuses on a new and unexpected opportunity offered by MacLaren Enterprises—an opportunity that will put him on a direct collision course with Cassie.

Will pride and self-preservation control their future? Or will one be strong enough to make the first move, risking everything, including their heart?

Redemption's Edge – Book One
Redemption Mountain – Historical Western Romance Series

"A heartwarming, passionate story of loss, forgiveness, and redemption set in the untamed frontier during the tumultuous years following the Civil War. Ms. Davies' engaging and complex characters draw you in from the start, creating an exciting introduction to this new historical western romance series."

Dax Pelletier is ready for a new life, far away from the one he left behind in Savannah following the South's devastating defeat in the Civil War. The ex-Confederate general wants nothing more to do with commanding men and confronting the tough truths of leadership.

Rachel Davenport possesses skills unlike those of her Boston socialite peers—skills honed as a nurse in field hospitals during the Civil War. Eschewing her northeastern suitors and changed by the carnage she's seen, Rachel decides to accept her uncle's invitation to assist him at his clinic in the dangerous and wild frontier of Montana.

Now a Texas Ranger, a promise to a friend takes Dax and his brother, Luke, to the untamed territory of Montana. He'll fulfill his oath and return to Austin, at least that's what he believes.

The small town of Splendor is what Rachel needs after life in a large city. In a few short months, she's grown to love the people as well as the majestic beauty of the untamed frontier. She's settled into a life unlike any she has ever thought possible.

Thinking his battle days are over, he now faces dangers of a different kind—one by those from his past who seek vengeance, and another from Rachel, the woman who's captured his heart.

Wildfire Creek – Book Two
Redemption Mountain – Historical Western Romance Series

"A passionate story of rebuilding lives, working to find a place in the wild frontier, and building new lives in the years following the American Civil War. A rugged, heartwarming story of choices and love in the continuing saga of Redemption Mountain."

Luke Pelletier is settling into his new life as a rancher and occasional Pinkerton Agent, leaving his past as an ex-Confederate major and Texas Ranger far behind. He wants nothing more than to work the ranch, charm the ladies, and live a life of carefree bachelorhood.

Ginny Sorensen has accepted her responsibility as the sole provider for herself and her younger sister. The desire to continue their journey to Oregon is crushed when the need for food and shelter keeps them in the growing frontier town of Splendor, Montana, forcing

Ginny to accept work as a server in the local saloon.

Luke has never met a woman as lovely and unspoiled as Ginny. He longs to know her, yet fears his wild ways and unsettled nature aren't what she deserves. She's a girl you marry, but that is nowhere in Luke's plans.

Complicating their tenuous friendship, a twist in circumstances forces Ginny closer to the man she most wants to avoid—the man who can destroy her dreams, and who's captured her heart.

Believing his bachelor status firm, Luke moves from danger to adventure, never dreaming each step he takes brings him closer to his true destiny and a life much different from what he imagines.

Sunrise Ridge – Book Three
Redemption Mountain – Historical Western Romance Series

"The author has a talent for bringing the historical west to life, realistically and vividly, and doesn't shy away from some of the harder aspects of frontier life, even though it's fiction. Recommended to readers who like sweeping western

*historical romances that are grounded
with memorable, likeable characters and
a strong sense of place."*

Noah Brandt is a successful blacksmith and
businessman in Splendor, Montana, with few
ties to his past as an ex-Union Army major and
sharpshooter. Quiet and hardworking, his
biggest challenge is controlling his strong desire
for a woman he believes is beyond his reach.

Abigail Tolbert is tired of being under her
father's thumb while at the same time, being
pushed away by the one man she desires.
Determined to build a new life outside the
control of her wealthy father, she finds work and
sets out to shape a life on her own terms.

Noah has made too many mistakes with Abby to
have any hope of getting her back. Even with the
changes in her life, including the distance she's
built with her father, he can't keep himself from
believing he'll never be good enough to claim
her.

Unexpected dangers, including a twist of fate for
Abby, change both their lives, making the
tentative steps they've taken to build a
relationship a distant hope. As Noah battles his

past as well as the threats to Abby, she fights for a future with the only man she will ever love.

Dixie Moon – Book Four
Redemption Mountain – Historical Western Romance Series

Gabe Evans is a man of his word with strong convictions and steadfast loyalty. As the sheriff of Splendor, Montana, the ex-Union Colonel and oldest of four boys from an affluent family, Gabe understands the meaning of responsibility. The last thing he wants is another commitment—especially of the female variety.

Until he meets Lena Campanel...

Lena's past is one she intends to keep buried. Overcoming a childhood of setbacks and obstacles, she and her friend, Nick, have succeeded in creating a life of financial success and devout loyalty to one another.

When an unexpected death leaves Gabe the sole heir of a considerable estate, partnering with Nick and Lena is a lucrative decision...forcing Gabe and Lena to work together. As their desire grows, Lena refuses to let down her guard, vowing to keep her past hidden—even from a perfect man like Gabe.

When revealed, Gabe realizes Lena's secrets are deeper than he ever imagined. For a man of his character, deception and lies of omission aren't negotiable. Will he be able to forgive the deceit? Or is the damage too great to ever repair?

Survivor Pass – Book Five
Redemption Mountain – Historical Western Romance Series

He thought he'd found a quiet life...

Cash Coulter settled into a life far removed from his days of fighting for the South and crossing the country as a bounty hunter. Now a deputy sheriff, Cash wants nothing more than to buy some land, raise cattle, and build a simple life in the frontier town of Splendor, Montana. But his whole world shifts when his gaze lands on the most captivating woman he's ever seen. And the feeling appears to be mutual.

But nothing is as it seems...

Alison McGrath moved from her home in Kentucky to the rugged mountains of Montana for one reason—to find the man responsible for murdering her brother. Despite using a false identity to avoid any tie to her brother's name, the citizens of Splendor have no intention of sharing their knowledge about the bank robbery which killed her only sibling. Alison knows her circle of lies can't end well, and her growing for Cash threatens to weaken the revenge which drives her.

And the troubles are mounting...

There is danger surrounding them both—men who seek vengeance as a way to silence the past...by any means necessary.

Reclaiming Love – Book One, A Novella
Peregrine Bay – Contemporary Romance Series

Adam Monroe has seen his share of setbacks. Now he's back in Peregrine Bay, looking for a new life and second chance.

Julia Kerrigan's life rebounded after the sudden betrayal of the one man she ever loved. As president of a success real estate company, she's built a new life and future, pushing the painful past behind her.

Adam's reason for accepting the job as the town's new Police Chief can be explained in one word—Julia. He wants her back and will do whatever is necessary to achieve his goal, even knowing his biggest hurdle is the woman he still loves.

As they begin to reconnect, a terrible scandal breaks loose with Julia and Adam at the center.

Will the threat to their lives and reputations destroy their fledgling romance? Can Adam identify and eliminate the danger to Julia before he's had a chance to reclaim her love?

Our Kind of Love – Book Two
Peregrine Bay – Contemporary Romance Series

Selena Kerrigan is content with a life filled with work and family, never feeling the need to take a chance on a relationship—until she steps into a social world inhabited by a man with dark hair and penetrating blue eyes. Eyes that are fixed on her.

Lincoln Caldwell is a man satisfied with his life. Transitioning from an enviable career as a Navy SEAL to becoming a successful entrepreneur, his days focus on growing his security firm, spending his nights with whomever he chooses. Committing to one woman isn't on the horizon—

until a captivating woman with caramel eyes sends his personal life into a tailspin.

Believing her identity remains a secret, Selena returns to work, ready to forget about running away from the bed she never should have gone near. She's prepared to put the colossal error, as well as the man she'll never see again, behind her.

Too bad the object of her lapse in judgment doesn't feel the same.

Linc is good at tracking his targets, and Selena is now at the top of his list. It's amazing how a pair of sandals and only a first name can say so much.

As he pursues the woman he can't rid from his mind, a series of cyber-attacks hit his business, threatening its hard-won success. Worse, and unbeknownst to most, Linc harbors a secret—one with the potential to alter his life, along with those he's close to, in ways he could never imagine.

Our Kind of Love, Book Two in the Peregrine Bay Contemporary Romance series, is a full-length novel with an HEA and no cliffhanger.

Colin's Quest – Book One
MacLarens of Boundary Mountain – Historical Western Romance Series

For An Undying Love...

When Colin MacLaren headed west on a wagon train, he hoped to find adventure and perhaps a little danger in untamed California. He never expected to meet the girl he would love forever. He also never expected her to be the daughter of his family's age-old enemy, but Sarah was a MacGregor and the anger he anticipated soon became a reality. Her father would not be swayed, vehemently refusing to allow marriage to a MacLaren.

Time Has No Effect...

Forced apart for five years, Sarah never forgot Colin—nor did she give up on his promise to come for her. Carrying the brooch he gave her as proof of their secret betrothal, she scans the trail from California, waiting for Colin to claim her. Unfortunately, her father has other plans.

And Enemies Hold No Power.

Nothing can stop Colin from locating Sarah. Not outlaws, runaways, or miles of difficult trails. However, reuniting is only the beginning.

Together they must find the courage to fight the men who would keep them apart—and conquer the challenge of uniting two independent hearts.

Brodie's Gamble – Book Two
MacLarens of Boundary Mountain – Historical Western Romance Series

Brodie MacLaren has a dream. He yearns to wear the star—bring the guilty to justice and protect those who are innocent. In his mind, guilty means guilty, even when it includes a beautiful woman who sets his body on edge.

Maggie King lives a nightmare, wanting nothing more than to survive each day and recapture the life stolen from her. Each day she wakes and prays for escape. Taking the one chance she may ever have, Maggie lashes out, unprepared for the rising panic as the man people believe to be her husband lies motionless at her feet.

Deciding innocence and guilt isn't his job.

Brodie's orderly, black and white world spins as her story of kidnapping and abuse unfold. The fact nothing adds up as well as his growing attraction to Maggie cause doubts the stoic lawman can't afford to embrace.

Can a lifetime of believing in absolute right and wrong change in a heartbeat?

Maggie has traded one form of captivity for another. Thoughts of escape consume her, even as feelings for the handsome, unyielding lawman grow.

As events unfold, Brodie must fight more than his attraction. Someone is after Maggie—a real threat who is out to silence her.

He's challenged on all fronts—until he takes a gamble that could change his life or destroy his heart.

Find all of my books at:
http://www.shirleendavies.com/books.html

Avalanche Ranch Press, LLC
PO Box 12618
Prescott, AZ 86304